GHOST MAN

by
Nathan Roden

The Casper Halliday NYPD Series
Ghost Man

Copyright © 2019 by Nathan Roden

www.nathanroden.com

One

27 Months Later

Casper Halliday showered and dressed for the trip home. It was still strange having his own apartment, but he knew moving out of his parent's apartment was the right thing to do. They had rekindled their relationship after a trying fourteen-month separation. Casper was now a rookie NYPD officer with a steady paycheck and a hectic schedule. The last thing he wanted to do was disrupt the lives of Kathy and Bobby Halliday when everything was going so well.

Casper stepped out of the locker room and faced three different hallways. He scratched his head and took the hallway with the exit sign at the end. He walked through the door and stared out across the parking lot. Casper had just finished his third day on the job. Everything was new to him, including the inside and outside of the precinct station. He couldn't remember if he had parked on this side of the building or not. Casper sniffed. He smelled something burning.

"Are you lost?"

The voice made Casper jump. He turned and saw a woman standing beneath an awning. She appeared to be mid-thirties, with long, dark hair. She had big, hypnotic blue eyes and the face of a movie star. The lady wore a black leather short-coat over a striped blouse, a form-fitting black skirt, and athletic shoes. Casper's first thought was that she might be an aerobics instructor—except for the cigarette burning in her right hand.

"I'm not *exactly* lost," Casper said. "But I might have to try all four sides of the building before I remember where I parked this morning."

"Maybe I can help," the lady said. She craned her neck and stood on tip-toes to look out over the parking lot. Casper noticed the favorable effect this had on her legs.

"What are we looking for? Corvette? Camaro?"

"A white Crown Victoria," Casper said.

The woman laughed, choking slightly on her last puff.

"You're kidding me, right?"

Casper stared at her.

Something…

"Are you the dispatcher?"

"I'm one of several," the woman said.

"Are you…Charlie?"

The woman dropped the cigarette butt to the pavement, ground it out with her foot, and disposed of it in a garbage can. She held out her hand.

"Yes, I'm Charlie Tall-Butt. Pleased to meet you."

This time, Casper's eyes flicked toward the woman's backside. He looked up and realized he had been caught. Charlie laughed. She turned sideways and smacked her left hip.

"Well, what do you think?"

"Uh…about what?"

Charlie rolled her eyes.

"I am fully aware that I am known throughout the precinct as 'Charlie Tall-Butt'." Charlie swished her hips.

"So, what do you think?"

"It's…nice. Very nice," Casper said.

"It damned well better be," Charlie said. "I work my ass off on this ass."

Charlie narrowed her eyes.

"I think I know who you are but I would hate to be wrong."

Casper lifted his hand, but remembered they had already done that.

"I'm Casper Halliday."

Charlie threw her arms around Casper and hugged him tightly. Casper had no idea what to do with his hands so he stood as still as a statue. Charlie backed away but held onto Casper's arms.

"You've changed some in…what has it been? Two years?"

Casper shook his head slowly.

"I…"

"Come *on*, Casper Halliday," Charlie said. "Your picture was *everywhere*—especially around here. Oh. My. Gawd. A nineteen-year-old hero! You saved all those girls—and the Chief's daughter!"

"I was just one part of that whole thing, Ma'am."

Charlie put her palm against Casper's face.

"And modest, too. Just like Captain America. Why, I believe you're blushing, Mr. Halliday."

"I'm sure I am," Casper said.

"The young lady," Charlie said. "Officer Hampton. How is she?"

Casper paused.

"I hate to speak for Blair. She was a huge part of taking those guys down. But it was...it took its toll. I mean, she was new to the job—and it happened so fast. Detective Freeman was her first partner, but he was also her friend and her mentor."

Casper blinked and looked away.

"And...when she looks at me, I think it makes that night real all over again."

"I'm sorry, Casper," Charlie said.

Casper looked around.

"So, is this the designated smoking area?"

"It is for me," Charlie said. "I don't even know if there *is* a designated smoking area. I'm not a real smoker. I only smoke when I drink."

"You're...drinking?" Casper said.

"Not yet," Charlie said. "But I will be in about fifteen minutes." Charlie motioned with her head. "Come on. I want to buy our resident hero a beer."

She took a step away.

"I have to drive home," Casper said. "And I just got my own place. I got lost yesterday."

Charlie grabbed Casper's arm.

"I didn't say I was going to pour a fifth of tequila down your throat, honey. I said I want to buy you a beer."

"Well..."

"How many days have you been on the job?"

Charlie asked.

"Three."

"And you haven't been to a cop bar yet?"

"No."

Charlie pulled on Casper's arm.

"Then it's time to pop that cherry. Let's go."

Casper gave up and followed.

"Why do they call you Charlie? What's your real name?"

"Celeste."

"That's a pretty name," Casper said.

"It's not bad," Charlie said. "But it doesn't work on the radio. No hard consonants. Celeste is a good name for stuff like tea parties, and wedding showers, and maybe figure skating. But when you're communicating about shots fired, officer needs assistance, burglary in progress; you want a name that cuts through the bullshit."

"You have a way with words, Mrs. Talbot."

"Oh, *puhleeze!*" Charlie said. "Mrs. Talbot sounds exactly like an English teacher; glasses on a chain and the whole nine yards."

"Where is this bar?" Casper asked.

"Right around the corner, of course," Charlie said.

"Are you sure this is cool?" Casper asked. "I've been here three days. What is it going to look like when I show up in a bar already?"

Charlie stopped. She raised her arms to her side and then pointed at herself with both thumbs.

"You're with *me!* Now, if you walked in there and

took a seat in the dungeon and drank until Max threw you out, you might have something to worry about."

"The dungeon?"

"You'll see."

They turned the corner. Casper looked up at the neon sign.

"Max's Cigar Lounge."

He looked at Charlie and shrugged.

"It's the only kind of place you can still smoke and drink in public anymore," Charlie said. "You may have to burn your clothes later."

Charlie opened the door, exposing a cloud of smoke and an old Rolling Stones song. She waved for Casper to step inside. As soon as the twenty-two customers saw who had arrived, a chorus of "Charlie!" filled the room.

Charlie was obviously popular with the off-duty policemen and the bartender. She was slightly less popular with the four women customers and two barmaids.

"Where do you want to sit?" Casper asked.

"Pfft!" Charlie said. "At my table, of course."

Two off-duty cops stood at a table in the back of the room. They stepped behind the chairs and held onto the backs.

"Thank you, Brad," Charlie said. "Thank you, Harpo."

Brad helped Charlie move the chair up to the table. Casper looked at the other chair and the large, silent man who held onto it.

"Please, take your seat, Harpo," Charlie said. "I'm afraid our new friend is a little nervous."

The men walked away.

"His name is Harpo?" Casper asked.

"That's his nickname," Charlie said. "He can talk. But he would rather not."

"He's huge," Casper said. "And kind of scary. So, what's the deal? Do you have your own table? Do you own this place?"

"Good God, no," Charlie said. "Designating this as my table started as a joke a few years ago. It stuck. When I walk through the door, this is my table. I swear if I sat anywhere else some of these men would have to go in for counseling. It's a tradition now. And in case you didn't know it, when it comes to cops you don't screw with tradition."

"Okay," Casper said. "But it feels a little weird sitting here. I feel like the teacher's pet."

"Dammit, Casper!" Charlie snapped. "Cut it out with the English teacher shit or I swear I will cut you."

"I didn't mean—"

Charlie put her palms flat on the table and took a deep breath.

"Men," she snarled. "Men are the reason I drink. And therefore…the reason I smoke."

She reached for her purse and lit a cigarette. After such a grand entrance, Casper was surprised no one seemed to be in a hurry to wait on them. The barmaids didn't seem particularly busy. The bartender had disappeared. He walked through the kitchen door a few minutes later and walked up to their table. Casper didn't recognize the burly man for a moment until he realized the man had changed his shirt and his hair was freshly combed. He also smelled strongly of cologne. The man ignored Casper.

"Hi, Charlie,"

"Hello, Max. How's life treating you?"

"Aw, like a one-eyed hunting dog, Charlie."

Max winked and pointed a finger at Charlie.

"But *you* are always the bright spot in my day."

Charlie feigned embarrassment.

"Oh, you're so sweet, Max."

"What can I get for you?" Max said.

"What would you like, Casper?" Charlie asked.

"Just a beer," Casper said.

"A beer," Max said. He put his hands on his hips. "You know I'm sure that after a long day of chasin' down cattle rustlers and assorted other mangy varmints, a man just wants to mosey down to the saloon and have himself a beer. But this is the twenty-first century, son. I sell fifty-six beers—"

"Fifty-six beers!"

The other customers raised their mugs, bottles, cans, or glasses and sounded off in unison.

Yet another cop bar tradition.

Max rolled his eyes and shouted over the music.

"You're going to do that shit until I drop dead, aren't you?"

"Yes, sir!" the room sounded off. Max turned back to Casper.

"I'll have a Budweiser," Casper said.

"A Bud. Yeah, we got that believe it or not."

Max turned to Charlie and his whole demeanor changed.

"What can I get for you, love?"

Charlie closed her eyes and rubbed her chin.

"What was the one I tried last week? The label is yellow and red and there's a sheep dog and a windmill—"

Max rattled off a seven-syllable name that sounded like it had originated in the farthest corner of Holland. He retreated to the bar.

"Max is such a sweetie," Charlie said. She leaned closer to Casper and whispered.

"I think he likes me."

"Ya think?" Casper said.

Casper and Charlie clinked their bottles together and took a drink. When Casper put his bottle down, Charlie grabbed his right arm.

"*Rrowrrr,*" she purred. "Now that's a bicep. But you don't walk like a gym rat. You walk like a cat. Like a panther."

Casper squirmed in his chair.

"You didn't think I noticed, did you?" Charlie asked.

Casper didn't know what to say. Charlie patted his hand.

"Drink your beer, honey. I'll stop bothering you."

"I'm only having one," Casper said. "How long are we staying here?"

"Oh, I don't know," Charlie said. "Are you not having a good time?"

"I'm having a great time," Casper said.

Charlie squeezed Casper's hand and took a long drink. Casper shivered and felt goose bumps rise on his arms. He took another sip of beer. Max walked by and left two more bottles on their table just as Charlie finished hers. Charlie shrugged.

"He knows my pace."

Casper pointed at the full bottle in front of him.

"I'm not drinking that. I have to drive home."

Charlie waved her hand.

"Don't worry about it."

Charlie finished her second beer quicker than the first. Max was right there with another. Casper looked around.

"So, where is the dungeon?"

Charlie pointed across the room.

"There are two booths and a table on the other side of the bar—behind the pool table."

Casper stood and squinted.

"It's really dark over there. I can't see anything."

"That's the whole point," Charlie said. "Not everyone who walks in here is having a good day. Cops can have some high highs and some low lows—and it's not always about the job. Maybe there's trouble at home. Sometimes you might just want to have a few drinks. Or a lot of drinks—where you can be around your people but you really don't want to talk. You just don't want to be alone. You know, when you have a gun strapped to your hip all day, being alone isn't always a good thing."

"Have you ever been in the dungeon?" Casper asked.

Charlie smiled.

"Let's talk about happy things, okay?"

She took a long drink.

"I can't pronounce the name of that beer," Casper said. "Is it good?"

Before Casper could think or react, Charlie put her hand behind his head and pulled him into an open-mouthed kiss. Charlie pulled away, laughing hysterically at the look on Casper's face. The nearby officers whooped and cheered and clapped.

"Well?" Charlie said.

"Huh?" Casper said.

"The beer. Does it taste good?"

"Uh…yeah."

Casper hadn't noticed the front door opening, but he heard it close.

He turned and looked into the stunned face of Officer Blair Hampton.

Two

Robert Ferrill pulled down on the bill of the baseball cap. It rested on top of large black-framed glasses with thick clear lenses. Ferrill merged into the morning sidewalk traffic, his hands in the pockets of a dark gray windbreaker. He bumped into the shoulders and elbows of strangers without a look or comment.

Ferrill held open the door to the crowded bakery for two young women. They nodded and walked to the counter to place their orders. Ferrill followed and ordered a coffee and a cinnamon roll. He took his items and turned. The women had taken his coveted booth — the booth in the far corner of the small dining room. Ferrill forced himself to stay calm.

He sat at the table nearest to the two women. He took a sip of coffee and stared intently at the woman sitting in the seat he considered his. Three times the woman's eyes caught Ferrill's stare. Ferrill did not look away. The woman leaned across the table and whispered to her friend. They stood and left the building.

Ferrill stood and hurried to the vacated booth. He

bumped into a man and woman who had the same destination.

"Really?" the man said. Coffee splashed onto his hand.

"Some *people*," the woman snapped. "Let's just go."

Ferrill sat back and sipped his coffee. His eyes found the woman he came to see. Her name-tag read "Liz". All five waitresses at the bakery wore identical uniforms; short beige dresses trimmed in scarlet red. All wore sheer stockings.

But none of them were as exquisitely perfect
As Elizabeth.

Her smile was bright. And engaging. And genuine. She did not project the same aura that the others did. Some of them were tired. Bored. They wished they were somewhere else. Still in bed, without a doubt.

No. Liz is not like the others.

Ferrill had seen the Health Department certificate behind the register.

Owners and Proprietors.

Cristian and Elizabeth Cappelletti.

Ferrill sipped his coffee and pinched a tiny bite from the roll. It was far too sweet for his taste but that meant nothing to him. Ferrill watched every move Liz made. She fussed with the waistline of her dress.

She's gained five pounds. It bothers her.

It is not a problem, my love. You are perfect.

A man walked out of the kitchen. He was

handsome and well-dressed. The hem of his slacks rested against expensive Italian loafers. He whispered something to the girl at the register and they shared a laugh. The man approached Liz as she delivered a tray to a table.

Liz turned and threw her arms around the man. She kissed him on the mouth. She even raised her right leg at the knee the way actresses did in old movies. This made Ferrill squirm in his chair. The other employees and a few of the customers clapped their hands and laughed.

Cristian Cappelletti looked exactly like Ferrill thought he would. Handsome. Virile. Cocky. This made it easy for Ferrill to hate him.

Robert Ferrill dabbed the corners of his mouth with a napkin.

He left the bakery, knowing he would only return one more time.

Ferrill unlocked the front door to his house with two keys and stepped inside. He walked into the bathroom and washed his hands thoroughly. He took an emery board from the medicine cabinet and smoothed his nails. He worked a pumice stone methodically against his palms and fingers. The whole process took almost an hour. Ferrill removed his shirt. He moved his hands over his hairless torso. Ferrill had his body hair removed by electrolysis years ago in a European clinic.

The clinic burned to the ground the next day along with five employees and six patients. Ferrill patted his hands dry and walked into his bedroom.

The bedroom was perfectly normal except for one unique piece. In the middle of the room, atop a ten-inch pedestal, stood the bottom half of a female mannequin. The mannequin was dressed in lace panties and a garter belt affixed to sheer stockings. Ferrill placed his hands on the mannequin's hips. He slid his hand around to the hard plastic buttocks. His smooth hands created minimal resistance. The heightened nerve endings in his palms and fingers allowed the feel of the silk to arouse him as it always did. Ferrill moved his hands to the toes of the stockinged feet. He inched his hands up to the calves. The knees. The thighs.

Ferrill undressed and showered in preparation for a busy night.

****

Liz Cappelletti silenced her alarm clock. It was two A.M.

She kissed her husband's cheek. He moaned softly but did not open his eyes. Liz smiled. She would let him sleep. He deserved it.

The past six years had been like a fairy tale. Liz met Cristian Cappelletti while she was on a second date with someone else. Her date impressed her with his choice of restaurants. But Liz knew their relationship would never progress any further. As she would say to her closest friends; he is a choice cut of beef, but there is no *sizzle*.

The dinner was magnificent. When they finished, Liz asked to speak to the chef. The moment she saw

Cristian Cappelletti, chills ran through her. Her skin buzzed like she had touched a bare electric wire.

Liz returned to the restaurant two nights later. Alone.

She ordered a different dinner from the menu. It was just as good as her earlier experience. Once again, she asked to speak to the chef.

Once again, the chef was Cristian.

Cristian smiled.

"Ah, we meet again."

He offered his hand.

"It is very good to see you."

The way he said it conveyed much more than a common pleasantry.

Moments later, he asked her out—his dark eyes staring deep into hers. She accepted.

"Where could we possibly dine that could compare with this?" Liz asked.

Cristian smiled.

"Nowhere, of course. But I have tickets to a popular play. Perhaps that will be enough to make the night worthwhile."

After a lovely dinner and a Broadway play, Liz was mesmerized. The taxi pulled up in front of her apartment. She looked into Cristian's eyes.

"I don't do things like this," Liz said. "Would you like to come up?"

Cristian smiled as he gazed into her eyes.

"Would that be taking advantage of you?"

"Absolutely not."

They made love with reckless abandon—clothes and bedsheets were strewn about Liz's bedroom. Dawn found them sprawled and sweating, lying naked on her bed. Their chests heaved as they caught their breath.

"I think this went fairly well," Liz said. "For a first date."

"I tend…to agree," Cristian said, struggling for air. "Is it safe to assume…that your date…the night we met…is not serious?"

Liz laughed so heartily that her back bowed off of the bed. She rolled over, crossing her leg over Cristian's torso. She pressed her finger against Cristian's lips.

"I want *you*, Cristian Cappelletti."

"And I want you, Elizabeth. Oh, my God! I don't know your last name!"

"Liz Kennedy."

Cristian froze.

"Holy…You're not related to—"

Liz laughed.

"No! Calm down, Cristian."

He blew out a long breath.

"This is happening so fast," he said.

"I was thinking the same thing," Liz said.

"So, what do we do?" Cristian asked.

Liz smiled. Her fingers walked down Cristian's torso.

"I can think of something."

****

Cristian Cappelletti proposed to Elizabeth Kennedy three months later. She accepted with a squeal, a hug that left Cristian unable to breathe, and a shout of *"Yes!"*

At the wedding reception, Elizabeth's grandmother hugged Cristian with tears in her eyes.

"Bless you, my son," she said. "Take good care of our baby."

"I will, my lady," Cristian said.

Elizabeth's grandfather shook hands with Cristian.

"Do you know about the accident with Elizabeth's parents?" Devin Kennedy asked.

"Yes," Cristian said.

Devin sighed.

"There was never any question that Elizabeth would live with us. We've thought of her as our own daughter. She has brought us nothing but joy."

"I believe it, sir," Cristian said.

"She tells me you are a gifted chef."

"I have worked hard to earn that reputation, sir."

"Elizabeth believes you will one day open your own restaurant—perhaps even a *chain* of restaurants."

"It is my dream, sir. Maybe after a few years—"

"I believe in hard work and talent, Cristian. And I believe in being open to opportunities. I also believe in my granddaughter."

"Yes, sir," Cristian said.

"Do you know what I do, Cristian?"

"You work at a bank," Cristian said.

Devin chuckled.

"That sounds very much like Elizabeth. I am president of a bank, Cristian. And as such, I constantly have my finger in the wind for good investments. What do you think of the prospects for a fine eating establishment known as, say…'Cappelletti's'?"

Cristian almost choked on his drink.

"Well, sir. I could put my full faith and confidence behind such a venture."

Three years later, the *second* Cappelletti's restaurant opened to rave reviews and hard-sought reservations. Celebrity appearances drove the popularity of both locations.

The night before Liz's next birthday, she came out of the bathroom toweling her freshly washed hair. Cristian stood by the dining room table. On the table, in the middle of a large dish, there was a cinnamon roll with a single lit candle in the middle.

Liz laughed.

"What is this?"

Cristian held out a small gift-wrapped box.

"Your dream, my dear."

Liz opened the box. Inside was a single large key.

"Oh, my. A key. I'm…curious, yet confused."

"What is your dream?" Cristian asked.

"*You* are my dream."

"No, silly. You told me about the hours you spent with your grandmother in her kitchen—baking pies and cakes and—"

Liz sucked in a breath. She covered her mouth. Cristian laughed.

"The key—to Elizabeth's Bakery."

The bakery was a success from the beginning. After two years, Cristian and Liz made plans to step back from their hectic schedules. They planned to hire a management team to handle the everyday aspects of their businesses. They had worked long and hard to get their businesses up and running. Now, they looked forward to enjoying the fruits of their labors—and having their first baby.

Maybe within a year…

****

Liz hummed as she got dressed and put on her makeup. She peered into the bedroom three more times. Cristian was still asleep.

Good, Liz thought.

The night before had been magical. They had dinner with Liz's grandparents and the general manager for both Cappelletti's restaurants. The occasion was for Cristian to propose the opening of a third restaurant. This would mean more responsibility and a significant raise for the general manager. The idea put smiles on every face and led to a series of toasts.

Later, at home, Cristian opened an expensive bottle of champagne. Liz had one glass while Cristian finished the rest of the bottle. They made love. A few minutes later, Cristian's hands began to roam again, in spite of Liz's objections that she had to be at the bakery in a few hours. Cristian laughed. Liz laughed. They made love again.

Cristian had driven them to the bakery for the last two weeks. Their regular early prep baker had fallen off a ladder at home while painting. He would probably be out another month.

But Liz couldn't bring herself to wake Cristian that morning. He was such a good man, and a tenacious worker; he deserved to sleep in, especially after a night of celebration.

Liz left a note on the kitchen island and slipped out the door. She pulled it closed as quietly as she could and locked it.

Liz pulled into her normal parking space behind the bakery. It was one of only six available spaces; the same space where Cristian had parked their car for the past two weeks. Liz opened the car door just a little. She listened to the silence—the only sounds were far distant.

Liz stepped out of the car and set the alarm. She walked straight to the back door of the bakery and inserted her key. Liz heard the heavy tumblers of the lock fall into place. She pushed open the heavy door.

Liz sighed as she pushed the door closed behind her. She locked the door and dropped the security bar.

No problem. I'm inside. Safe and sound. Sleep well, Cristian. I love you.

Liz walked into the office. She placed her purse beneath the desk.

Safe and sound. Stop being such a baby.

But her senses told her something was wrong. She could sense it. Liz walked into the kitchen.

It's the oil. The oil is hot. The oil was not supposed to be hot at 2:30 A.M.

Liz checked the large fry vat. The temperature dial was set to 600 degrees.

Shit.

Someone had forgotten to turn off the vat burner the previous afternoon. They had not even placed the cover over the vat. And the deep fryer was never supposed to reach such a high temperature.

That was an *expensive* mistake. Burned oil can ruin multiple batches of pastry, resulting in dissatisfied customers. Those customers might never return. Worse, they might tell others of their substandard experience.

Liz fumed. She would have harsh words for the late crew. Rule number one was posted inside the kitchen. It was in bold print, all caps, and underlined.

IT IS VITAL THAT ALL BURNERS ARE TURNED OFF AND THE DEEP FRY VATS COVERED BEFORE THE DOORS ARE LOCKED!

God. It's always something.

****

Robert Ferrill stood perfectly still behind the broom closet. His pulse raced when he heard the car arrive. Ferrill knew there were no security cameras in the parking lot, the kitchen, or the dining room. He had more than enough skills to break into the bakery without leaving evidence of a forced entry. Inside, he found only a simple personal computer. No security monitors.

Ferrill moved his flashlight around the office. There were two pictures of Cristian and Elizabeth on the desk. One picture was from a ribbon-cutting ceremony in front of a Cappelletti's restaurant. The other photo was similar; a ribbon-cutting ceremony in front of this very building.

There was a large print on the wall behind the desk. A wedding photo. Ferrill raised a gloved hand and covered Elizabeth Cappelletti's head. Ferrill leaned close to the photo. His hot breath escaped the small opening of his rubber mask. He spoke to the smiling face of Cristian Cappelletti.

"She is mine now…"

Three

Liz emptied the bag of cake flour into the mixer. She checked the deep fryer again. The temperature had only come down thirty degrees. Liz swore again. There was no time to change out the oil. She wouldn't know if the oil was damaged until she tested the first batch of pastries. She envisioned finding the person responsible for the mistake and firing them on the spot. Liz took a deep breath. She didn't want a reputation as a ruthless employer,

But, dammit...

Liz opened the heavy stainless door to the walk-in cooler. She stepped inside and reached for two cartons of eggs.

A gloved hand shot in front of Liz's face. A strong arm pinned her arms to her sides. Liz opened her mouth to scream. Another hand shoved a rag into her mouth.

The man shoved her against the back wall of the cooler, face-first. Liz felt cold steel against her right wrist. She heard a mechanical click. The man pulled Liz away from the wall far enough to handcuff her left wrist. Liz kicked backward with her right foot. She connected with the man's shin. She drew back her foot prepared to kick again until she felt the man's hot breath in her ear. Liz froze. The man shifted his feet. He pushed his right knee into the small of Liz's back and pinned her against the wall. Liz could hardly breathe. She heard a ripping sound.

Is that my…my dress?

No…

Liz recognized the sound. It was the sound of tape being pulled from a roll.

A hand appeared in front of her eyes. The tape went over the rag in her mouth. Forced to breathe through her nose, Liz gagged. When her stomach attempted to empty its contents, it had nowhere to go. Just before Liz passed out, the man removed his knee from her back. Liz lost her footing and fell to her knees. She sobbed from pain and fear. The man tied her ankles together.

The man wrapped his arms around Liz from behind. He lifted her as if she weighed no more than a child. He carried her out of the cooler. Liz heard the cooler door close as the man carried her through the kitchen. The man's foot slipped on spilled flour. He fell to one knee and lost his grip. Liz fell to the floor on her side. The man groaned like a wounded animal. He climbed to his feet.

Liz's eyes went wide when she saw the horrific creature.

Every inch of him was covered. He had trash bags tied over his shoes and the legs of his pants. The sleeves of a turtleneck sweater disappeared inside of long black leather gloves.

His head was covered with a hideous rubber mask.

Liz sobbed as the monster lifted her again. He carried her to the edge of a table and pushed her between her shoulders.

He's going to rape me.
Oh, please, let that be all there is…

Robert Ferrill reached down and gently gripped the hem of Liz's dress between his thumbs and forefingers. He lifted the dress and folded the hem across Liz's back. Liz felt the man behind her, his groin barely grazing against her pantyhose. He stepped back. Liz didn't want to look but she couldn't help herself. The man removed his gloves. This gave Liz a glimmer of hope.

He may have not have done this before. There will be fingerprints. He'll be caught! Doesn't he realize that? Maybe…maybe…

His next move took Liz completely by surprise.

Ferrill untied Liz's shoes and removed them. He touched her toes. Liz felt him tremble. Slowly, he moved his hands up Elizabeth's legs.

His *real* living and breathing doll. The object of his desire. His everything.

Ferrill's hands reached her hips. He pressed in against her. Fully clothed, Ferrill gently thrust himself against her. He did it again. And again. His hands moved up and down the sides of Liz's sheer stockings.

Liz felt the man shudder…and then his weight

collapsed against her, pushing her hips painfully against the table's edge.

What? Is that…is that it?

Oh, please, oh, please. Maybe…maybe he's through. Maybe…it's over!

Oh, God, what now?

Ferrill put on his gloves. He gripped the waistband of Liz's pantyhose. He pulled them down in one long, deliberate motion—keeping his hands at the outsides of Liz's legs.

Ferrill untied the silk scarf he had used to bind Liz's ankles. He removed the pantyhose, folded them, and laid them on top of Liz's shoes.

Liz didn't know how much more she could take.

This can't be happening…

What the hell is he doing?

Ferrill retied the scarf around Liz's ankles. He stood her up at the table and turned her to face him. Ferrill put his left hand behind her back. He put his right arm behind her knees and lifted her into a princess carry. With a show of incredible strength, Ferrill supported Liz with only his left arm. He clenched his right glove between his teeth and freed his hand. He gently pulled the tape from Liz's mouth.

Ferrill gripped the bottom of his mask and lifted it over his mouth and nose. Liz whimpered.

What the hell? What are you doing?

Ferrill moved closer.

He kissed Liz's chin. He kissed her bottom lip and then her upper lip.

Liz jumped when something splashed into her eye.

Oh, my God! Is he…is he crying? Is he ashamed? Is he sorry?

Please let me go…

Ferrill kissed the bridge of her nose. Finally he kissed her forehead. Tenderly, as a parent might kiss a child to comfort them.

Ferrill raised his head. Liz looked into the madman's eyes.

*He **is** crying!*

Ferrill slid his left arm up Liz's back. He grabbed a fistful of her hair.

Robert Ferrill lowered Elizabeth Cappelletti into the boiling oil.

Four

Casper rolled over and slapped the snooze button on top of his alarm clock. The ringing continued. Casper opened one eye. It was 4:15. The ringing came from his phone.

"Hello?"

"Halliday? Is this you?"

"Yeah. Who is this?"

"Sergeant Rice. Look, we have a bad situation over in Manhattan that calls for some serious crowd control. I need you to get here as quick as you can."

"What's going on?"

"I have more calls to make, Halliday. Get your ass down here."

The line went dead.

Casper and his friend, Mando, had attended a martial arts class the night before. Casper did not get to bed until eleven o'clock. He rolled out of bed, showered quickly and dressed. He craved caffeine but he had never tried drinking coffee while driving. It seemed like a bad day for that kind of challenge.

There was an unusual amount of activity outside the station house for 4:55 in the morning. Casper parked and walked inside.

"You look lost, Rookie."

The voice came from behind him. Casper turned and grinned.

"Hey," Casper said to Mando Gonzalez. Casper and Mando became friends at the police academy.

"This isn't my 'lost' look, Mando. This is my sleep-deprived look. Take a look in the mirror, Bro. You have it too."

Mando yawned.

"No shit. So much for an easy first week on the job."

"What happened?" Casper asked. "Have you heard anything?"

"I just got here," Mando said.

They walked into the briefing room.

Sergeant Rice got everyone's attention.

"Listen up. There was a homicide a couple of hours ago in a high-traffic retail section of East Village. The victim and the victim's family are prominent members of the community. Headquarters has shut down a two square block area that includes at least forty-two businesses. They've asked for our help to set a perimeter for at least the next few hours. If you were called to report early, let's get to the garage. We'll travel four to a car."

Twenty-four officers formed a line in the garage. Sergeant Rice walked down the line counting off groups of four. Casper opened a car door and looked across the roof. He saw Blair Hampton staring at him.

"Hi," Casper said.

"Hello," Blair said. Her face showed no

expression.

Mando Gonzalez rode in the front with Sean Kelly, a seven-year veteran and Blair's latest partner. Mando turned in his seat. Blair stared out the side window. Casper drummed his fingers on the armrest.

"How are you doing, Blair?" Mando asked.

"I'm okay," Blair said, flatly. "Thanks, Mando."

Mando looked at Sean.

"This must be some bad shit, huh?"

"Yeah," Sean said. "They don't shut down that much real estate for a regular old homicide."

"Do you know more than we do?" Casper asked.

Sean followed the car ahead out onto the street.

"You'll find out soon enough," Sean said. "A lady was murdered inside her own bakery. If Manhattan asked for extra manpower, it must have been really ugly."

"Wow," Mando said. "A bakery. Ovens. Giant knives—"

"Mando," Casper said.

"What?"

"Shut the hell up."

"Forty-two businesses," Mando said. "On a weekday morning? That's a lot of shopkeepers and customers that are gonna be pissed."

They met with officers from the ninth precinct. There were tables stocked with coffee and water placed around the police perimeter. Two flatbed trucks off-loaded portable toilets.

Mando stepped next to Casper.

"What's up with you and Blair? I can't believe you, man. Three days on the job and you've got some domestic head-game shit going on?"

"It's no big deal," Casper said.

"It looked like a big deal to me," Mando said. "You could cut the air in that car with a knife, bro. What the hell happened?"

"It was just some bad timing," Casper said. "This other...this girl was kind of flirting with me and Blair saw it."

"That doesn't sound like Blair," Mando said.

Casper sighed.

"We were having some problems before that happened."

"This ain't cool, man," Mando said.

"Do you think I don't know that?" Casper snapped. "How would you like it if every time your girlfriend looked at you it reminded her of the most horrible night in her life?"

"I know that sucks, Caz, but you're in the spotlight now. And that means *both* of you are in the spotlight. I hate to sound like your dad or something, but neither one of you needs any more pressure right now."

"I don't know how to fix this," Casper said. "I'm not a psychologist."

"Is Blair still seeing Dr. Phillips?"

Casper shook his head.

"She did for a while; until she got paranoid."

"Paranoid?"

"She swears people were whispering about her. Other cops. Like she was a hopeless mental case."

Mando glanced at Blair.

"You should go talk to her."

"Now?" Casper said.

"Come on, Caz," Mando said. "I don't mean start a fight. I mean let her know you care. Let her know you're there for her—whatever happens."

"When did you get so smart?" Casper asked.

Mando smirked.

"I have always been wise in the ways of love, my friend. Didn't your first Kung Fu Master teach you anything about women?"

"No," Casper said. "But I did get a late start. And we were in prison, so it would have been a little weird."

"I'm going to have a talk with Master Kim," Mando said. "I don't need help, of course, but a Master should see that his pupils aren't entirely clueless when it comes to the opposite sex."

"I'm not clueless," Casper said.

"Okay," Mando said. "Whatever."

"I'll be back," Casper said.

"Cool. Take your time," Mando said.

****

"Hi," Casper said.

Blair sipped her coffee.

"Hello. Again."

"Did you get any sleep?" Casper asked.

"A couple of hours."

Casper pointed to the street.

"The barricades are working so far."

"It's only five-thirty," Blair said. "Things will change."

Casper lowered his voice.

"Look, Blair—about yesterday—"

"I don't want to talk about it," Blair said. She shuffled her feet and kicked a rock.

"I had nothing to do with it," Casper said.

"Really?" Blair said. "From where I was standing you looked like a participant."

"Charlie was playing with me like a cat with a mouse," Casper said. "She knew I was a nervous wreck."

"Yeah," Blair said. "You were so nervous you were sitting next to her in the back of the bar. You must have been *terrified.*"

"I met her outside the station when I was trying to find my car. She wanted to buy me a beer and she wouldn't take no for an answer. I didn't want to look like an asshole."

"Maybe you just have a thing for older women," Blair said.

"I didn't want to be there," Casper said.

Blair shook her head.

"Now you're trying too hard. I guess you're going to tell me you didn't want her tongue down your throat."

"I didn't see it coming, all right?" Casper said. "What was I supposed to do? Punch her in the mouth? Shove her off her chair? Dammit, Blair—I have three days on the job. I'm trying not to make any enemies, okay?"

Blair looked away.

"Welcome to my world."

"What is that supposed to mean?" Casper asked.

"It's not like everything was lollipops and rainbows before yesterday," Blair said.

"So you think we're broken," Casper said. "Do you think we can be fixed? I'll do anything."

Blair closed her eyes.

"It's going to start all over again—and you don't even know it."

"I don't know what you're talking about," Casper said.

"The freaking media hasn't found out you're in uniform yet," Blair said. "It's going to happen any day now."

"*What's* going to—?"

Blair faced Casper. She ground her teeth and her nostrils flared.

"I didn't bother you with everything I went through. I didn't complain and cry on your shoulder. They were *relentless!* This entire city—hell, the entire country tried to make me the poster child for every female from birth to the grave. Everybody wanted a piece of me. I was asked—sometimes *begged* to give commencement speeches. To speak to high schools. Junior Highs. Elementary schools. Private schools. Even the freaking Girls Scouts. And all this time, I can't sleep—I wake up seeing that bullet rip through Chris's neck…"

"I'm sorry, Blair," Casper said.

"You killed three of those men," Blair said. "Three out of four. But only a handful of people on the planet know that. The world thinks I'm Little Miss Rambo because we *lied*."

"We didn't have a choice," Casper said.

"So what?" Blair said. "We lied and my life turned to shit."

"But—"

Blair held up her hands.

"You didn't want to look like an asshole to Charlie Talbot. Big freaking deal. What do you think I looked like when I said, 'No, I'm not going to speak to your fourth-grade girls? No, I'm not going to speak at your graduation'. What was I supposed to do, Casper? Stand up on a stage and lie my ass off again? I can't do that! All you had to do was say you fell on top of one man. Bad man go **Boom!**"

Casper stared at the ground.

"I'm sorry," Blair said. "You didn't deserve that."

"It's okay," Casper said.

Blair blinked and bit her lip.

"I don't...I don't think we can do this anymore, Casper. I'm a mess—and I don't want to hurt you."

"I can't turn my back on you, Blair. I care about you. A lot."

Blair looked away.

"I've had four partners in less than three years. Nobody wants to work with me. Who can blame them? Who wants to work in the shadow of the Woman Super-cop? No one trusts me. I can see it. I can feel it. They think I'm a mental case. And they're right. I've only had to draw my gun three more times, and every time I thought I was going to pass out."

"Maybe you need—"

"Don't, Casper. Just don't. Don't tell me I need more time. Or that I need to have more counseling."

Blair cleared her throat.

"My parents have offered to pay for me to finish school. My father knows people at the FBI. I'm thinking about an office job; psychological profiler, something like that."

Blair stared at Casper.

"I'm going to resign from the department."

Their radios crackled with the sound of a frantic voice. They could hear the sounds of confrontation both from the radio—and from nearby.

"*Officers need assistance at the bakery! No weapons! Repeat! No weapons!*"

Five

Cristian Cappelletti woke with a headache and a dry mouth. He smacked his lips, rolled from his left side to his right side, and put his arm over the space where his wife was supposed to be.

Cristian opened his eyes. He sat up and looked at the alarm clock. It showed 3:55. Cristian hurried out of bed.

"Liz? Elizabeth?"

Cristian checked the bathroom and the kitchen. He found Liz's note and called her cell phone. After four rings the call went to voice-mail. He called the bakery's phone. There was no answer. Cristian dressed and hurried to his car. He tried calling again.

"Come on, honey. Pick up."

Cristian ran red lights and ignored speed limits. *Something is wrong.*

Cristian's stomach clenched when he saw the line of barricades and the flashing lights of police cars. He stopped in front of a barricade and got out of his car. A police officer ran to meet him.

"I'm sorry, sir. We can't allow anyone inside the barricades. There's been some trouble."

"What kind of trouble?"

"I don't have that information, sir."

Cristian pointed.

"I have a business here. A bakery. My wife is there."

"I understand, sir. We have strict orders from headquarters. No one is allowed in until we hear differently. It's for the best, sir. Have you tried calling your wife?"

"She's not answering," Cristian said. "I have to go to her."

The officer discreetly moved his hand to his holster.

"I'm sorry, sir. Please be patient and try calling again. Just as soon as we get the word we'll let you through."

Cristian climbed into his car. The tires squealed when he backed away from the barricade. Cristian drove two blocks, turned a corner, and parked. There were police officers everywhere. The last time Cristian had seen this kind of police presence was New Year's Eve. Cristian moved in the shadows. He stood against the side of a building and stared at the line of police. A few minutes later, three officers walked away. One stepped inside a portable toilet. The other two walked toward a table on the sidewalk. Cristian hurried through the vacated space.

He moved toward the bakery, sprinting from shadow to shadow. Twice he was almost caught.

Cristian pressed his back against a wall. There were fewer shadows here. He leaned forward. There. He could see the front door of the bakery. He saw four officers. They were huddled together; looking at a cell phone.

Cristian froze when the bakery door opened. A police officer stepped out, held the door open and looked in all directions. He turned and went back inside.

No...oh, God...

Cristian sprinted toward the door at top speed. He was almost to the door before an officer saw him. Three officers ran to intercept him while another radioed for help.

****

Casper and Mando matched each other, stride-for-stride. Blair and Sean were right on their heels. Four police officers were trying to tackle a man who had reached the front door of the bakery. The man swore at the top of his lungs and fought with his feet and his fists. One officer fell to the sidewalk, holding his knee. The crazed man jerked open the door. An officer's head struck the door frame. He crumpled to the ground, out cold. Casper and Mando dove at the man's legs at the same time. They slid across the bakery floor in a heap of thrashing limbs.

The five men froze in place. They stared at the same spectacle.

A fragment of beige and scarlet fabric. A pair of legs. Bare feet. Above the knees, the legs ended abruptly in bone, tendons, and charred flesh.

Cristian Cappelletti went berserk.

"Elizabeth! Elizabeth! Noooooo! Noooooo!"

Cristian thrashed against the grips of the officers and tried to stand. More officers arrived. Nine of them held Cristian. They pushed and pulled him toward the door.

"Get the paramedics!" Sean shouted.

They carried Cristian into the street. He sobbed and screamed, flailing his arms and legs. Foam ran down the sides of his mouth. Two paramedics arrived. They knelt beside Cristian.

"What happened?"

"He's out of his mind," Sean said. "You need to knock him the hell out before he kills himself."

Cristian was sedated and strapped to a gurney. The paramedics and three police officers loaded him into an ambulance. The ambulance raced away, it's siren and lights making a path through the chaos.

Casper and Mando sat on the curb, breathing heavily.

"Holy shit," Mando whispered.

"Yeah," Casper said. He looked at Blair. She stood alone with her arms wrapped tightly across her chest. Casper wondered if she might be in shock, too. He wanted to put his arms around her and hold her head against his chest.

But he couldn't. Not here. Not now.

Maybe never again.

Six

Shane Murphy stopped his car in front of the secluded restaurant. Two very large men stood by the double doors. One of them offered Murphy a valet slip. Murphy did his best to remain calm.

Even their valets can snap your neck.

The second man held open the restaurant door. Light classical music provided ambiance. The dining room featured rich woodwork and quality leather. The hostess was a beautiful Asian girl with black hair that fell to the small of her back.

"Table for one?" she said in a sultry voice.

"I'm Shane Murphy."

The hostess motioned to her right. A barrel-chested man walked toward them. He offered no pleasantries but motioned with his head.

"This way."

A door opened from the inside just as they reached it. Murphy surveyed the surrounding walls. He did not see a camera, but he knew there was one. Probably several of them.

Murphy flinched when he heard a **crack!** He relaxed when he realized the sound came from a pool table. A tall, thin man with swept-back hair and steel-blue eyes circled the table holding a cue stick. His eyes bored in on Murphy.

Murphy walked toward the man with his right hand extended.

"I'm Sha—"

The man raised his hand to signal "stop". He turned to the bar where two beautiful young women sat on stools, drinking from tall glasses. The man motioned toward the door. The women exited without a word, followed by a man who placed his cue stick into the wall rack.

When the door closed, the man waved toward a large mahogany desk.

"Sit, Mr. Murphy."

Murphy stood in front of a chair and extended his right hand across the desk. The man shook his head.

"We will never be friends, Mr. Murphy. Ours is a business relationship of mutual benefit only."

Murphy lowered his hand. He was angry and insulted, but he would not show it.

"Fair enough, Mr. Glazkov."

Glazkov made a sour smile.

"Your friends are prone to accidents…"

"That was very nice work, Mr. Glazkov," Murphy said. "Thank you for—"

Glazkov sat forward and slapped the top of his desk. He pressed a button on the phone.

"Ivan. Pyotr. Come."

Two men entered the room. Glazkov stood.

"Remove your jacket," Glazkov said. "Unbutton

your shirt and drop your trousers."

Murphy gripped the arms of the chair.

"What the hell?"

"You politicians are all alike," Glazkov said. "You talk too much. You would not know discretion if it bit your ass."

"Do you think I would be stupid enough to come here wearing a wire?" Murphy snapped.

"I know you are impetuous, Mr. Murphy," Glazkov said. "You act impulsively without considering ramifications. You are a dangerous man."

"And you're not?" Murphy asked.

Glazkov smiled.

"Of course, I am. But I am not foolish enough to believe I am invincible. Your status and your presumed 'destiny' will not protect you, Mr. Murphy. Destiny is earned one day at a time."

Murphy glared at Glazkov as he loosened his belt and dropped his trousers.

"Should you ever visit my office, be prepared for the same treatment."

Glazkov shook his head.

"I do not foresee that happening. There is a good reason that sharks and crocodiles do not swim in the same waters."

The men performed their search. Murphy got dressed. He waited until the men left the room.

"Tell me about David Hatch."

"He's clean," Glazkov said. "A regular Boy Scout. We've uncovered no skeletons. No girlfriends. No boyfriends. No drugs. No questionable affiliations."

"What about the kids?"

"His daughter is in her first year at Cornell," Glazkov said. "Her 'wildest' activities are limited to attending movies and pizza establishments. His son is top of his class at Harvard."

Glazkov leaned back. He drummed his fingers on the desk.

"If you wish to unseat the District Attorney, you will have to do so at the ballot box."

"Shit," Murphy said. "I can't beat him. Unless something unfortunate—"

"No," Glazkov said. "There will be no more 'accidents'. Perhaps if you had shown more patience with Mr. Williams…"

"I told you," Murphy said. "He was going to walk. I know it as sure as I'm sitting here. I couldn't trust him."

"I will not lie to you, Mr. Murphy," Glazkov said. "Having ties within the legal system is valuable to me. Perhaps you could set your sights even higher; say, the State Senate. Or even Attorney General."

Murphy smiled.

"I like the sound of that."

"We have people who can help," Glazkov said. "But we will not meet like this again. Mr. Williams performed a valuable service as liaison. He must be replaced."

"Of course," Murphy said. "After an appropriate period of mourning."

"Do you have someone in mind?" Glazkov asked.

"Yes," Murphy said. "A University classmate."

"Leave me his contact information," Glazkov said. "I'll have him checked out."

"Oh, yeah?" Murphy said with a smirk.

"A University classmate," Glazkov said. "This raises questions. Let me tell you a little of what I know about you, Mr. Murphy: mid-western upbringing. Lower middle-class parents. University grades barely above average. Tuition paid for in cash earned from unofficial employment by one Rocky Pensado. These 'services' including but not limited to extortion, illegal gambling, and assault. Will I find more of the same from your classmate?"

"You're real funny, Glazkov," Murphy said.

Glazkov held up his hands.

"It is only good business, Mr. Murphy. You come from humble beginnings. So do I."

Glazkov tapped a fist against his chest.

"The struggle builds a fire inside you can get no other way. In this way, we are similar. Tell me about this man."

"He has a degree in accounting," Murphy said. "And a brother at a Washington D.C. law firm. Currently, my friend holds a management position with the TSA in D.C."

"I take it your friend has similar…motivations?" Glazkov asked.

"He's smart," Murphy said. "And we are similar in important ways."

"Such as?" Glazkov said.

"If you were not born with a silver spoon," Murphy said. "You take one from someone else."

"Goodbye, Mr. Murphy. I'll be in touch."

Seven

The crime scene was cleared, and the barricades removed at ten A.M.

Back at Precinct Sixty-Seven, Casper was given the option to go home or finish his shift and take the next day off. He and Mando chose to stay. Blair chose to go home. She did not attempt to speak to Casper.

"Aren't you sleepy?" Casper asked Mando.

Mando shook his head.

"Man, I don't want to be by myself staring at the ceiling after seeing that shit. How freaking sick would you have to be to do something like that?"

"Yeah," Casper said. "And he's still out there."

"Not for long," Mando said. "This is going to be one massive man-hunt."

Casper stared at the ground.

"Her poor husband. I can't even imagine what that would be like."

"He loved her a lot," Mando said. "You could tell."

"No doubt about it," Casper said. He narrowed his eyes.

"I hope the sick bastard gets caught in a state that has the death penalty."

"How did it go with Blair?" Mando asked.

"Not so great," Casper said. "Don't say anything, but she said she's going to resign and finish school. Her dad has connections at the FBI. She wants to be a profiler."

Mando thought for a moment.

"Maybe it's for the best, Caz. This job ain't for everybody. You know the numbers. Lots of divorces. And suicides."

"Are you trying to cheer me up?" Casper asked.

"I'm just saying maybe it's better if you two don't work together."

"I don't know," Casper said. "That thing at the Port was just a freaking mess—and not for the reasons everybody thinks."

"I want to ask you something, Bro," Mando said.

"Go ahead," Casper said.

"Was the official story true?"

Casper looked away.

"We don't have time for this discussion. I have to find my partner."

"Yeah, me too," Mando said. "I guess I need to get a few beers in you sometime."

"It wouldn't hurt," Casper said. "We'll see you later."

"Take care, amigo."

****

Casper joined Leo, his training partner, for lunch. At 2:45 PM they received a call that two suspicious looking males were loitering outside the playground of a junior high school. A few minutes later they spotted the men. Leo pulled the car to the curb. The men ran. Casper and Leo gave chase. Casper caught up to the first man and shoved him in the back. The man tumbled to the ground. Leo jumped on the man and cuffed him. Casper caught up to the other man and grabbed his arm. The man spun around and threw a punch at Casper's head. Casper ducked, jumped up and kicked the man in the face. The man went down. Casper rolled him onto his stomach. He pinned the man to the ground with his knee and cuffed him. Casper pulled the man to his feet.

"We didn't do a damn thing," the man protested. "I'm pressing charges against you, asshole!"

"Yeah. Good luck with that," Casper said. He leaned in close to the man's ear.

"You picked a really bad day to screw with me."

Leo held up a clear plastic bag that contained an assortment of pills, capsules, and powders.

"It looks like our friends here have been talking some kids out of their lunch money."

"That's *bullshit!*" the men screamed together.

Casper and Leo walked the men to their car and loaded them into the back seat.

Leo leaned against the car.

"I heard about that thing in Manhattan. That was pretty ugly, huh?"

"Yeah," Casper said. "Really ugly."

"Well," Leo said. "You've got your first arrest now—and it's a good one. Too bad it didn't happen on a better day."

Casper nodded.

"You'll make a helluva partner," Leo said. "You're fast as hell. I would have had to shoot one of those guys in the leg."

"That's a joke, right?" Casper asked.

"Yeah," Leo said. "Probably. My daughter goes to a junior high just like this one. Let's book these scumbags and call it a day."

Casper showered, dressed, and climbed into his car. He took out his phone and stared at it. He keyed Blair's number.

"Hullo?"

"I'm sorry, Blair. Were you asleep?"

"Yeah. No. I don't...know," Blair mumbled. "I took some...something to make me sleep."

"I was wondering if you'd like to go out for dinner," Casper asked.

"Hold on," Blair said. Casper heard Blair's phone clatter against a hard surface. She was gone for a full minute.

"I'm back," she said.

"Would you like to go to dinner?" Casper repeated.

"No. No, I'm a mess," Blair said.

"I could bring you something," Casper said. "Are you at your apartment?"

"Yes. I don't...I don't want anything. Thank you."

"I wouldn't have to come in—"

"No," Blair said. "I don't want to fix my hair. I don't want to get dressed. I don't want to *think*."

They were silent.

"I'm here for you if you need anything," Casper said. "I'm here for you if you just want to talk—or listen to each other breathe."

"You're sweet, Casper. I'm sorry."

There was another lingering silence.

"Blair?"

"Blair, are you still there?"

Casper listened until the call was disconnected.

****

Casper rested his forehead against the steering wheel. He sat up, sighed, and got out of his car. He walked to the back of the station. Casper waved to someone he didn't know as they drove out of the parking lot.

Charlie Talbot's smoking section was unoccupied, but Casper thought he smelled cigarette smoke. He walked to the trash can. He looked in all directions and then lifted the lid. Right on top he saw two cigarette butts with lipstick on them.

Charlie had apologized many times when she learned Blair had seen her kiss Casper.

"It was just a *joke!* It didn't mean anything. I don't even *know* you, for God's sake. I might as well have given a wedgie to a freshman."

Casper had assured Charlie it was no big deal, although he wasn't sure if it was or not. He didn't want Charlie to feel bad about it. She couldn't have guessed that Blair was about to walk through the door. It was just bad timing. Casper turned and walked toward Max's Cigar Lounge.

If he found Charlie there, he would assure her again—maybe have a beer with her to show her everything was cool.

Who are you trying to fool? You just had the day from hell and you don't want to be alone. And don't bullshit yourself, Mister. You are more than fascinated by Charlie Talbot. And that kiss...it scared the hell out of you at the time—but you've thought about it some more since then. A LOT more.

So what? We work together. And she's cool. I'm not stupid. She's almost twice my age. And she's married to a Wall Street hot-shot who was a college quarterback.

She likes to have a beer or two or three and a smoke or two or three before she goes home. Maybe she's not all that happily married.

Shut up, Casper. Get in your car and go home.

YOU shut up. I'm going to have a beer. With a friend.

Eight

Casper opened the door to Max's Cigar Lounge. The thirteen people inside looked to see who it was, but quickly returned to their drinks.

Charlie's table was empty. Casper walked to the bar.

"You come into town for another beer, Marshall?" Max said.

"Maybe," Casper said. "I was hoping to talk to Charlie. But I guess she's not here."

Max put both hands against the counter and sighed. He pointed to his left with his thumb. Casper leaned across the bar.

"She's in the dungeon?"

Max motioned toward the kitchen door.

"Come back here."

Casper stepped inside.

"What the hell's going on?"

"Charlie's got..." Max stammered.

"It looks like she's got a shiner."

"A—you mean a *black eye?*" Casper said. "What the fu—?"

"Shh!" Max snapped. "Keep your voice down, dammit! I'm not a hundred percent sure—she wears makeup, you know."

Max paused and rubbed his face.

"It happened once before—a couple of years ago. There wasn't much doubt about it that time. Her left eye was swollen almost shut. You can't fix that with Maybelline."

"This place is full of cops," Casper said. "And nobody's doing anything?"

Max jabbed his finger at Casper's chest.

"You listen to me, boy. If Charlie gave the word, me and a hundred and fifty cops would be on Mister Matt Talbot like flies on *shit!* Do you hear me?"

"But—"

Max shook his head violently.

"No! There ain't no '*but*'! You better learn this and learn it good, son. Cops don't get into each other's business. Everybody has their own shit to deal with."

"But...he freaking *hits her?*" Casper said. "I can't believe it."

"Go home, kid," Max said. "Get yourself a case of beer and keep drinking until you think about something else."

Casper sighed.

"Thanks for telling me, Max. I'm going home."

Casper reached for the door.

"You do that," Max said. "And don't even think about trying to talk to her. You take one step toward the dungeon and me and everybody else in here will throw you out on your ass. And you don't come back for a year."

"You have tough rules," Casper said.

"You gotta have rules and you gotta make them

stick," Max said. "Didn't you just swear an oath like that?"

"Yes, I did," Casper said. "We'll see you later, Max."

Casper had beer in his refrigerator, but he had no desire to use alcohol for a crutch. It was hard for him to picture a successful career beginning with becoming an alcoholic the first week on the job. Still, the silence inside his apartment was unnerving. He knew his mother was covering one of her friend's shifts at the diner. He decided he would have dinner there.

Kathy Halliday's face lit up when she saw Casper. Two of Kathy's long-time friends were working as well. They congratulated Casper on his new job and told him what a fine young man he had become.

Casper blushed and smiled.

"Did you just stop by or are you eating?" Kathy asked.

"I'm eating," Casper said. "I'm starving. It's been a helluva day."

"I hear the meatloaf is excellent," Kathy said.

Casper held up his hands.

"Say no more. Meatloaf it is. Make it a big slice and there just might be an extra-special tip involved."

"I'll see what I can do," Kathy said.

Casper sat in a booth toward the back. He faced the door. As he sipped his glass of tea, three loud and burly men came in and sat at the bar. They all wore dirt-caked boots.

Construction workers.

"You're looking might delicious, Kathy."

The man who called Kathy Halliday by name was the ringleader of the three. Casper stared at the men. He felt a familiar tingle at the back of his neck.

In the next few minutes, Casper learned that the ringleader's name was "Dutch". Dutch talked almost constantly and referred to Kathy as "Honey", "Babe", and "Sugar". Kathy ignored the men as much as possible.

As a waitress put the meatloaf plate in front of Casper, Dutch spoke again.

"Kathy, doll-face, when are you gonna run away with me and make all our dreams come true?"

Kathy glanced at Casper. She knew from her son's scowl that he heard everything Dutch said.

A man sitting in a booth with his wife raised his hand to get Kathy's attention.

"Miss?"

Kathy stepped around the counter. She had to pass by Dutch.

"Whoa," Dutch said to his friends. "Is that the best legs you've ever seen or what?"

As Kathy passed, Dutch put a finger beneath the hem of her dressed and raised it a few inches. Kathy squealed and slapped Dutch's hand.

"*Oh, no,*" she whispered.

Casper was coming.

Casper paused and grabbed another waitress by the arm. He whispered in her ear.

"Get my mother out of the room. Now."

The woman hurried and pushed Kathy through

the kitchen door.

Dutch put up his hands.

"Hey. Where you goin', Babe?"

"Let's take a walk, Dutch," Casper said.

Dutch looked Casper up and down.

"I don't know you."

"No. You don't," Casper said. "Let's take a walk."

"Fuck off."

Casper pulled his badge from his pocket.

"I'm not asking."

Dutch swore under his breath. Casper followed him out to the sidewalk.

"What the hell do you want?" Dutch asked. "I was eating."

"What you were doing was harassing a waitress and that last little move could get you arrested for assault."

"Assault?" Dutch said. "Who are you kidding, sonny boy? We were just havin' a little fun. Women like to know they're attractive. And appreciated. It's a public service."

"You need to leave your cave and say hello to the twenty-first century, Dutch."

"Pfft!" Dutch said. "What the hell do you know about women? The last time you saw a cootch was when you fell outta one."

Casper paused.

"Take your friends and get out of here. Don't come back."

Dutch laughed.

"I swear. This can't really be happening. Are you messing with me? Did Artie put you up to this?"

"Believe it," Casper said. "I am as serious as the heart attack you're gonna have within the next five years. Get lost."

Dutch jabbed his finger within an inch of Casper's chest.

"You wait until Artie finds out you're trying to run off his best customers."

Casper stared at the finger.

"I think that's the same finger you used to lift my mother's skirt."

"Your mother?" Dutch said. "Bullshit."

Casper stepped forward until he was inches away from Dutch's face.

"I told you to get out of here."

Dutch shoved Casper away and charged. He threw a punch. Casper dodged to the side and kicked Dutch in the hip. Dutch crashed into the wall. Casper pinned Dutch's left arm behind his back. He grabbed Dutch's right fist and pried his index finger away from the others.

"If I find out you've stepped one foot inside this diner again, I'll hunt you down. And I will make sure you never use this finger again. And if you ever touch my mother again…

"I'll break them all."

Nine

Robert Ferrill opened the hotel room door. He checked the hallway in both directions. He saw no one; heard no one. Ferrill hurried through the exit. He crossed the parking lot, toward its darkest corner. He unlocked his car and climbed inside. The old car held onto a musty smell that matched its age.

Ferrill drove for over an hour. He pulled the car into the half-full parking lot of a recently opened restaurant/bar. He had checked out this restaurant the week before; lured by a billboard just outside of town. The billboard clearly displayed the unique feature of the new business. Three buxom and beautiful waitresses smiled down at the highway, dressed in skin-tight tops bearing the restaurant name over tiny, glossy shorts. The six perfect legs glowed with the sheen...

Of sheer stockings.

Ferrill entered the restaurant on a Wednesday evening. The dining room was half-full. Every seat around the bar was taken. A cheerful hostess directed Ferrill to a table and handed him a menu. Ferrill felt conspicuous. He glared at the backs of the men seated at the bar. He knew why the seats were full. The men who were here by themselves did not want to stand out as the lonely, dirty men they were.

Ferrill's waitress was stunningly beautiful. Ferrill recognized her from the billboard. Chills ran through him. The girl introduced herself with a dazzling smile.

"Hi! I'll be your waitress. My name is Karin."

She pointed to her name tag.

"Karin with an 'i'."

"Karin with an 'I'," Ferrill repeated.

"Are you ready to order?"

"Yes," Ferrill said.

Ferrill thought the food was mediocre and overpriced.

Twice the price to stare at tits and ass.

Ferrill didn't care. He would never come back.

When Karin brought his ticket, she had written a note on it.

Thanks! Have a great night! Karin.

Her handwriting was big and round and curvy—full of youth and joy and confidence. She had replaced the dot over the "i" in her name with a tiny heart.

Five hours later, Ferrill had everything he needed. He knew the apartment building she lived in. He knew the location and number of her parking space in the parking garage.

C-45.

Karin with an "i".

Sweet as pie.

Karin with an "i".

The next to die.

He loved her. And he hated her.

Ferrill parked and surveyed the parking lot. He was not too close, and not too far away from the restaurant. He watched a group of three young men and a young woman exit the restaurant. They exhibited the effects of a few drinks—laughing and talking loudly. They got into a car and left.

Ferrill lifted a scope to his eye. It took only a few seconds to get his answer.

Karin was working.

Karin with an "i".

Ferrill checked his watch. He had a little over two hours to kill.

Ferrill pulled into the parking garage at 1:15. He drove up to the "C" level. There was a block of ten empty spaces between C-45 and the elevator. Ferrill parked in C-23. He checked his watch again; He closed his eyes and willed his breathing to slow.

Ferrill saw lights flash against the walls of the lower level. He heard the squeal of tires turning against the concrete surface.

Ferrill pulled on his rubber mask. He pulled the hood of his jacket over his head. A black SUV turned the corner. It stopped behind Ferrill's car. A man stepped out, leaving the vehicle running. He walked to Ferrill's car and tapped on the driver's window.

Ferrill reached into the center console. His gloved fingers slid through the rings of a knuckle knife. The man tapped harder on the window.

"Hey, buddy. You're in my parking pla—"

Ferrill pulled the door handle and slammed his shoulder into the door. The man stumbled backward.

"What the hell—?"

His eyes bulged when he saw the horrible mask. He ran for the SUV.

Ferrill closed the distance. He shoved the blade into the man's back. A scream began just before Ferrill clamped his hand over the man's mouth. The man crumpled to the ground. Ferrill opened the rear hatch of the SUV. He dragged the man and lifted him inside. The man's eyes opened.

"Please..." he whispered.

Ferrill shoved the blade into the man's mouth. He pulled the knife back and wiped the blood on the man's jacket. Ferrill closed the hatch and drove the SUV into the C-24 parking space. He climbed out, keyed the remote to lock the doors, and pocketed the keys.

Ferrill hurried to his car. He took a jug of water from the back seat and washed down the man's spilled blood. The diluted stream ran down the banked concrete floor.

Ferrill saw another flash of headlights. He hid between his car and the SUV. The approaching car turned the corner and parked.

In the space marked C-45.

Karin climbed out of her car and removed a duffel bag from the back seat. She pulled the strap over her shoulder and walked toward the elevator. Ferrill moved silently between the vehicles. He crept up behind the girl.

He grabbed her around the waist with his left

hand.

Karin's four years of self-defense training kicked in automatically. She drove her right elbow into the attacker's ribs.

"*Oooof!*"

Ferrill struggled for breath. The chloroform-soaked rag in his right hand fell to the ground. Karin grabbed Ferrill's left wrist with both hands. She dropped her head and spun, twisting Ferrill's arm behind his back.

"*You bitch!*" he hissed.

Karin pushed Ferrill toward the rear of the SUV. She tripped him and threw her weight against him as he fell. Ferrill's head struck the corner of the steel bumper, slicing open the rubber mask and opening a deep cut over his right eye. Karin leapt to her feet. She bounced on her toes—adrenaline coursing through her. She held her hands in front of her, ready to strike again.

"Get up, you son-of-a-bitch! I will *kill* you!"

Ferrill's right eye was filled with blood. He did not register a word Karin said. He blinked his left eye and focused on the concrete beneath him.

Blood. HIS blood.

Evidence.

Ferrill shook with rage. He pushed to his feet. Karin jumped forward and launched her knee into Ferrill's gut. With his one good eye, Ferrill saw Karin preparing to kick him again. He jumped to the side. Her foot only grazed him.

This gave him the access he needed. Ferrill leapt

forward and fired his stun gun beneath Karin's perfect breasts. She crumpled to the ground.

Ferrill was exhausted but had no time to spare. He had his objective. Ferrill loaded Karin's limp body into the trunk of his car. Her duffel bag went into the back seat. He took a gallon of bleach and splashed it over the bumper of the SUV and the concrete where his blood had dripped.

Ten

Karin opened her eyes. It took her several seconds to focus. She sat on a cold concrete floor. Every muscle in her body ached.

Karin stared ahead at her legs and feet. Her shoes and socks were gone but her feet were not bound. She pulled her hands in front of her. Her heart sank when she heard the tinkle of chain against the concrete. The shackles around her wrists were attached to the concrete wall at shoulder height, with several feet of slack between them.

Karin jumped when the duffel bag landed in her lap.

"Put it on," the hideous monster said.

Karin did not immediately understand. Seconds later, she knew what he wanted.

He wants to rape me in my uniform. Isn't that what we're selling? The goddamn fantasy?

Karin swore silently at herself.

You didn't have to take the stupid job. Of course, it paid more money—the cost of staring at your body was added to the freaking menu! But that money isn't worth much when you're about to be raped...

Or worse.

Karin stood. She looked around the dimly lit

room. She was certain they were underground. The place smelled of old earth and grease.

"I can't change without my hands."

Ferrill approached her carrying a wide leather belt attached to yet another chain. He stopped five feet away and held up the knuckle knife.

"Touch me with a foot—I will take your toes—one at a time. Touch me with a hand—I take your fingers."

Karin nodded.

Ferrill attached the chain to the wall. He fastened the belt around Karin's waist, his gloved hands moving steadily. He barely touched Karin's skin.

Ferrill stood to the side and stared into Karin's eyes. She could hear him breathing—it sounded more like an animal than a man.

"Lift your hand."

Ferrill removed the left shackle and then the right. He moved away.

Karin changed her top. She peeked to see if the masked man was watching. He was not. He was busy clearing the top of a wooden table.

So that's where it will happen. Will he tie me up? Of course he will. He's strong, but he's not a skilled fighter. Should I try to take him down? He'll torture me if I fail.

But is he going to let me go?

No. One of us is going to die in this place.

Karin took off her shorts. She pulled the uniform shorts from the bag.

"No!"

Karin jumped. The shorts fell to the floor.

"All of it," Ferrill snapped. His voice broke—coming in a tense, primal growl.

Karin froze. The only thing left in her bag was...

The pantyhose.

She took them from the bag, watching for his reaction. She saw him lick his lips behind the mask. This frightened Karin more than anything. It didn't make sense. Why did he want her layered in clothing if he was going to rape her?

Because he's insane.

Karin no longer cared about rape. She did not want to die. She made up her mind. When the time came, she would try to execute the most lethal offensive attack she knew. She rehearsed the moves in her mind until—

Ferrill retrieved the left shackle and stepped toward Karin.

"Lift your arm," he said.

Karin raised her arm. At the same time, she slid her left foot between Ferrill's legs. She hooked her foot around his ankle. She launched a front kick at Ferrill's knee with every bit of strength she had. Ferrill moved just enough to avoid having his kneecap shattered. He screamed and fell on his back.

Karin fell to her knees and grabbed the ankle of Ferrill's injured leg. He screamed again. Karin felt the chain tug at the belt around her waist. She pulled on Ferrill's leg in panic and desperation. He was almost too far away. Ferrill kicked with his good leg. He missed twice and then connected with Karin's shoulder. Her hands slipped, but she did not let go of the ankle. Karin pulled him closer. One inch. Two. And then, four.

Just a little closer and I'll kick this asshole's balls up between his eyes…

Ferrill's next kick hit Karin in the jaw. She lost her grip on his ankle as she fell backward. Ferrill pulled himself out of Karin's reach. Both of them lay on the floor, breathing heavily.

Karin moaned and rolled her head to the side. She spit out two teeth and a mouthful of blood. Ferrill struggled to get to his feet. He stood, supporting most of his weight on his uninjured leg. He shook his finger at Karin.

"You will *pay* for that! I warned you. I told you, Mommy. I *told* you!"

Karin tried to focus her eyes.

Mommy? Oh, my God…he's out of his mind!

Ferrill disappeared down a dark tunnel. Karin heard the sound of a car door. Ferrill returned carrying a portable torch. He lit it, producing a five-inch flame. He crossed the room.

"Get up."

Karin stood.

"Back against the wall," Ferrill said.

Karin shook her head.

Ferrill grabbed the top of Karin's shirt and yanked it down. He moved the torch toward her breasts. Karin backed away until she bumped into the wall. Ferrill grabbed the left wrist restraint.

"Put it on," he said.

Karin looked into the flame. She took the metal

shackle from Ferrill with trembling hands. She held it against the back of her wrist and reached for the clasp. The shackle fell and swung out of reach.

Ferrill roared like a wild animal.

"I warned you! I told you! It's all your fault, Mommy! I told you!"

Ferrill jabbed the torch at Karin's breast. She screamed and grabbed the torch, burning her hand. She threw the torch to the ground. Karin fell to her knees, sobbing.

"Please…please…"

Ferrill grabbed the shackle and cuffed Karin's left wrist. He pulled her to her feet. He gripped her left arm and reached into his pocket with his other hand.

"I warned you."

Ferrill drove the knife through the palm of Karin's hand. She screamed even louder. Ferrill shackled her other wrist. He picked up the torch, turned it off, and moved it to the other side of the room. He pushed a table toward Karin, stopping a few feet away. Karin's cries became weak whimpers. She leaned against the taut chains, her head hanging lifelessly. Ferrill threw a glass of water into her face. He removed the belt and pushed Karin's shoulders, bending her over the table. He pulled on her shorts, but became frustrated and cut them off with the knife. Ferrill removed his gloves. His hands shook in anticipation. He rested his hands on Karin's hips and then slid them down the outside of her thighs.

A fresh blast of pain shocked Karin from her catatonic state.

"Help! Help me! Please help m—!"

Ferrill shoved Karin's shorts into her mouth. He stroked her legs again and could wait no more. He thrust his groin against her. He had never known such pleasure.

It was over in seconds. Ferrill put on his gloves. He peeled off Karin's pantyhose while she sobbed. He picked up the torch, the water jug, and the glass, and returned them to his car.

Karin remained on the table. Jolts of pain racked her body. Her thoughts were erratic.

And then a single thought formed in her consciousness.

She was bound and virtually naked—but she had not been raped.

Karin bolted upright when cold liquid splashed against her head.

But this was not water. The smell was unmistakable.

Gasoline.

"No!" she screamed.

Karin ran to her right, pulling the chain of the left shackle taut. She jerked her arm against the cuff. The blood from the knife wound lubricated her hand and wrist. Her ruined hand slipped through the shackle. Karin ran in the opposite direction, willing to break every bone in her hand for a chance at freedom.

She looked up.

Karin saw the strike of the wood match and its flight through the air.

The last thing she saw was the monster walking

away behind the wall of flames.

throw up. I'm not going to be able to make it."

"One moment please."

"Mr. Ferrill, we have a scheduled departure in fifty minutes."

"Check my record," Ferrill snapped. "I have *never* called in sick. Never!"

"That is commendable, Mr. Ferrill. However, I know you understand the nature of our business—"

"Look," Ferrill said. "Say the word and I will come in. I'm only minutes away. Maybe when I puke all over some passengers you will realize your mistake. What is your name? I need it for my records."

"I'm sorry, Mr. Ferrill. You're putting us in a terrible bind."

Ferrill ended the call and dropped the phone onto the passenger seat.

****

Casper closed the door behind him. He switched on a tiny flashlight. He was in the kitchen. It was spotless; no dishes in the sink. The stainless steel dish drainer next to the sink was empty. A dish towel hung perfectly level from the handle of the oven. Casper moved through the doorway.

He opened the door into a half-bath. It was also spotless.

What kind of bachelor is this? Maybe he has a maid. A maid who wears pantyhose.

Stop it. Finish the search and get the hell out of here.

The living room was neat and tidy. So was the

main bathroom. The first bedroom he came to was empty. The closet held coats and other winter clothing. There was one room left.

Ferrill's bedroom was just what Casper expected. The furnishings were plain and sparse. The full-sized bed was made. Only one door remained. The closet.

The closet had double doors.

Strange. A walk-in-closet in a house this small?

The tickle.

The tickle at the back of his mind. It felt like a fingernail…scratching the back of his neck.

From the inside.

Casper gripped his pistol and pulled it from the pocket of the windbreaker. He opened the door.

He jumped when automatic lights activated.

His knees grew weak. His vision swam. He was nauseous.

Casper ran to the bathroom, dropped to his knees, and emptied his belly into the toilet. He exhaled three deep breaths, flushed away the evidence, leapt to his feet, and ran back to the closet.

Casper stared in disbelief at the half-mannequin. The pantyhose. The small, white shoes.

I've seen those shoes…

Casper turned and looked at the far wall. Pairs of pantyhose hung clipped to hangers. And above them…

Casper stepped closer. Four pairs of athletic shoes lined the top shelf. Casper's gaze was drawn to one pair. He picked them up. Pulled them in front of him.

These were Kathy Halliday's shoes.

Casper's lips trembled. He shook all over. He

And then my friendship with Cheng Sun and his son-in-law, Jonathan Kwan, brought my dream back to life.

Casper looked into the sky as a cloud covered the sun.

"I made it, Sonny Cheng. I'm a police officer. I wish you could have been here to see it. I would have been lost without you."

Casper climbed out of the car and brushed donut crumbs from his jeans and sweatshirt. He was dressed casually. He had no desire to flaunt his freedom to anyone here.

Casper checked in at the desk and filled out the necessary paperwork. The lady behind the counter called a guard to escort him. Casper recognized the guard immediately. The guard cocked his head and stared.

"Is that you, Halliday?"

Casper laughed and offered his hand.

"In the flesh, Wombat."

Wilbur Orlon Batch did not care for his first and middle names. Inside Fishkill's walls, he was "Wombat" if he liked you and "Mr. Batch" if he didn't.

Batch shook Casper's hand heartily.

"Is this your first trip back?"

"My fourth," Casper said. "I must have come on your days off."

"You're looking good, man," Batch said. "We heard all about you helping the cops bust those kidnappers."

"I was just a little part of that," Casper said.

"Sure, you were," Batch said. "Are you still working at the port for old Cheng?"

Casper's smile faded.

"No. Sonny Cheng passed away a little over a year ago."

"I'm sorry to hear that," Batch said. "Personally, I think the guy should have got a medal instead of a jail term. You two were pretty tight, huh?"

"Yeah," Casper said. "Pretty tight. I had to resign from the job at the port. I got a new one."

Casper showed Batch his badge.

"No waaaay!" Batch said. "Is that thing real?"

Casper produced his other credentials.

"Well, I'll be damned," Batch said. "Whoever heard of such a thing? An ex-con with a badge."

Casper held up his finger.

"An ex-con with a clear record."

"I bet Shane Murphy *loves* you," Batch said.

"He hates me," Casper said. "Even more than the day I hit him in the head."

Batch shook his head.

"You should have hit him harder. I don't like that guy."

"You and me both," Casper said.

"So, are you here to see Tinsley?" Batch asked.

"Yes, sir."

Batch smiled.

"Just wait 'til you—nah, I'm not saying any more."

"Okay," Casper said. "You have me curious. Let's go."

They walked into the visiting room. Batch showed Casper to a booth. Batch opened and Tinsley walked through wearing a broad grin. Casper's jaw dropped. They shook hands and embraced while Batch looked on. They sat.

"Holy crap," Casper said. "Dude, you are a *monster*."

Mo had gained at least twenty pounds of muscle since Casper saw him last. Mo pushed back his sleeve and flexed his right arm.

"Hasta la vista, baby," he said in a bad impersonation of Arnold Schwarzenegger.

"This is all thanks to you, Caz," Mo said.

"Me?" Casper said. "What did I do?"

"I don't know what you did or said to Jerome Slade, but you sure got in his head, man," Mo said.

Casper shrugged.

"I don't get it."

"A little while after you left, Slade waved me over to his table at breakfast," Mo said. "He moved over and made room for me to sit down. That scared the shit out of me. I thought he was going to tell me I was about to eat my last meal. But he told me to meet him at the weight pit and he would show me some stuff. I thought his posse was gonna fall in the floor."

"Wow," Casper said. "All I did was tell him he was going to blow his parole."

"Well, he didn't blow it," Mo said. "He's gone."

"I know," Casper said. "You told me last time I was here."

"I'm kind of surprised he didn't look you up," Mo

said.

Casper laughed.

"Come on, Mo. It's not like we were friends."

"You showed him that you gave a shit," Mo said. "This place is full of dudes that never had that."

Casper leaned forward.

"What about you?"

Mo stared at Casper for several seconds.

"I got three brothers, man. Aunts and uncles, and more cousins than I can count. Them, and everybody else in my hood cares about one thing above everything else—how much of a bad-ass they are. That ain't a good thing. People act tough because they're *afraid.* You act tough to survive—because there are people around every corner who prey on the weak. The helpless.

"People been calling me 'Queer', and 'Homo', and 'Fairy' all my life. They didn't even know if it was true. On my eighteenth birthday, my brothers and a couple of my cousins told me they had a surprise for me. We went to this apartment building, climbed some stairs and stopped outside a door. They held me down, stripped me naked, and threw me inside. There was a whore in the room wearing nothing but panties. She came over and grabbed my...my thing. I...I *couldn't,* man. I was scared and I felt sick...I threw up on her arm. She started screaming and hittin' me on the head. She picked up a lamp and swung it at me. The lamp broke. "

Mo lifted his right forearm, revealing a six-inch scar.

"She swung it again and sliced me open. Then she was screaming about me getting blood all over her carpet."

Casper bit his lip.

"In two-and-a-half years you never told me any of this."

"It ain't exactly my favorite story," Mo said. "I made it out the door. At least that crazy woman didn't chase me. My brothers and cousins were gone. When I got home, they wouldn't let me in. My old man was long gone by then and my mom had to have my brothers' money to get by. They said I had shamed them and I was no longer a part of the family."

"Ouch," Casper said.

"Yeah," Mo said. "I didn't have anywhere to go, man. I had to hide at night. I got food at the mission, but there were some scary people there. Finally, I begged my way into working as a mule for a drug pusher. Shit, the cops were already watching that dude. I got busted in two weeks. So here I am. That's enough depressing shit. Are you finished with cop school yet, or did you flunk out?"

Casper raised his badge.

"I'm officially a rookie."

Mo laughed.

"I knew that already. Hell, I've already met part of your fan club."

"Who's that?" Casper asked.

"This fine looking blond woman from the TV news paid me a visit just a few days ago. All she wanted to talk about was you—well, you and your girlfriend the lady cop. Man, you work fast, son."

Casper was as confused as he looked.

"A reporter was here? Asking about me?"

"I don't think she's trying to make you look bad," Mo said. "We talked about you and those kidnappers and the Chief's daughter and your girlfriend—she sounded like a fan to me. She asked me if I called you by your nickname—Ghost Man."

Mo smiled.

"I told her I call you Sugar-Pants."

"You didn't," Casper said.

"I guess you'll have to watch the news," Mo said.

"I don't like this," Casper said.

"Everybody loves a hero, Ghost Man," Mo said.

Twelve

Dwight Livingston removed his reading glasses and massaged his temples. The Chief of Detectives' morning had gotten off to a good start despite the pressures associated with the East Village murder. Two strong cups of coffee lifted his spirits until he received the fax lying on his desk.

Another grisly murder occurred the night before, this one fifty miles west of Baltimore, Maryland. This was well out of Livingston's jurisdiction, but the information in the fax led him to believe the cases were related. Livingston fully expected his people to be involved in the investigation.

Livingston jumped when his secretary's voice sounded over the intercom.

"Chief, the gentlemen are here for your briefing."

"Good. Send them in."

Livingston stood and shook hands with Senior Detectives Miller and Washington. They sat. Livingston spun the fax paper around in front of the detectives.

"I guess you've seen this?"

Miller and Washington nodded.

"It came in right after six this morning," Detective Washington said.

Livingston looked both detectives in the eyes.

"What do your guts tell you? Is this the same guy?"

"Christ, I hope so," Miller said. "I don't want to think there are two psychos out there who could do things like this."

Livingston tapped the sheet of paper.

"This latest victim was eight years younger than Mrs. Cappelletti. What else do we know?"

"They were both very attractive," Washington said.

"Baltimore PD forwarded two photos of Karin Armstrong," Miller said. "She and two other young ladies are featured on billboards for a new restaurant chain called 'Babes'. Their waitress uniforms don't leave much to the imagination. This girl was smokin' hot."

Detective Washington winced.

"Ouch, Dan!"

"What? Oh. Shit. I'm sorry," Miller said.

Chief Livingston scowled.

"Let's not make mistakes like that in front of the media."

"Of course not, sir," Miller said.

Livingston tapped his pen against a legal pad.

"The Cappelletti case. What do we know?"

The detectives shared a look.

"We don't have jack shit, sir," Miller said. "Whoever this guy is, he had every base covered. No fingerprints. Not even a freaking *hair*, Dwight."

"There was a dusting of cake flour on the floor of the bakery kitchen," Washington said. "We should have at least gotten a partial footprint."

"He was wearing a cover over his shoes," Miller said. The detective leaned forward.

"You know what this means, sir."

Livingston leaned back in his chair.

"Yes. These are not crimes of passion. He's done his homework—and he does not intend to get caught."

"And he won't stop," Washington said. "Until we stop him."

Detective Washington's phone rang. He stood, answered the call, and walked to the corner of the room. He listened and made only short replies. Washington ran a hand through his hair and over his face. Livingston and Miller waited. Washington ended the call.

"That was my contact with Baltimore PD. The killer took Karin Armstrong in the parking garage of her apartment building."

"How do we know that?" Livingston asked.

Washington blew out a breath.

"Apparently, another tenant got in the way. A Caucasian male, age thirty-two, was found murdered in the cargo area of his late-model SUV—stabbed in the back and through the mouth. The second wound was the cause of death. The vehicle was parked near Armstrong's car."

"Shit," Livingston said. "Anything else?"

"Yeah," Washington said. "The dead guy's blood on the floor was diluted—washed down with water. There's a high concentration of bleach around the SUV."

"Every move is premeditated," Livingston said.

"Yes, sir," Washington said.

"But why bleach?" Livingston asked. "Unless the killer had reason to believe he was leaving behind evidence?"

Washington shrugged.

"Maybe Miss Armstrong was not a helpless victim," Livingston said. "Check that out."

Washington and Miller nodded and made notes.

"Where did they find the body?" Livingston asked. "Do we know?"

"It was a rural area, outside the city," Miller said. "In an old abandoned service tunnel. There are lots of these things left over from fifty to a hundred years ago—before the highways filled up with eighteen-wheelers."

"Who found her?" Livingston asked.

"We don't know. 9-1-1 got an anonymous call from a gas station pay phone," Washington said.

"Great," Livingston said. "We need to get some people down there—"

"We have that covered, sir," Miller said.

"Who are you sending?" Livingston asked.

Miller and Washington pointed at each other.

"We're driving down as soon as we leave here."

"Good," Livingston said. "I'm going to have the DA, the Governor, and the mayor up my ass—"

The secretary's voice over the intercom interrupted Chief Livingston

"I'm sorry, sir. The mayor is on line one."

Chief Livingston sighed.

"Good luck, gentlemen."

Thirteen

Robert Ferrill walked into the cafe. Eddie Bailey waved him over to the table where he sat alone with a cup of coffee. Eddie stared at the bandage over Ferrill's eye.

"Holy crap, Bob. What happened to you?"

"It was my own damned fault," Ferrill said. "I was going back to my room last night and my foot slipped on the top step. My forehead hit the corner of the brick wall."

"Ouch!" Eddie said. He leaned closer. "Did you go to the emergency room?"

"Nah," Ferrill said. "It's just a cut. I'll have a little battle scar, that's all."

"That's what insurance is for, Bob," Eddie said. "The hotel has plenty, I bet. Maybe there's something wrong with the stairs—"

"No," Ferrill snapped. He stared at Bailey's smart-ass grin. He thought of how much he would love to watch the shock on Eddie Bailey's face when he shoved his knife between the man's stupid lips.

Bailey's eyes narrowed.

"Are you going to be okay today?"

Ferrill yawned.

"Of course."

It had been a long night for Ferrill. The cut was deep and bled considerably. He would not risk a doctor visit. He only had to make it to the end of the day—a day where he would have to answer the same stupid questions over and over again.

Ferrill had only had about three hours of sleep. He took his car to a self-service car wash and cleaned it thoroughly. In his hotel room, he worked on the cut above his eye for over an hour. He showered three times.

Ferrill lay back on the bed, thoroughly exhausted. *Stupid bitch…*

He would not make the same mistake again; assuming every female was weak and defenseless. For a moment, Ferrill admired the girl's resourcefulness. But only for a moment.

Now, with the trouble caused by her resistance, he wished he had cut off her head.

Karin with an "i".

She didn't just die.

She had to fry.

Ferrill closed his eyes. Sleep would come, he had no doubt.

But not before the memories.

When puberty arrived for young Robert Ferrill, his father had been gone for six years. The last time Robert saw his father he was fighting his way through the front door of their tiny house with a butcher knife protruding from his left shoulder. The knife was the work of Robert's deranged mother. His father made it to his old pickup truck and disappeared forever.

Years before, Robert's father had begged his mother to seek medical help for her violent outbreaks. She was diagnosed with severe bipolar disorder and prescribed medication to control her manic depression and rage.

But Mrs. Ferrill despised the way the medication made her feel and refused to take it. She bought illegal street drugs that made her condition even worse.

Young Robert never knew or understood how his mother and he survived financially. There was never a lot of food in the house, but the electricity and heating continued. His mother left the house often without explanation, particularly at night. Robert fended for himself when it came to attending school. He liked learning, although he hated the social aspect. He was picked on by others his age. He would have suffered physically if not for the fact that something about the look in Robert's dark eyes made the other children stay away.

Robert's mother opened his bedroom door one night. He pretended to be asleep but his mother was not fooled. She yanked the blankets off of him and screamed.

Robert was touching himself—while wearing a pair of his mother's pantyhose.

His mother beat him with her hands. She beat him with anything she could reach. Their neighbors had given up on calling the police long ago. Nothing seemed to change and the people of the neighborhood wanted nothing to do with the crazy Ferrill woman.

Robert's mother stayed at home more. She spent most of her waking hours with glazed-over eyes—often talking to herself. She entertained lots of men, who neither knew nor cared that Robert existed. Mrs. Ferrill disappeared into her bedroom with these men.

One night, Mrs. Ferrill took a handful of pills. She beckoned Robert to sit next to her on the sofa. She took his hand and told him to touch her. Her head lolled backward and fell against the back of the sofa. She moaned. Seconds later she sat up and looked at Robert's naked erection.

She leapt to her feet; spit flying from her lips in a fit of rage. The beatings came again.

The next night, Mrs. Ferrill opened the door for yet another strange man. They disappeared into the bedroom. Robert heard another knock at the door moments later. Mrs. Ferrill let another man inside.

But this time, the man opened the door to Robert's room. He turned off the light.

"W-who are you?" Robert asked. "What are you doing?"

The man undressed.

"You're a handsome little bitch," the man said, quietly.

The man pulled back the covers and climbed into the bed. Robert tried to get away. The man grabbed him by the hair and whispered in his ear.

"You will do exactly what I say, or I'm going to press this pillow over your face until you can't breathe anymore. Do you understand?"

Robert nodded through his tears. He did things. He had things done to him. Things that hurt. But when the man got dressed and left, Robert was still alive.

He lay on his side, wide awake, until the morning sun lit his room. Robert stood, wincing. He tiptoed to his mother's room. He pushed open the door and began to cry. His mother was sprawled across her bed, a sheet covering only part of one leg. She opened her eyes to find Robert standing at her bedside. He stood board-straight with tears dripping from both cheeks.

"What?" his mother hissed between clenched teeth.

"Mom. That man…he made me—"

His mother bolted from the bed with her hands flailing. A backhand connected with Robert's jaw. He fell to the floor, sobbing even louder. His mother kicked him.

"What's the *matter*, Robert? It's okay for *me* to do whatever I have to do to keep a roof over our heads and food on the table while you lie around like a little prince? Well, not any more, Prince Robert. If you're not willing to earn your keep, then get the hell out!"

She kicked him again.

"Get out! Get out of my sight!"

The same man returned the next night. Robert did not resist. He did as he was told. The man talked constantly, whispering in Robert's ear. He spoke in great detail of the many ways he would murder Robert if he ever caused any trouble.

The man finally climbed out of the bed. He turned on a lamp and dressed.

"Tell your old lady I'll be back tomorrow night," the man said. "I have to go out of town for four days and then I'll be back."

Robert clutched a blanket against his neck and nodded.

The man returned the next night at the same time. He undressed. Robert moved to the side of the bed. The man slid beneath the sheet. Robert rolled onto his side to face the man and smiled.

And then he drove a pair of scissors through the man's neck.

The man clutched his throat and made gurgling sounds as Robert diverted the spurting blood with a pillow.

Robert leaned closer.

"I could hold this pillow over your face until you can't breathe. But that's no fun, is it?"

Robert leaned closer, staring into the man's bulging eyes. Robert giggled. He kissed the man on the nose. He giggled again.

"It's funny, you know? You are about to die...

"And I've never felt more *alive...*"

Robert crept down the hallway. He put his ear against his mother's door and listened. He heard the unmistakable sounds of sex. Robert took a chair from the kitchen and wedged it beneath the doorknob. He hurried through the front door and circled to the back of the house where he had hidden two gasoline cans he stole from neighbors.

Robert doused the outside walls of his mother's bedroom with gasoline. He entered the front door of the house and poured the remainder of the gasoline beneath his mother's bedroom door. He dropped the lit match and ran.

Police found young Robert Ferrill two blocks away. He was sitting on the curb wearing his pajamas and one shoe. He clutched his knees against his chest, rocking back and forth and staring at the flames.

"Is that your house, son?" A policeman asked.

Robert continued to stare. He nodded.

"Do you know what happened?" the policeman asked.

Robert shook his head. He coughed.

"I woke up. Couldn't...breathe. I ran..."

Two policemen held out their hands.

"Come on, son. We'll take you somewhere warm."

"My mother?" Robert said in a whisper.

"She's gone, son. I'm sorry."

Robert nodded, relishing the moment all alone.

****

A child psychiatrist interviewed thirteen-year-old Robert Ferrill. He offered little information. Most of the doctor's questions he met with a blank stare and would not answer at all. He was taken to a clinic and given a physical examination. The doctor phoned the police and demanded they send a representative to her office immediately. A sergeant and the department psychologist arrived within a half hour. They made introductions, and the doctor closed her office door. She rubbed her face with both hands.

The physician lay four x-rays on her desk. She used a pen as a pointer.

"Here. Here. Here. And here. These are broken bones that were never treated. As far as we can find, the boy has no medical history since birth other than mandatory vaccinations. He has more cuts, bruises, and abrasions than I can count. I took photographs. Lots of photos."

The doctor paused to catch her breath.

"And he's been sodomized. Repeatedly."

She stared at her visitors with narrowed eyes and flaring nostrils.

"Please tell me whoever did this is in custody."

"We don't know where his father is," the psychologist said. "No one has seen or heard from him in years. The boy's mother died when their home burned down."

"It was arson," the sergeant said. "Gasoline."

"Do you think the boy did it?" the doctor asked.

"We don't know," the sergeant said. "We can't prove it. The neighbors we interviewed described Mrs. Ferrill as 'crazy', and probably mentally ill. She screamed a lot—even after her husband disappeared."

"Crazy enough to commit suicide by fire?" the doctor asked.

"She wasn't alone," the psychologist said. "She and a 'friend' were found together."

"Where her bedroom used to be," the sergeant said.

The doctor shook her head.

"This boy needs help. He's suffered more abuse than—I'm sorry. I've run out of comparisons. This case makes me *ill*. Whoever did this to this boy needs to suffer the death penalty."

The sergeant sighed.

"Not in our fair state, Doctor."

Robert was housed in an orphanage not far from his former home. He had weekly appointments with a child psychologist. The psychologist was amazed at Robert's condition. Robert was calm and focused and seemed untroubled after the tragedy. Robert never missed another day of school.

After two months, Robert was placed with a foster family. This family had fostered four different teenagers through junior high and high school. Three of the four had gone on to college. The other joined the military. The couple had no children of their own and derived great joy from providing a solid home for older children that so many were not interested in fostering.

The couple drove to the office of the social worker that had handled the foster case. They left their house just as soon as Robert got on the school bus.

"Is there a problem?" the social worker asked.

"Yes," the man said. "We—we can't keep this boy."

"Uh…I'm sorry?" the social worker stammered. "It's only been three days—"

"Four," the distraught foster mother said. She sat on the edge of her chair, wringing her hands.

"This is most unusual," the social worker said. "We're not able to—"

"Don't tell me what you're not able to do!" the man snapped. He took several deep breaths.

"I'm sorry. It's just—"

"I've been missing…clothing," the woman said. "No. I've been missing underwear. Not my bras. My…panties. And my pantyhose."

"The boy took them," the man said.

"I didn't want to look for them." The woman said. She began to cry.

"I found them. Folded. In the back of Robert's closet. And he's…he's different somehow. Different from when we met him here. In only a couple of days, his eyes…his face they're…*darker*. He stares at me…like he's looking into my soul."

The man pulled his wife to her feet and pressed her head to his chest as she sobbed.

"We bought clothes for Robert," the man said. "I'll leave them with you. He's not setting foot in our home again. Do you hear me?"

The social worker slumped into her chair.

"I'll have to make some calls."

"You do whatever you have to," the man said. He looked at his watch.

"We have to go. We're to meet the locksmith in twenty minutes."

****

Robert Ferrill had three hours left in his workday. He made his way to the dining room, taking his usual table in a far corner. He placed his cup of coffee and opened his briefcase. Here, he would take at least an hour to complete paperwork that required less than half of that time. The paperwork was only an excuse.

The kitchen and dining staff arrived. The majority were women between the ages of twenty and forty-five; fourteen women in all. They wore matching uniforms and comfortable shoes

And sheer stockings.

Fourteen

Sergeant Rice stepped behind the podium and called the meeting room to order. He referred to the white-board to his right and the short list of information they had on the Cappelletti murder. Rice then referred to the white-board to his left. This board listed the information from the Armstrong murder.

"There has been no official statement connecting these murders, but every precinct is on alert and expected to cooperate with the Baltimore authorities until that determination is made official. We certainly don't want to think there are multiple psychopaths operating simultaneously.

"In both cases, the lack of physical evidence shows a high level of planning and execution."

Sergeant Rice took a moment to look at faces around the room.

"In spite of our efforts to guard this information, some members of the press have taken it upon themselves to refer to the killings as 'serial-style'. This is the kind of thing that drives ratings, sells advertising, and makes news careers. We know that. But it doesn't make our jobs any easier. They're already referring to the killer as 'Specter' and 'Phantom'."

Sergeant Rice made brief eye contact with Casper Halliday before dismissing the room full of officers. He would not repeat aloud the other name he heard on the late night news.

The Ghost Man.

Casper and Leo Sanchez, his training partner, had an uneventful morning until eleven-thirty. A young Caucasian man burst out of the door of a small shop. He slipped to the ground, got to his feet and ran up the sidewalk in the same direction as the patrol car. A short Oriental man wielding a sawed-off shotgun chased the young man, screaming at the top of his lungs. People on the sidewalks ran or dropped to the ground. Sanchez turned on lights and siren and raced ahead of the young man. Sanchez halted at the next intersection. The young man was fast and motivated. He ran around the patrol car as Casper and Leo climbed out.

"I've got the gun!" Leo shouted.

"Roger!" Casper said. He chased down the runner in the next block and wrestled him to the ground.

"He was gonna blow me away, man!"

Casper pulled the man's hands behind his back and cuffed him.

"I'm guessing he had a reason," Casper said.

The young man began to cry.

"I'm sick, man. If I don't get a shot I'm gonna die."

Casper frisked the man and found a knife in his jacket pocket. He helped the man to his feet.

"I'm gonna die, man."

"You're not going to die," Casper said. "You're just going to feel like shit for about a month."

Sanchez arrived with the shop owner. Sanchez held the shotgun.

"This gentleman says this young man attempted to rob him while holding a knife."

"Like this one?" Casper said.

The Oriental man pointed.

"That's it! That's it!"

"Casper, if you'll take the prisoner to the car, I'll escort Mr. Li back to his place of business. His son will watch the store while Mr. Li comes to the station to make his statement."

"Got it," Casper said.

"You keeping my gun?" Mr. Li said. "That's not fair!"

Sanchez looked around. He leaned down and whispered.

"I'll give it back when we get in your store. Try not to pull it out every chance you get, Mr. Li."

Mr. Li spat on the ground and glared at the would-be robber.

"Worthless cur dog junkie boy! Nobody takes my money! You hear me? You tell your junkie friends!"

Sanchez pulled on Mr. Li's arm.

"Let's go, sir."

Leo Sanchez parked behind the precinct station. A silver Mercedes-Benz drove past and stopped in front of the station door. Casper recognized the passenger.

"Leo, would you mind taking the suspect into the station? I need to check on something."

"Not a problem," Leo said.

A broad-shouldered man in an expensive suit hurried from the driver's side of the car to the passenger side. The door opened before he got there.

Charlie Talbot ignored her husband's outstretched hand and climbed out of the car. Matt Talbot put his hands on Charlie's shoulders and leaned forward to kiss her. Charlie turned her head, allowing only a brush of his lips against her cheek. She stepped past Matt and walked into the station.

Matt slammed the passenger door and returned to the driver's side. He paused when he noticed two young women approaching on the sidewalk. He said something. The women stopped. They shifted their feet and smiled.

Matt said something else and the women laughed before waving and continuing on their way. They giggled and whispered. Matt stood there long enough to admire their departure.

Casper wanted to give Mr. Matt Talbot a black eye of his own.

What an asshole.

Casper pushed through the back door of the station at the end of his shift. He looked to his right in time to see Charlie Talbot crush out a cigarette butt with her shoe. She smiled politely and turned toward Max's Cigar Lounge. Casper ran to catch up with her.

"Hi," Casper said.

Charlie kept walking. She did not turn her head.

"Have we turned you into an alcoholic already?"

"No," Casper said. "I just wanted to see how you're doing."

Charlie stopped. She turned toward Casper while trying to keep the right side of her face out of his sight.

"Please don't turn into a guard dog, Officer Halliday. I have too many of those."

"I'm just trying to be a friend," Casper said.

"Thank you for your concern," Charlie said. "I am fine. Right as rain."

She continued walking.

Casper did not move. He knew it was dangerous to say anything more.

But he couldn't help it.

"You're better than this."

Charlie spun to face him.

"What? What did you say?"

Casper swallowed.

"You're better than him. You deserve better."

Charlie put her hands on her hips and laughed.

"You don't *know* me, Casper! Just who the hell do you think you are?"

"I *do* know you," Casper said. "You do a difficult, stressful job. An *important* job. And you don't need the money. You do it because you're a good person with a good heart."

Charlie's hands balled into fists. Her hands trembled and then relaxed. Her face changed from a look of rage to one of sadness. She blinked rapidly and looked down.

"I'm sorry," Casper said. "I shouldn't have—"

Charlie turned and walked away.

"Fuck off, Casper."

Fifteen

Casper unlocked his car. He heard someone calling his name. It was Sean Kelly.

"I've been trying to catch you," Sean said. "I heard Blair is going to resign. Is that true?"

"I think so," Casper said.

"What do you mean, you think so?" Sean said. "You don't know?"

"That's what she told me," Casper said.

Sean shook his head.

"That's crazy. She's been a good partner, man. She's smart. She could be a great detective. Hell, taking down those kidnappers and everything—I just don't get it."

"Yeah," Casper said. "It's too bad. Hey, are you hungry?"

"Famished," Sean said.

"Do you like burgers?" Casper asked.

"Are you kidding?" Sean said.

Sean spread the fingers of his left hand and ticked them off with his right.

"Donuts. Coffee. Burgers. Beer. I check off all the cop boxes."

"I know just the place," Casper said. "My treat. Climb in."

"You're on," Sean said.

Casper held open the door of the "A Simpler Time" diner while Sean walked through the door. Moments later, Mona Casey saw Casper. She ran on her tiptoes across the floor, threw her arms around his neck, and kissed his cheek.

"Hi, Mona," Casper said. "How are you?"

"I'm great," Mona said. She pretended to scowl. "What's in that sack, you *beast*?"

Casper laughed.

"Maybe I'll tell you and maybe I won't."

Mona smiled at Sean.

"Is this your friend?"

"Yes," Casper said. "Mona Casey, I would like you to meet my friend and co-worker, Sean Kelly."

Mona extended her hand. Sean shook it.

"It's a pleasure to meet you, Mona," Sean said.

"Likewise," Mona said. "A friend of Casper's is a friend of mine."

Mona swept a hand to her side.

"Your booth awaits you, gentlemen. Would you like to see the menu?"

"Actually," Casper said. "I've been telling Sean about the Mona-Special Burger. Would that be possible?"

"You got it," Mona said.

"Great," Casper said. He opened the bag in his hand. He took out a small windbreaker and a little pair of athletic shoes.

"I got these for Cody. I thought he might want to wear them to the zoo on Tuesday. His feet are growing."

"Casper—"

Mona looked at Sean.

"Your friend is *relentless*. He's going to turn my sweet little boy into a spoiled brat."

"Come on!" Casper said. "That's not possible. Cody is my homey."

"I can't believe you haven't put that on a t-shirt," Mona said.

Casper rubbed his chin.

"Hmmm…"

"Don't you *dare*, Casper Halliday," Mona said. "Let me get started on those burgers before you boys starve to death."

Casper handed the bag to Mona.

"Thank you, Casper," Mona said. She walked through the kitchen door.

Casper looked at Sean.

"She's cool, huh?"

"Very cool," Sean said. "And pretty, too."

"I met her and her son right here in this booth," Casper said. "Right after I got out of prison."

Sean smiled and shook his head.

"You know how weird that sounds, right?"

Casper shrugged.

"Yeah, I guess it does."

"Can I ask you something?" Sean said.

"Sure."

"I thought you and Blair were…you know. Dating, or something."

"Wait," Casper said. "You thought Mona and I— no. It's not like that. I hit it off with her little boy. We're like brothers now."

Casper leaned across the table.

"And Mona's a little bit older. She's like *your* age."

"Thanks a lot, young man," Sean said. "Blair is older than you, too."

Casper paused.

"As for Blair and me, I don't know what to tell you. The thing that went down at the port kind of messed us up. Blair was under a lot of pressure after it happened. Too many people wanted her to fill the role of 'Rookie-Woman-Super-Cop'."

"I'm sorry to hear that," Sean said. "I've never asked her about it, and she's never brought up the subject. She has seemed pretty...distracted lately."

Yeah," Casper said. "She thinks it's going to start all over again when people find out I'm with the department. I don't know how to deal with this."

Casper stared out the window.

"She hasn't been happy in a long time."

"I'm sorry, Caz," Sean said. "I hope things work out."

"Yeah," Casper said. "Look. The burgers from heaven have arrived."

Mona sat the two large platters on the table. Each contained a huge burger surrounded by fresh steaming French fries.

"Oh, *wow*," Sean said. "I've heard about burgers with a fried egg on top but I've never tried one."

Casper grabbed his burger with both hands.

"Hold on to your taste buds, Buddy."

Sean took a bite. He chewed three times. His eyes closed as his head rolled back. He spoke with his mouth still full.

"Oh, my God. I am in love."

Sean opened his eyes. He was looking right into Mona Casey's smiling face.

Casper fought to keep from laughing when Sean's face flushed red.

"You like it?" Mona asked.

Sean saluted.

"Ma'am, you are an artist beyond compare."

"That means yes, I think," Casper said.

"Thank you," Mona said.

"Now, Sean," Casper said. "Mona doesn't work in the kitchen. This is very special treatment."

"It certainly is," Sean said. "I am honored."

Mona waved her hand.

"Oh, stop it—both of you. You're embarrassing me."

She looked at Casper.

"So, what time do we need to be ready on Tuesday?"

"How about ten-thirty?" Casper said.

"We'll be ready," Mona said. "Cody is so excited."

"How about Wednesday?" Casper said. "I thought we might check out that place with the go-carts and bumper cars. They're supposed to have pretty good pizza, too."

"You don't have to spend all your free time with Cody," Mona said.

"I...don't have a lot going on right now," Casper said.

"We'll see," Mona said. "I'd better get back to my real job. It was a pleasure meeting you, Sean."

"The pleasure is all mine," Sean said. "All the way down to my stomach."

Mona laughed and laid her hand on Sean's arm.

"We'll see you later," Mona said. She walked toward the counter.

Sean took another bite and wiped his mouth. He looked at Casper.

"You're going to the zoo, huh?"

Casper nodded with his mouth full.

"Man, I haven't been to the zoo since...junior high, probably."

Casper swallowed.

"Do you want to come with us? You're more than welcome."

"Well...yeah. Sure," Sean said. "I'd like to go."

"I'll pick you up," Casper said. "I'm not real good with addresses, yet. But I could use the practice."

"Cool," Sean said. "I'll stand outside so you can't miss me."

Sixteen

Casper walked into his dark and empty apartment. He switched on the lights and the television. He tuned the TV to a food channel, lowered the volume, and took a beer he really didn't want from the icebox.

Casper never watched the programs, but the background provided a pleasant distraction. There was never any bad news on a food channel. Casper leaned against the bar that separated the kitchen from the living room.

What a strange day.

He had witnessed the signs of the continuing storm that was Charlie Talbot's marriage. And a short time later he had seen what he expected was the budding romance of two of his friends.

As for my own love life?

Casper didn't want to think about it. He wished he had a dog. Or a cat. But neither of those was practical.

Maybe I could get some fish. Or a turtle.

Casper looked at the television, where a room full of loud and happy people devoured platters of barbecued ribs. Casper raised his beer bottle.

"Am I pitiful or what?" he asked the crowd. "I should get a turtle. At least he could hear me."

Casper opened another beer and fell backward

into the sofa. He stared at his phone. He muted the television and dialed a familiar number.

Blair Hampton answered her phone without looking at the display. Casper heard Blair laugh. The sound filled him with warmth. It was a sound he had not heard in a long time. Conversation, laughing, and music filled the background.

"Hello?" Blair said.

"Hi, Blair. It's Casper."

"Oh."

Casper's heart sank. He heard the change in Blair's voice.

"Hang on a sec, okay?" Blair said. "It's noisy in here."

A few seconds later, Casper heard a door close. The background noise disappeared.

"There," Blair said. "That's better."

"It sounds like you're having a good time," Casper said.

Blair sighed.

"My parents are having another one of their Society Bashes. They threw a party for the son of their friends who just graduated in Europe—"

"Yeah, I remember," Casper said. "Bentley Moneywallet the Third or something like that."

"Why are you insulting someone you don't even know?" Blair said.

Casper was sorry he'd said anything.

"I was just kidding around," he said.

"He's actually a very nice young man," Blair said. "He's not *nearly* as pretentious as most of the people here right now."

There was an uncomfortable silence.

"What are we doing, Blair?" Casper asked.

"I don't know," Blair said. "You called me, remember?"

"I need to know where we stand," Casper said.

"Why?" Blair snapped. "Do you have somebody on the back burner?"

"No," Casper said. "Do you?"

Casper did not like the silence that followed. Blair's voice cracked.

"Casper...this...it's not going to work."

Casper knew she was crying.

"It's not your fault. It's mine. It was *my* decision to attend the academy. It was *my* decision to join the department..."

"I want you to be happy, Blair," Casper said.

"I don't know if I'll ever be happy, Casper. And that has nothing to do with you. It's just...

"I can't do this anymore. I've given notice to the department. One week from today will be my last day. This might be my last chance to start over. I'm almost twenty-six. I won't have opportunities forever. My father is seventy-five."

"I understand," Casper said. "It hurts, but I can't bear making you sad, Blair. I don't ever want to make you cry again."

Blair said something that Casper could not understand over her sobs.

"I want the best for you, Blair. I mean that.

"Goodbye."

Seventeen

Robert Ferrill pushed the shopping cart down the first aisle of the market. He saw an attractive young woman cross the end of the aisle ahead of him. He followed her at a distance until she turned and gave him an annoyed glance. Robert placed two cans of soup into his basket and turned his basket in the opposite direction.

You're safe for now, bitch.

Too close to home.

Ferrill waited in line at the register. The magazine rack to his left was filled with tabloid newspapers. A headline caught his eye.

Ghost Man Kills Again.

Another brutal murder leaves police baffled…

Ferrill put the paper into his basket.

****

Casper had a day off before he and Leo Sanchez moved to the evening shift for a week. Casper got dressed and looked up the address of the Private Investigation service where his father worked. The simple thing to do would be to ask his dad, but Casper preferred that Bobby Halliday not know what he was doing.

Casper entered the office of Mark Novak

Investigations. The receptionist was on the phone. She waved Casper toward a chair.

"Good morning," she said. "How may I help you?"

"I was hoping to speak to Mr. Novak," Casper said.

"Is he expecting you?"

"No, Ma'am."

"What is your name?"

"Casper Halliday."

The receptionist smiled.

"Are you Bobby's son?"

"Yes, Ma'am."

The receptionist stood and walked around the desk.

"Come on back. Mark will be thrilled."

She tapped twice on the office door and pushed it open.

"You'll never guess who's here."

Mark Novak raised his head.

"An angry philanderer."

"Not yet," the receptionist said. "But don't give up. The day is young. This is Casper Halliday."

Novak stood and crossed the room with his hand extended.

"Well, well, well. It's *Officer* Halliday, right?"

"Yes, sir," Casper said. "For almost a whole month."

"Yeah," Novak said. "I was with the department with your dad for a while. Did you know that?"

"Yes, sir. He told me."

Novak shook his head.

"I couldn't stick with it. I'm a little bit of a hot-head—"

"A little bit?" the receptionist said.

"Are you still here?" Novak said. He waved his hands at her.

"Shoo."

The receptionist winked at Casper.

"Good luck. He has issues."

"Yeah," Novak said. "I need a new receptionist."

"Good luck with that," she said.

"Have a seat Casper," Novak said. "Like I said, I get a little wound up and I sometimes have problems with authority; not the best combination for a cop. What can I do for you?"

Casper took a piece of paper from his pocket.

"Two things, really. First of all, I don't know how much surveillance costs. But I would like to know if this guy is…you know. Screwing around."

Novak looked at the paper. He narrowed his eyes.

"Matthew Talbot. Isn't that…? The hotshot quarterback? From the West Coast?"

"Yes, sir," Casper said. "He was drafted by the Giants but never played in a regular season game. He blew out a knee—"

Novak nodded.

"Yeah, I remember. He could have been a great one until he took an arrow to the knee."

"Excuse me?" Casper said.

Novak waved a hand.

"Never mind. That joke is older than you and me put together."

Novak stared at Casper.

"You're acting in the interest of his wife? What are you getting yourself into?" Novak said.

Casper fidgeted in the chair.

"He hits her."

Novak sat back and rubbed his chin.

"Are you sure?"

Casper nodded.

"She could turn him into the police and have him arrested for that," Novak said. "And bring twenty cops to his door. But she doesn't. That ought to tell you something."

"If he's cheating on her, maybe she doesn't know," Casper said.

"You're going to burn yourself out, Casper," Novak said.

"What does that mean?" Casper said.

"You're the guy who walks by the dog pound, sees all those poor puppies locked up, and takes them all home," Novak said. "But you know what? The next day the cages are full again."

Novak leaned forward.

"You can't save everybody. And worse than that, not everybody *wants* to be saved. I see it every day. If you prove to this woman that her old man not only hits her, he's boinking every sweet young thing he can get his hands on, she's not going to love you. She's not going to *thank* you. She's gonna hate your guts."

"I don't care what she thinks about me," Casper said. "She deserves better than this."

Novak shook his head.

"One month on the job and you wanna jump neck-deep into the middle of a domestic hell-hole?"

"I don't want to," Casper said. "I wish they could live happily ever after. But they can't."

"What do you want to do?" Novak asked.

"I don't want my dad to know about any of this," Casper said.

Novak laughed.

"Yeah. I guess not."

"I was thinking maybe watch him between two in the afternoon until about nine," Casper said. "Just on weekdays. That's when he can use the excuse of working late."

Casper pointed at the paper.

"That's where he works."

"I see that," Novak said. "Big brokerage house. Big cars. Big house. Big money."

"Big head," Casper said.

Novak sighed.

"And how long do you want him under surveillance?"

Casper shrugged.

"A week or so. If my guess is correct, he thinks he's untouchable."

"What about photos?" Novak said. "Do you want the down-and-dirty?"

"You mean, in the act?" Casper said. "No. I just want proof that he's cheating."

"Good," Novak said. "In-the act photos are expensive. And dangerous. I'm gonna take care of this myself, Casper. I'll even give you the family discount. I should tell you to get lost, but you'd just hire somebody else."

"Yes, sir. I would," Casper said.

Novak stood and put out his hand.

"Thank you, Mr. Novak," Casper said. "It was nice to meet you."

"Good luck," Novak said.

"Say, do you need any more investigators?" Casper asked.

"Don't tell me you're looking to give up the badge already," Novak said.

"No," Casper said. "But I have a friend who will be looking for work pretty soon."

"Tell me about him," Novak said.

"He used to be my cellmate," Casper said.

Novak laughed.

"I don't hear that every day. Tell him to come see me."

Eighteen

Casper and Leo took their lunch break at eight P.M.

"This feels weird," Casper said. They sat at an outdoor patio table overlooking a busy street.

"If you think this seems strange, wait until two weeks from now," Leo said. "We'll be doing lunch at three in the morning."

"I can't wait," Casper said.

"Yeah, right," Leo said. "The good thing about midnights, besides the few extra bucks, is that the shift goes by quick—thanks to the 'people of the night'."

"Ooooo," Casper said. "Coming soon. The People of the Night in the City that Never Sleeps…"

"Laugh it up, kid," Leo said. "You ain't seen nothing yet."

A man and a woman interrupted them. The man carried a portable video camera. The woman held a wireless microphone.

"Excuse me, officers," the woman said. "I'm Kit Callaghan with WNYX News."

Kit flashed a dazzling smile. She looked at Casper's badge.

"Are you Officer Casper Halliday?"

Casper looked at Leo for a reaction. He couldn't

read one.

"Yes, Ma'am."

Kit's smile broadened.

"So polite! Please, call me Kit. I'm not *that* much older than you."

Casper didn't know what to say.

"I know you gentlemen are here for dinner," Kit said. "If it's not too much trouble could I get a couple of minutes with you? The city will *love* knowing that one of her true heroes is carrying the badge of New York's Finest and guarding our streets."

"Ma'am, I probably shouldn't—"

Kit motioned to the cameraman to start filming.

Casper leaned close to Leo.

"What the hell do I do?"

"I don't know," Leo said. "Just be nice."

Casper stood. He could feel every eye in the room boring in on him. He knew he was blushing. And he was afraid he would start to sweat buckets.

"Ladies and Gentlemen," Kit Callaghan said. "This is Kit Callaghan, WNYX News. I know you all remember the night—right here in the city, when two members of the NYPD and one nineteen-year-old young man took down the ringleaders of a human trafficking ring. Eight young women were rescued that night, including the daughter of Chief of Detectives, Dwight Livingston.

"Well, you'll be happy to learn that that young man, Casper Halliday, is now a member of the NYPD."

Kit faced Casper.

"Officer Halliday, you now wear the uniform of our team of local heroes. But you made a major contribution toward making New York safe before you were old enough to attend the police academy."

Callaghan held the microphone in front of Casper.

"I was at the right place at the right time that night, Ma'...Miss Callaghan. The real heroes were in uniform that night; including—"

Callaghan moved the microphone.

"I understand that you are not only a co-worker with Officer Blair Hampton, but that you and Officer Hampton are romantically involved. Is that correct?"

Oh, God...

"We've gone out together," Casper said. He thought his voice might have cracked. He wasn't sure.

"We've been friends for a few years. Blair gave me my first driving lesson."

Callaghan laughed.

"That's so *cute!*"

Callaghan faced the camera.

"Our city not only has true heroes, but committed young people who give us feel-good stories at the same time. And we need those now more than ever.

"Officer Halliday, as you well know, we face a new threat. Brutal murders in the East Village and outside of Baltimore have left many in fear of where the killer might strike next—"

Casper held up his hands.

"Ma'am, I am in no position to comment—"

"Officer Halliday, I understand that you

sometimes go by the nickname, 'Ghost Man'. Is that correct?"

Leo pushed back his chair. He grabbed Casper by the arm.

"We have to go, Caz…"

"I spoke with a few friends of yours, Officer Halliday," Callaghan said. "Are you aware that the same nickname has been given to the serial-style killer currently terrorizing the northeast? Do you have a comment?"

Casper spoke quietly through clenched teeth.

"Turn the camera off."

"I'm sorry," Callaghan said. "I didn't get that."

"This is not a *game*, Ma'am. And it's not a freaking reality show. Two women are dead. They may have been raped and tortured. Is that what you want to hear?"

Kit Callaghan made a slashing motion across her neck to the cameraman.

"He said freaking, right?" she said. "We won't have to edit that out."

Leo dragged Casper across the floor toward the door.

"Keep your mouth shut, Casper," Leo said.

Kit Callaghan showed her best sarcastic expression.

"Thank you so much, officer. I have a job to do, too, you know. You didn't have to be a *dick* about it."

****

Robert Ferrill read the tabloid article for the

second time. He laid the paper on the table and turned on the television. He sat forward when he saw the pretty young reporter standing next to a police officer.

Lie to the people. Tell them you're hot on my trail. Tell them how you'll catch me.

Tell them how you and your pretty little friends will somehow unravel the tale of the Ghost Man…

Ferrill was shocked at what he learned in the interview.

*This young punk…this child is also called Ghost Man? No. No…this is not permissible. This is **my** time. The reign of Robert Ferrill. This city is mine. Millions of people will live in fear of me—every hour of every day. Their lives are mine.*

Ferrill's hand shook as he slipped his smooth fingers through the handle of the knuckle knife. He stabbed the blade into the tabletop.

Look at you, little boy.

Ferrill laughed at the screen.

*A little girl with a microphone controls the narrative? How do you expect to stop **me**? Is this how you respond to pressure? Do you have any idea what **I** would do with her, Officer?*

I would make her my slave—and then she would die in ashes—begging and screaming.

You are not prepared to face me, boy…

*You will **never** get the best of me.*

Officer Halliday,

There is only one…

Ghost Man.

Nineteen

The receptionist smiled and lifted the receiver from the desk.

"Mr. Butler is here."

Bradley Butler walked into Shane Murphy's office. He looked around the room and whistled.

"Wow. Looks like you've made the big-time, Shane."

"Just another step of the journey, Brad."

Butler held up his thumb and forefinger like a gun and pointed it at Murphy.

"That's my old pal Shane talking, right there."

"You expected any different?" Murphy asked.

"Absolutely not," Butler said.

Murphy sat behind his immense mahogany desk. Butler slumped into a stuffed leather chair. He loosened his tie, removed his stylish glasses, and rubbed his temples.

"My God," Butler said. "Bowing at the feet of the government dogs is sucking my soul out through my ears."

Shane Murphy leaned forward.

"Are you ready for a better game? The kind we used to dream about?"

Butler smirked.

"You mean the kind we dreamed up when we

were passing a joint?"

Murphy straightened his posture.

"Rule number one, my friend. What happened in our past—stays in the past."

Butler lifted his hands.

"Nobody cares about that stuff anymore, man. We were young and dumb and broke—"

Murphy's face darkened.

"Do you intend to stay that way?"

Butler sat back. He gripped the arms of the chair and looked around to gather his thoughts.

"Look, Shane. I know we talked some serious shit back in the day.—"

"It wasn't shit, Brad," Murphy said. "We came from nothing. No money. No influence. And no future."

"I think we turned out all right," Butler said. "Especially you."

"We did what we had to do," Murphy said. "I got you in with Pensado. If that hadn't happened, you would have been on a midnight bus back to Kansas before—"

"Come on, man," Butler said. "I'm from Indiana—"

Murphy leapt to his feet and leaned across the desk.

"Who gives a *shit* where you're from?"

Butler shook his head.

"Man, maybe you should smoke a joint or something. You have gotten *way* too intense…"

Murphy took a deep breath and rolled his neck on his shoulders.

"I'm sorry. I was out of line."

Butler pointed at himself.

"You asked *me* here, remember?"

Murphy blew out another breath and sat.

"I remember. I need your help, Bradley. And the stakes are higher than any we talked about in that crappy apartment."

"Sure," Butler said. "I figured that. If you're aiming higher than this Assistant DA gig—"

"Listen to me, Bradley," Murphy continued. "Everything I told you back then is true. It may seem that the privileged few have endless good fortune—but only up to a certain level. Above that...it comes down to the never-ending fire in a man's belly and what he will do to achieve his goals."

"I know what you're saying, Shane. I really do. I'm still the guy who looked into the future with you. That's why I'm here. What are we doing?"

Murphy's intercom buzzed. Murphy slammed his hands on the desk and rolled his eyes. He pushed the button.

"What?"

"I'm sorry, sir. You told me to notify you immediately if you received a call from a man named Andrew Glass."

"Yes," Murphy said. "I'm sorry. Put it through."

Andrew Glass was the code name for Glazkov.

Murphy lifted the receiver.

"This is Murphy."

Murphy listened for a few moments.

"Very well." He hung up the receiver, stood, and crossed the room. He turned on a corner-mounted television and switched to a news channel.

The lovely news-woman introduced herself and then turned the microphone to a tall and very young NYPD officer. Shane Murphy watched the short interview, unaware that he had a pencil in his hand. At the end of the broadcast the pencil snapped in two. Murphy switched off the television and returned to his desk, visibly disturbed.

"I'm sorry, Shane," Butler said. "I am totally lost."

Murphy forced himself to focus.

"What are we doing? We're climbing the ladder, Brad. My original thought was to displace the District Attorney. That is no longer the plan."

"Then what is the plan?" Butler asked.

"In case you haven't been watching the news," Murphy said. "We have a psycho serial killer in the area. Do you know what that means?"

"Yeah," Butler said. "I've heard about that."

"That means the bosses in the ivory towers get stormed by the press. I've got connections that can make that happen. And fast."

"If you want my help, you need to speak in English," Butler said.

Murphy sighed and pushed himself to his feet. He walked slowly around his desk. Butler stood, warily. Murphy put his arm around Butler's shoulder and squeezed.

"I'm going after the mayor's seat," Murphy said. "And I need a liaison between me and the man that can help make that happen."

"Okay," Butler said. "I can do that. What's his name?"

"Andrei Glazkov."

Murphy felt Butler shudder beneath his grasp.

"Oh, Jesus…"

Twenty

Casper woke to the alarm clock. The weekend on the evening shift had been exhausting. He and Leo had been called to a total of five domestic disturbances, during which Casper had to separate three angry couples and wrestle crazed men to the floor. Leo did not fare much better with the women.

Casper realized that missing his martial arts classes with Master Kim was not a good idea. He was rusty. And rusty might not be good enough.

Casper got out of bed and brewed a pot of strong coffee. He showered and dressed.

This was not a work day. It was Tuesday, and Cody Casey was on spring break from first grade. Today, he would take Cody and Mona to the zoo.

Along with Sean Kelly.

Casper stopped in front of Sean's apartment building. Sean was ready and waiting. He was also dressed up more than Casper had ever seen him. That made Casper smile. Sean got into Casper's car.

"Dang, you smell delicious," Casper said.

"You've made this weird already," Sean said.

"That's what I do," Casper said. "It's gonna be a great day."

Casper waved his hand at the sky.

"Look. The sun is shining. There's a cool breeze blowing. The animals will be frisky and happy. And we'll be in excellent company."

"I agree," Sean said. "It's gonna be a great day."

Mona and Cody waited in front of their little house. Casper and Sean got out of the car. Cody ran to Casper, who dropped to one knee. Cody leapt into Casper's arms.

"Hey, Buddy, how you doing?" Casper said.

"I'm on spring braked! We're going to the zoo!" Cody said.

"That's right," Casper said. "My friend is going with us. His name is Sean. He's a policeman, just like me."

Cody ran toward Sean. Sean bent over and held out his hand. Cody ran past it and wrapped his arms around Sean's legs. Sean lowered himself to one knee. He hugged Cody and squeezed him tight.

"It's good to meet you, Cody," Sean said. Sean stood and wiped his eyes.

Casper didn't say anything.

"Hi, Sean!" Cody said. "We're gonna have a great day at the zoo! Do you know what they have at the zoo?"

Sean sniffed and looked at Casper.

"Wow. I went to the zoo a long time ago, Cody. Do they have animals there?"

Cody clapped his hands.

"They have a million billion animals! Tiny ones and giant elephants!"

"I can't wait," Sean said.

"Me neither," Cody said.

"I'm looking forward to this myself," Mona said.
Sean looked at Mona and struggled to find words.
"Hi, Mona. You look great."

"Thank you," Mona said. "So do you. I'm glad
you're coming with us."

"Uh…me too," Sean said.

Casper spent the better part of the first two hours
trying to keep up with Cody. Casper didn't mind
because Mona and Sean were enjoying their time
together.

After they ordered lunch and sat down, Casper's
phone rang.

"Hello?"

"Yeah, Caz. This is Leo."

"Hey, Leo. How's it going?"

"I have some news for you," Leo said. "It's not
very good news."

"Yeah?" Casper said.

"You're no longer off-duty tomorrow," Leo said.
"You have an appointment with Captain Willis at three
P.M."

"Why?" Casper said.

"You can't guess?" Leo said. "You and Kit
Callaghan are all over the airwaves."

"Oh, no," Casper said. "Really?"

"Yeah," Leo said. "You're famous again, partner.
And it's not so good this time."

Casper closed his eyes. He stood.

"What's up?" Sean said.

"Three o'clock," Casper said. "All right. I'll be there. I'm sorry, Leo."

"Don't worry about it," Leo said. "She blindsided you. She knew what she was doing."

"Yeah, but I should have just walked away," Casper said.

"We work for the people, Casper," Leo said. "We don't get to walk away."

"I doubt that's what the Captain is going to say," Casper said.

"We'll see," Leo said. "Don't let it get to you."

"I've got one month on the job, Leo."

"But you're no ordinary rookie, Casper," Leo said.

"Thanks, Leo," Casper said.

Casper ended the call and faced the others.

"Bad news?" Sean said.

"That was Leo. I have to go in tomorrow."

Sean raised an eyebrow.

"Because of…?"

"Yeah," Casper said. "My interview didn't play too well with the Captain."

"Ouch," Sean said. "The Captain?"

"What are you talking about?" Cody asked.

Casper sighed.

"I'm sorry, Cody. I'm not going to be able to take you to the amusement park tomorrow. I have to go to work."

Cody patted Casper's shoulder.

"That's all right, Casper. We're having fun at the zoo, huh?"

"You bet we are."

Sean cleared his throat.

"Hey, Caz. Uh…I could take them tomorrow, if you and Mona don't mind."

Casper shrugged.

"I don't mind. If you want to…"

Mona smiled.

"You don't have to do that, Sean. Cody will be out of school soon and he'll have all summer to play."

"I'd loved to go—if it's okay," Sean said. "That's the place with the go carts, right?"

Cody nodded. Sean tickled him.

"Those things are fun," Sean said. "I used to go there when I was a kid."

"Well, let's do it, then," Mona said.

"Thanks, Sean," Casper said. "You're the best."

"Oh, please," Sean said. "I think I'm getting the best deal tomorrow."

"Yes," Casper said. "I think so, too."

Twenty-One

Casper's cell phone woke him at eight-thirty the next morning. The call came from Mark Novak.

"Good morning, Casper. I think I have what you wanted."

Casper sat up in bed. He was wide awake now.

"Already?" Casper said. "What has it been, two days?"

"It only took one," Novak said. "Apparently, Mr. Talbot is a busy man. You're working the afternoon shift, right?"

"Yes," Casper said.

"If you have the time, I'll be in my office until noon," Novak said. "You can look over the photos and see if we're done here."

"Yeah," Casper said. "I'll be there in an hour."

Casper rubbed his face with both hands.

So this is it. The guessing game is over. Matt Talbot is a cheating husband who hits his wife. In an hour, I'll have the proof in my hands.

Then what?

What have I done?

Casper stared at the six eight-by-ten photos lying on Mark Novak's desk. Two photos showed the parking lot of a Holiday Inn. Matt Talbot and a young, very attractive blond woman were in the picture along with Talbot's car. They walked toward the bank of hotel rooms holding hands.

The other four pictures showed the couple outside a hotel room door. A high-quality zoom lens captured the scene. Talbot and the woman engaged in a passionate kiss—with a hotel room number clearly visible behind them.

1103.

"What do you think?" Novak said.

"These don't leave a lot to the imagination," Casper said. "And that's not the bastard's wife."

"Nope," Novak said. "You know, this was the easiest job I've ever done."

Casper looked away from the photos. His mind raced.

Breathe, my son. Learn from my mistakes.

"Cheng...?"

"Excuse me?" Novak said. "Are you okay?"

"Oh. Yeah," Casper said. "It's just...it's *real*, now."

"I know what you mean," Novak said. "I've seen every reaction under the sun—and then some."

Casper offered his hand. Novak shook it.

"This is exactly what I asked for," Casper said. "How much do I owe you?"

"Two hundred bucks," Novak said.

Casper opened his wallet.

"I hope you take cash. I'd like to avoid a paper trail."

"Not a problem," Novak said.

"It should cost more than two hundred dollars to break up a marriage," Casper said.

"Is that what you're going to do?" Novak asked. "Never mind. Don't answer that. We provide a service. What you do with the information is up to you. Just promise me you'll think long and hard about this, son. I know you're a police officer now. You've had gun training and your dad tells me you know some of that...uh, it's Kung Fu, right?"

"Yes, sir."

"Domestic situations can be extremely dangerous," Novak said. "Sometimes more dangerous than facing down hardened criminals. Some guys lose their minds when they get caught with their pants down. And the women...sometimes they kick and cry and scream and break shit—but then they want to kiss and make up. And if *that* happens—everybody will turn on *you*. Are you ready for that?"

"He hits her, sir," Casper said.

Novak rubbed his chin.

"Shit. Are you willing to bet your life on that?"

"Yes, sir."

"This will be an ugly one, Casper," Novak said. "I would almost guarantee you she knows he's sleeping around. If she's in denial after being physically abused, she's going to be in denial about infidelity. Who really knows what goes on inside someone else's head? Maybe she's afraid of divorce more than being mistreated. Maybe she has childhood issues. Maybe she's afraid he would come after her and hurt her bad. Maybe her self-esteem ain't what it used to be."

Casper shook his head.

"I don't think it's self-esteem, sir. Mrs. Talbot turns heads all day long."

Novak narrowed his eyes.

"Wait a minute...is this the woman that—is she a police dispatcher?"

"Yes, sir."

"Oh, my God," Novak said. "She started after I quit, but I went by the station to see some of the guys after that...they called her 'Charlie', I think."

"Yes, sir."

"How long have you known this woman?" Novak said.

Casper bit his lip.

"A few weeks."

Novak let his head loll backward.

"Jesus," he said.

"Please don't say anything to my dad," Casper said.

"Oh, trust me, kid," Novak said. "I don't want Bobby to know I had anything to do with this. He'd probably walk out on me after he beat my ass."

"Thank you, Mr. Novak," Casper said.

"You don't have to thank me," Novak said. "Loose lips aren't allowed in this line of work. You get a reputation for turning your clients into gossip; you might as well lock the doors. I just have one more thing to say. I know you're young and full of piss and vinegar and you have a strong sense of justice. But there are ten million people in this city, Casper. You can't save them all."

"I'll remember that, Mr. Novak."

****

Robert Ferrill had the information he required. After his next conquest, his fame would know no equal.

Ferrill wore padding beneath his shirt that added twenty pounds to his appearance. He wore a fake mustache and a brown wig beneath a Yankees baseball cap. Ferrill settled back into the cushioned bench of the booth. The coffee was very good, as was the hot apple pie. But the electric feeling that coursed his skin was caused by the fresh, clean, and delectable scent of the lovely lady who served his table.

It was a bonus that she was so desirable.

Beautiful face. Full lips. Exquisite body. Outstanding legs…wrapped in luxurious sheer silk stockings.

The lovely…

Kathy Halliday.

Twenty-Two

Casper checked his watch. He had time to join Sean, Mona, and Cody at the amusement park, but it didn't seem like the right thing to do. Casper shook his head when he realized he felt a slight twinge of jealousy. Not about Sean and Mona. No, a part of him was jealous of Sean spending time with Cody.

Casper laughed out loud.

"Stop it, dumbass."

Casper knew he would never be more to Cody than a good friend—a stand-in big brother at most. But Sean could very well become something more.

*And that is a **good** thing.*

Casper and Sean were little more than acquaintances and co-workers. But Sean had played an important part in Blair Hampton's life. He had become Blair's partner and friend at a time when few others wanted to do so.

Blair had confided to Casper the reason Sean Kelly was single and unattached at twenty-seven-years of age. Sean was engaged to his high school sweetheart when she was killed in an automobile accident. Sean was twenty-two at the time, and had just entered the police academy.

Casper wanted do everything in his power to encourage his friends and whatever relationships might be on the horizon. He smiled into the rear-view mirror.

In fact, I may just become the greatest matchmaker on the East Coast.

Casper wore slacks, a white shirt, and a casual sports coat. He thought wearing a tie would be too much and make him look like he was on trial.

Which maybe I am.

Casper walked into the precinct station and met with the usual wall of sound. There were conversations, laughter, crying, and banter between police and complainants or the recently arrested. He made his way toward Captain Willis's office. Everyone who saw and recognized Casper fell silent or reduced their voice to whisper level.

Uh-oh. This can't be good.

Casper entered the Captain's office. Captain Willis looked up from behind the desk. His steel-blue eyes peered over reading glasses.

"Ah. Officer Halliday. Come in and have a seat."

"Yes, sir."

Willis shuffled a few papers.

"You have had a rather eventful first month, Officer."

"I'm sorry, sir—"

Willis held up a hand.

"You responded at the murder scene when the victim's husband got by the barricades. Did that bother you?"

Casper shrugged.

"It was the most horrible thing I've ever seen, sir.

But we're the NYPD. We're the last line of defense. It's what we signed up for."

Willis nodded.

"I know you didn't go looking for the press, son. But they're not going to leave you alone—especially after all this 'Ghost Man' talk."

"Am I supposed to ignore them?"

"More or less," Willis said. "Standard procedure is to say you're not allowed to comment on an ongoing investigation."

"I understand, sir," Casper said. "That lady caught me off-guard. I asked Officer Sanchez—"

"You stop right there!" Willis snapped.

Casper swallowed hard and moved back in his seat.

"One thing we do not do in this department is pass blame. If you make a mistake—you *own* it."

"I'm sorry, sir. I didn't mean—"

"What are you saying now, Officer Halliday? That you're a sworn member of the finest law-enforcement organization in the land and you say things you don't mean?"

Casper had no reply.

Willis leaned back.

"I didn't bring you in here to break your spirit, Halliday. This was not all your fault. But you're going to have to grow up fast. You're a special case. You have to harness your emotions and think before you speak."

Willis walked around the desk and sat on its corner.

"Do you know where this hurt us?"

Casper looked into the Captain's eyes.

"I'm not sure I understand."

"You mentioned rape and torture. None of that had been mentioned to the press."

Casper looked at the floor and mumbled.

"Shit."

Willis returned to his chair.

"It's not the end of the world. It just gave them a little more ammunition. But that bit of news, and the 'Ghost Man' thing, coupled with your role in saving those girls—"

"I was only a small part of that, sir," Casper said.

Willis looked at Casper with a wry smile on his face.

"Save your breath. I am familiar with the case, Officer Halliday. I take it you are aware that Officer Hampton has submitted her resignation?"

"Yes, sir."

"I've spoken to Miss Hampton a few times over the years," Willis said. "I've also spoken with her superior officers. Officer Hampton is intelligent, with excellent analytical instincts. She is a good marksman. By every indication, she was a prime candidate for detective promotion. But then…the incident at the port occurred. Apparently, it was more than she could deal with. What do you think?"

Casper nodded.

"I believe that's what happened—"

"Bullshit," Willis said.

Casper's lips moved without a sound.

"S-sir?"

"Officer Halliday," Willis said. "I have been with this department for twenty-nine years. I'm no rocket scientist, but I *have* worked a lot of investigations. First of all, Chris Freeman's service weapon was a Glock 17. Do you know how many rounds Chris put through that gun at our range?"

"No, sir," Casper said.

"I do," Willis said. "Yet, in response to a live gunfire situation, in the dark and the rain, he chose to use a side-piece. A revolver."

Casper shrugged.

"Officer Hampton made high scores on the psychological and ethical tests," Willis said. "Make no mistake about it, Officer Halliday; only a damaged person can kill another human and it have no effect on them. However, the department goes to a great deal of trouble to see that our recruits are prepared to deal with traumatic situations. Do you see what I'm getting at?"

"No, sir," Casper said.

"I'm saying I know when I'm having smoke blown up my ass."

Casper cleared his throat.

"I still don't—"

"I'm saying I don't think Blair Hampton is resigning because she can't get over killing two pieces of human garbage."

"You don't?"

"No," Willis said. He leaned forward and steepled his fingers.

"I believe Miss Hampton cannot deal with being complicit in a batch of lies."

"Lies, sir?"

Willis waved a hand.

"Don't worry about any of this, Casper. Nothing said today will leave this room. Do you really think I would accuse the Chief of Detectives of such a thing? Dwight and Maggie Livingston are the finest people I've ever met. When Brooke disappeared—"

Willis sniffed and rubbed his eyes.

"Well, it just about killed them. It was terrible. If you hadn't been on your toes and showing remarkable detective skills at nineteen-years-old—those girls would have been lost forever. And God only knows how many more might have followed. So, Casper, between you and me, what you did was a good thing. It wasn't by the book and didn't follow the letter of the law—but it was a good thing. A *damn* good thing."

Casper avoided the Captain's eyes.

"I don't know what to say, sir."

"You don't need to say anything," Willis said. "Especially to the press."

"Yes, sir."

"I don't want you to lie to me," Willis said. "Ever. But if you happen to save my life or the life of someone I care about, you come and see me. We might need to get our stories straight."

Casper nodded. Willis stood and extended his right hand.

"You are dismissed, Officer Halliday. Enjoy the rest of your day off."

Casper reached for the door handle.

"One more thing," Willis said. "Your dad was a good cop."

Casper turned and smiled.

"He still is, sir."

Twenty-Three

Casper walked through the lobby. His knees were trembling. He saw a familiar face.

"Ooo. Who's that man in the fancy pants?" Mando Gonzalez said.

"Yeah," Casper said. "I had to go to the Principal's office."

"So I heard," Mando said.

"I'm sure *everybody* heard," Casper said.

"You're not surprised are you?" Mando said. "After your network television premiere?"

"Yeah, I screwed up," Casper said. "And I have the chunk missing from my butt to prove it."

"It's a bummer that we work different shifts," Mando said. "We never get to hang out anymore."

"That'll probably change when we get new partners," Casper said.

"I'm sure it will," Mando said. "We'll both be on duty midnights and weekends."

"Stop crying," Casper said. "You're breaking my heart."

"I'm not crying. You're crying," Mando said. "Hey, do you work next Saturday?"

"I'm off," Casper said. "Leo and I start midnight shift on Sunday."

"Good," Mando said. "We're having a party for

my sister. She's graduating from NYU."

"That's great," Casper said. "Is it at your house?"

"Hell, no," Mando said. "I got lots of family, bro. That's not enough room. We rented a banquet hall. I'll make you a map."

"Cool," Casper said.

"Uh-oh," Mando said. "My partner is giving me the stink-eye. Gotta go."

Casper was alone again, and aware of the roomful of stares and whispers. He hurried through the back door. The sky had grown cloudy. Casper stopped at the edge of the awning. A gust of north wind blew dust into his eyes. He rubbed his arms against the chill. Another wind gust brought the smell of tobacco smoke. Casper looked into the trash can and saw the remains of a burning cigarette. He took a half-full cup of coffee from the trash and doused the smoldering butt. He shivered and walked to his car.

Casper climbed in and closed the door. He leaned back and closed his eyes.

When was the last time I felt this lousy?
When Cheng Sun died?
The day I went to prison?
The day I got arrested?
The night my father left us?

Casper sat up and put the key into the ignition. He saw the manila envelope on the floor on the passenger side.

She only smokes when she drinks.

So she's drinking. Probably in the dungeon.

Casper picked up the envelope.

If she's at her table, I'll turn around and leave. I'll take these photos home and burn them.

And that will be the end of it.

Casper opened the door to Max's Cigar Lounge. He counted eleven people. Two men lifted their chins to acknowledge his presence. Max was nowhere to be seen.

Charlie Talbot's table was empty.

Casper took a deep breath and stepped into the dungeon. Charlie sat alone at a candlelit table. Overhead, a single wall sconce shined its dimly colored bulb toward the ceiling. The table held five beer bottles. Charlie picked up a shot glass and downed its contents.

Charlie saw Casper from the corner of her eye. She slammed the glass onto the table.

"What the hell are you doing here? You know the goddamn rules!"

Casper's hands shook. He tried to swallow but his throat was dry.

"You have to leave him, Charlie."

Charlie shook her head and slammed her palms on the table. Two beer bottles toppled and hit the floor.

"Just who the *hell* are you? Huh? Answer me, boy! You'll never—you won't—! Jesus Christ, I can't even talk…Max! **Max!**"

Max ran in from the kitchen. He stopped when he reached the dark shadows of the dungeon.

"Holy *shit!* Get out of my bar this instant! And don't come back!"

Max pushed against Casper's chest. Casper tried to hold his ground. He spoke over Max's head.

"He hits you, Charlie…

"And he's cheating on you—"

"You…*bastard!*" Charlie screamed.

"Hey!" Max yelled. "I need some help in here!"

Four off-duty police officers ran into the darkness.

"Jesus, Halliday," an officer said. "What the hell are you doing?"

Three men pulled Casper toward the door. He had no intention of fighting them.

"I'm telling you the truth," Casper said.

"*Shut up!*" Charlie screamed.

"You heard the lady!" Max said. "Shut your mouth!"

"Please," Casper said. "Don't wait until he hurts you b—"

Max clamped his hand over Casper's mouth. The front door stood open. Two men pulled Casper onto the sidewalk. Max gave Casper one last shove in the chest. Casper went down hard on his back.

The door closed. Casper was alone. That was when he realized he no longer had the manila envelope.

An officer whispered to Max.

"So, do we…check on her?"

"No," Max snapped. "She's a grown woman. Go back to your table."

Charlie downed another tequila shot and a drink of beer. She noticed something on the floor and picked it up. It was a sealed letter-sized envelope with a metal clasp. Was Casper carrying this? Charlie didn't know.

She walked into the ladies' room and locked the door.

Charlie tried to avoid the mirror, but she failed. Her hair looked tired and limp. She noticed the sloppy job she'd done on her makeup that morning. Charlie raised her chin. She couldn't tell if there was still a hint of the bruise beneath her right eye or if the light was too poor.

Charlie walked to the corner of the room and leaned against the wall. She lifted the envelope with trembling hands. Charlie looked at her right hand. She had chewed the nails down to the quick. She squeezed her eyes shut against the onset of tears.

Charlie wiped her eyes and took a deep, ratcheted breath. She tore open the envelope and pulled out the photos.

Charlie slid slowly down the length of the wall. She hugged her knees to her chest and sobbed until she couldn't sob anymore.

****

Charlie showered and applied her makeup with great care. She put on her favorite dress, which also happened to be Matt's favorite. She stood in front of the wall mirror and smoothed the fabric. Charlie finished with her special-occasion perfume.

Twenty-five minutes later, Matt Talbot walked through the front door with his suit coat over his shoulder. His tie was loosened and the top two buttons of his shirt were unbuttoned. He tossed the coat over the back of a living room chair.

"Wow," Matt said. "You look great, babe."

Charlie glanced at the clock on the wall.

"Thank you. Another long day, huh?"

Matt sighed.

"They never seem to end."

He crossed the room and put his hands on Charlie's hips. He leaned in to kiss her. Charlie brushed his lips and lowered her head to Matt's shoulder.

"Mmm. Is that the cologne I gave you for Christmas?"

"Yes, it is," Matt said.

Charlie sniffed again.

"Something…else, though."

She stepped back and bent over at the waist until her head was level with Matt's crotch.

"Ah, I know what it is now. It's *sex*. You smell like sex."

Charlie rose. Her face looked set in stone. She turned her back on Matt.

Matt grabbed Charlie's arm.

"Celeste…"

Charlie pulled her arm away and stepped back. She pointed at Matt with her left index finger and held up her cell phone in her right hand.

"No," she growled. "Don't *ever* touch me again, Matthew. If I press my thumb against this screen, there will be a hundred cops here in two minutes. And they will be looking for the tiniest excuse to tear you into pieces so small your mother won't recognize them."

Matt Talbot froze. Charlie stepped into their bedroom and returned with a suitcase.

"I will be back here in exactly sixty hours," Charlie said, "with more than sufficient manpower. I suggest you do as I say. I also suggest you cut back on your expenses. I've hired an attorney who can't wait to get her hands on you."

That part was a lie, but Charlie didn't care.

"Get your shit and get out of my house."

Charlie slammed the door behind her. Matthew Talbot stared at the door for a full thirty seconds. He grabbed his suit coat and walked into the bedroom. He saw something lying on top of the pillow on Celeste's side of the bed. He picked up the photo.

"Shit…"

Twenty-Four

Casper stepped into his apartment. He took a beer from the refrigerator and dropped onto the sofa. His cell phone rang. Casper sighed and looked at the display.

"Hi, Mom."

"I'm just checking in on you, honey," Kathy Halliday said.

"Yeah," Casper said. "I guess you've seen me on the news."

"Well…it's been hard to ignore," Kathy said.

"I just came from a meeting with my Captain," Casper said. "The department didn't care much for my performance."

"I thought that might cause some trouble," Kathy said. "Do you want to come over and curl up on the couch? I made spaghetti. We could watch a cop movie or something. I'm working tomorrow night."

"I don't think so, Mom. I'm exhausted. It's been a hell of a day. I'm going to bed."

"Okay," Kathy said. "I understand. Try not to get old so fast."

Casper laughed.

"I'm trying, Mom."

****

Robert Ferrill slumped down in the seat of his car. He had seen the lights go out in two of the apartment windows. Ferrill knew Bobby Halliday worked as a private investigator. P.I.'s did most of their work at night—when people tend to do things that need investigating.

You have it all wrong tonight, Bobby-boy.

Ferrill knew Bobby Halliday's car. He waited to see it leave. Ferrill moved his car around the block. He removed a wheeled suitcase from the trunk, shouldered his duffel bag and entered the building. He looked like just another anonymous businessman returning home.

****

Casper stared out the passenger window. Leo Sanchez looked at him.

"You haven't said two words all day. Did the Captain rip you a new one?"

Casper waited for the exchange on the police radio to finish. Charlie Talbot usually worked the first two hours of Casper and Leo's afternoon shift, but the voice on the radio belonged to someone else.

"Not really," Casper said. "I'm just a little bummed out. And tired."

"Yeah," Leo said. "We could use a good bank robbery or something right now."

"Jesus, Leo," Casper said. "Why not a suicide jumper off a tall building while we're at it?"

"Now you're talkin'," Leo said.

"How long have you been doing training shifts with new recruits?" Casper asked.

Leo closed one eye and bit his lip.

"Uh…almost five years, I guess. Why?"

Casper smiled.

"Because you're not exactly stable."

Leo's head whipped around.

"What? Me? Kid, what makes you think *any* of us are stable? Anybody that applies to the academy is certifiably insane."

"Oh, really," Casper said. "I wish you had said that to Miss Kit Callaghan. I think you could have saved me from a lot of trouble."

"You got over thirty-five thousand brothers and sisters out here on the NYPD," Leo said. "Do you think they're all Boy Scouts and Girl Scouts?"

"Of course not," Casper said. "But I don't think they're all crazy."

"Actually," Leo said, "I like to think we're *all* crazy. Thirty-five thousand to police ten million. Those are shitty numbers, Caz. Crazy don't scare me, as long as the ones on our side have a strong sense of right and wrong—"

Leo slapped a hand against his chest.

"…and loyalty to this uniform. Because I'll tell you what. If I'm gut-shot and lying in the street in the middle of a gun fight, the only person that's gonna come and get me will be wearing the blue. Am I right or am I right?"

Casper nodded.

"I changed my mind. I like having you as a partner."

"Don't get attached," Leo said. "I've got you for four more weeks. And then it's fresh meat for the both of us."

"Yeah," Casper said. "I know."

"Your girlfriend's really quitting, huh?"

Casper winced.

"Yeah. Blair Hampton has resigned. Yes, we're friends and we've gone out together."

Casper looked down.

"But I don't think it was ever serious. At least for her."

"I'm sorry, man," Leo said. "You know how the rumor-mill goes…"

"Ha," Casper said. "Of course, I do. The human-interest story. That's what attracts people like Kit Callaghan."

"I screwed up, Casper," Leo said. "I should have gotten you out of there."

"Don't give me that crap," Casper said. "That was my mistake. All mine."

"You're a good dude, Caz," Leo said. "I'd like to have you as a partner full-time."

"Nope," Casper said. "You have more baby birds that need to know how to fly when you shove them out of the nest."

Casper leaned forward and looked up at the high-rises.

"Do you see any jumpers?"

Leo looked up.

"Not today."

Leo stopped for a traffic light that turned yellow.

A foreign sports car in the lane to their right sped through the red light.

"Do you wanna mess up someone's evening?" Leo asked.

"No," Casper said. "I might feel compelled to dump all my baggage in his lap."

Leo laughed.

"It was a girl. Beautiful. With long, dark hair."

"A girl?" Casper said. "Oh, God. No. Not today."

****

The evening remained uneventful. Casper checked his watch. One-and-a-half hours remained to his shift. Casper was glad Leo had engaged him in conversation. The scene from Max's Cigar Lounge played over-and-over in his mind. He was depressed and exhausted.

Charlie Talbot hated him. She had screamed at him like she wanted to tear him to pieces. She would hate him *forever*—especially if she found the envelope. The pictures proved he had invaded her personal life without her knowledge or consent.

What would Charlie do? She could very well go to the Captain or even higher—Casper had invaded her personal life without any right to do so.

For the first time, it occurred to Casper that he could be fired—removed from the ranks of the New York Police Department.

Just like his father.

His clean record, won by Cheng Sun's son-in-law Jonathan Kwan, might be wiped away. All because of his sense of justice.

Could he lose his career because he cared too much? For a woman he barely knew?

Maybe. Life didn't always make sense.

Man. Don't I know it.

The radio broke the silence.

"Dispatch to unit eight-six."

Leo sat up straight in the driver's seat.

"That's us, Caz."

"Eight-six to dispatch. Go ahead, over."

"Officer Halliday. Phone in to the desk sergeant immediately, over."

"What is this crap?" Casper asked Leo.

"Call in," Leo said. "Now."

The look on Leo's face concerned Casper.

"This is Halliday," Casper said into his phone.

"Come to the station," the desk sergeant said. "Immediately."

"Yes, sir," Casper said.

"Go to the station," Casper said to Leo.

Leo flipped on the lights and the siren. He did a U-turn in the middle of a crowded street and spun the tires.

"Damn," Casper said. "You act like this is something serious."

"Exactly," Leo said. He drove as fast as possible to the station. He squealed the brakes stopping at the front door.

"Go," Leo said. Casper ran into the building. He was met by the desk sergeant and six other officers.

"What the hell?" Casper said.

The desk sergeant laid down a folded sheet of paper.

"This was pinned to the bulletin board. No one knows how it got there."

The front of the paper was printed in standard printer type. It read

To the Fake Ghost Man

Casper unfolded the paper.

Mommy has been bad
The REAL Ghost man

"Oh, my God," Casper said.

He pulled his cell phone from his pocket. With trembling fingers he dialed his mother's cell phone. There was no answer. He dialed the home phone. No answer. He called the diner where she worked.

Kathy had been relieved an hour-and-a-half ago.

Casper turned to Leo.

"Give me the keys."

"What? What's going on?"

"GIVE ME THE GODDAMN KEYS!"

Casper snatched the keys from Leo's hand and ran for the door. Leo picked up the note from the floor.

Casper started the car and floored the accelerator. The car fishtailed away from the curb. Leo and several other officers ran after Casper.

"What the hell is going on?" an officer asked Leo.

"Oh, my God," Leo said. "I hope it's not what I think it is."

Casper flipped on the lights and siren. He tried his mother's cell phone again. No answer.

He called his father's cell.

"What's up, Cas—?"

"Dad! Go home NOW! This is not a joke! Go HOME NOW!"

Casper switched the radio to the outside PA speaker. Most motorists pulled to the curb when they heard the siren or saw the lights. The others made way after Casper swore at them over the PA.

When Casper reached the residential section, traffic was more difficult to avoid. Casper looked up at the windows of the apartment building. He clipped the rear bumper of a slow-moving car. He side-swiped a parked car and drove onto the sidewalk in front of the building. He leapt from the car and ran for the door. Casper was going to run the twelve flights of stairs, but the elevator door opened as he entered the building. He ran into the elevator along with five other people. He pushed the button for the twelfth floor. A man reached for the bank of buttons.

"No!" Casper growled. "Police business."

"What's going on?" the man asked.

Casper did not answer. His breath came in gasps of air. He unbuttoned his holster and drew his gun. A woman screamed.

"Shut up!" Casper snapped.

The elevator passed the eleventh floor.

"Don't follow me."

"No problem," the man said.

Casper ran through the elevator doors. The hallway was clear. He held his gun in the air and tried the door to his parent's apartment.

It was unlocked.

Casper threw the door open and leveled his gun.

"Mom! Mom! Where are—"

Casper smelled something burning. He hugged the wall of the entry and crept toward the kitchen.

"*Jesus...*"

In the middle of the kitchen stood a five-gallon gas can. Four holes had been bored into the top. Four tapered black candles dripped into puddles of wax.

Less than two inches separated the flames from the top of the gas can. Casper grabbed a bowl and filled it from the kitchen faucet. He doused the candles.

"Mom! Mom, answer me!"

Casper crept toward the living room—his pistol raised in his trembling hand.

"Oh, God. *No...*"

A dining room chair stood in the middle of the floor. Beneath a blood-stained white sheet, lifeless eyes stared through round holes.

Eyes...that Casper knew well...

No...no...

Casper crept closer. His right foot slipped in the pool of blood. With trembling fingers, he gripped the sheet. It wouldn't move.

No...

Casper bent and gripped the bottom edge of the sheet.

He didn't want to see what was beneath it — more than anything else in the world. But he had to. He pulled against the tug of congealed blood.

Casper thought his heart might explode.

Kathy Halliday was tied to the chair with duct tape around her mouth and head. Her waitress uniform was cut in dozens of places, as was almost every inch of her face and body. Casper dropped the sheet. Blood covered his shaking hands.

"Kathy! Kathy!"

Casper heard his father's voice. In seconds, Bobby would reach the open front door. Casper blocked the hallway.

"No, Dad. Don't — !"

"Kathy! Kathy!"

Bobby ran until he saw Casper's outstretched, bloody hands. Bobby froze.

And then he lowered his head and charged.

Casper wrapped his arms around his father. Bobby roared a wordless scream. Casper tripped him and they crashed to the floor.

"She's gone, Dad. She's gone."

Father and son squeezed until they were out of breath.

"No, no, no, *no...*"

Twenty-Five

Senior Detectives Burton and Riley sat across the table from Casper and Bobby Halliday.

"God, I'm so sorry," Burton said.

"Yeah. Me, too," Riley said. "We're gonna nail the bastard. I promise you that."

Bobby stared ahead, his eyes unfocused in an absent fog. He nodded.

"You know we have to ask you some questions," Burton said. "Anything you can't talk about right now, we can address later."

"The goddamn press," Bobby growled.

Burton leaned forward.

"I'm sorry? What was that?"

Bobby looked up—his bloodshot and swollen eyes blazing with rage.

"The goddamn *press*," Bobby said. "They couldn't wait to hang a nickname on this psycho mother—now look what they've done!"

"Dad—" Casper said.

Bobby honed in on detective Burton.

"Don't you see? They glamorized a goddamn *psycho murderer*. Well, you have some more information for your bulletin board now, don't you? This monster loves the attention. He's watching the news. He's famous. He's a star! A superhero! That bitch painted a target on my son's back so big that the bastard slaughtered…"

Bobby fell back in his chair and covered his face with his hands. He leaned forward, moaning in agony.

Detective Riley scribbled furiously on his pad.

"Oh, shit," Casper whispered.

"What is it, son?" Burton asked.

"I need a pen and paper," Casper said. He wrote down Mona Casey's name, address, and phone number.

He also wrote down Blair Hampton's information.

"He could have come after me," Casper said. "But he didn't. And…he might go after other people I care about."

Casper tapped the paper.

"We have to protect them. Blair's father might still have access to the Secret Service. I'm not sure."

"We'll take care of it," Burton said.

There were two knocks on the door. Chief of Detectives Dwight Livingston leaned into the room.

"Can I come in?"

Burton and Riley stood.

"Sure. Come in, Chief."

Livingston walked toward Casper. Casper stood and offered his hand. Livingston ignored it and pulled Casper into a hug.

"God, I'm so sorry, Casper."

"Thank you, sir."

Livingston shook Bobby's hand.

"I'm so sorry, Robert."

"Thank you," Bobby said.

"Casper, you're on indefinite paid leave," Livingston said. "Take your time—as much as you need."

Livingston looked at Bobby.

"Let me know if you need anything—anything at all. I mean that. Detectives, I'll let you complete your business here. Casper, your friends are waiting if you'd like to see them; Officers Gonzalez and Kelly, and his wife, I suppose. Or if you'd rather, Detective Burton can see you through a rear exit."

"Thank you, sir," Casper said.

Livingston left the room. The detectives resumed their questions. Burton produced a clear evidence bag.

"This note he left—can you tell me anything about it?"

"Note?" Bobby said. "He left a note? Where?"

Riley cleared his throat.

"Here at the station. On the employee bulletin board."

"Jesus," Bobby said. "He'll be on the surveillance cameras."

"Yeah," Burton said. "We should be getting data from the lab guys pretty quick."

Bobby looked at the note, front and back.

"Sick bastard."

"There were no fingerprints," Burton said. "All we know at the moment is that this came from a standard ink-jet printer. It could have been printed at a library, a copy store, or a million other places."

"He's not stupid," Bobby said.

Burton and Riley stood.

"Thank you for your cooperation," Burton said. "We're very sorry for your loss."

Burton handed business cards to Casper and Bobby.

"If you think of anything that might be useful, call us. Anytime."

"I need to talk to some people," Casper said to Bobby.

"Okay."

"It won't take long," Casper said. "Do you…want to wait for me?"

"If you want me to," Bobby said.

"We can't go home yet. They've booked us into a hotel. After that, maybe I could stay with you for a while, if that's okay."

"Sure," Bobby said. "As long as you want."

Casper shuffled his feet.

"Maybe…it would be better if we went to the apartment together. When it's time."

"Yeah," Bobby said.

Mona Casey threw her arms around Casper and buried her face in his chest.

"Oh, God. Oh, my God. I am so sorry…"

Casper held Mona tightly. Sean and Mando looked on. When Mona stepped away, Mando hugged his friend.

"I'm really sorry, bro."

"Thanks for being here, all of you," Casper said.

"It means a lot."

"We love you, Casper," Mona said. Mando nodded.

"I need to go," Casper said. "My dad's waiting for me."

"Of course," Mona said. "You do what you need to do, honey."

"Sean," Casper said, "could I talk to you for a second?"

"Sure."

"I don't want to scare anybody," Casper said. "But I asked for security for Mona's place. Blair's, too."

Sean nodded.

"This is kind of weird," Casper said. "But are you and Mona...a thing?"

"Yeah," Sean said. "I guess we are."

"That's great," Casper said. "Look, I'm going to stay away from Mona and Cody until we catch this monster. Would you explain that to her? I can't take the chance."

"Yeah," Sean said. "I understand. It sucks, but I get it."

Casper blew out a breath.

"I feel like a disease."

Sean clapped Casper on the shoulder.

"We'll catch him, all right," Sean said. "And the bastard will never see daylight again. You're a good guy, Caz."

"Thanks," Casper said.

"You introduced me to Mona on purpose, didn't

you?"

Casper took a few seconds. He was happy for Sean and Mona, but he could not show it now.

"Maybe."

Casper jumped when Sean hugged him.

Sean whispered.

"Thank you. I'm here for you if you need me, my friend."

Twenty-Six

Bobby Halliday stood in front of the apartment door. He looked to his left. The heads of two neighbors disappeared into their apartments, followed by the soft clicks of door latches. The same thing happened to his right.

Bobby fumbled with his keys. Casper held his breath and waited patiently.

Bobby pushed open the door. Casper followed him. Bobby stepped silently through the kitchen and into the dining room. Casper followed, trying his best to make no sound at all. Everything was just as Casper remembered, yet the apartment felt alien.

The rooms had been cleaned and sanitized and then cleaned again.

Casper could smell it. Soap. Disinfectant. Bleach. Deodorizer. Like a hospital room.

No sign of his mother's horrific death remained.

It was a good thing. And a bad thing.

There was no lingering presence of Kathy Halliday's last minutes on earth. No purse and keys on the kitchen counter. No shoes left just inside the door. No jacket draped over a barstool.

No lingering scent in the air from Kathy's favorite perfume.

Bobby disappeared into the half-bathroom. Casper entered when Bobby exited. Bobby sat on the living room sofa, rocking back and forth. Casper sat on the other end.

"Are you hungry?" Bobby asked.

"No," Casper said.

They sat in silence for a few moments. Casper took out his phone.

"I'll order pizza. For later. Maybe."

"Okay," Bobby said.

After a few more moments of uncomfortable silence, Bobby picked up the remote control and clicked on the television. It seemed that every channel was broadcasting news of the New York City serial killer. Bobby stopped switching channels when he reached a Cooking Channel.

Casper answered the door when the pizza was delivered. He put a slice on each of two plates and put them on the coffee table. There were eight bottles of beer in the refrigerator.

An hour later, the pizza had not been touched. Eight empty bottles sat next to the plates. Bobby's eyes closed as he leaned against the back of the sofa. Twice, his head snapped forward, and he moved forward on the seat cushion. The third time, he remained asleep and snored softly. Casper stared at his father's hand. Bobby's trigger finger twitched over and over.

Casper got up and took a blanket from the linen closet. He spread it across Bobby's lap. Casper carried the empty bottles to the kitchen. He stared at the chalkboard rectangle on the wall, where Kathy Halliday had last left a note for her husband.

There's Salisbury steak and potatoes in a Tupperware. I'll be home around ten.

I love you, Kathy.

Casper took a deep breath.

Should I erase it? This is...

How are we ever going to get over this?

Casper sniffed. He sniffed again. He felt tears welling up in his eyes.

No. Don't melt down. Not now.

Casper opened the door to his old room. The bed was made and everything was in place.

Always kept ready for him. Always.

Casper walked to the doorway to his parent's bedroom.

Will my father ever be able to sleep there? Knowing...

Casper was glad for one thing. He had stopped his father from seeing the place where Kathy Halliday died. That nightmare would be his alone.

Casper took another blanket from the linen closet, returned to the sofa, and closed his eyes.

Twenty-Seven

Shane Murphy and Bradley Butler sipped coffee and stared at the television. The grim-faced mayor of New York City turned the televised briefing over to the Police Commissioner. The Commissioner had little to add to the mayor's report. The Chief of Department stood behind; looking relieved that he would not be speaking to the cameras.

The Commissioner took several questions from a crowded group of journalists. His answers provided no real insights.

Yes, it did appear that the same individual committed the three murders. This came as news to no one. According to the Commissioner, this determination was not made because of physical evidence. It was made because of the *lack* of evidence.

Bradley Butler shook his head.

"Unbelievable. The kid who hit you with a baseball bat went to prison and spent thirty months in the pen. He walks out with a clean record, became a freaking *cop*—and his mother just got whacked by a serial-killer? Jesus, Shane. Hollywood can't make up this kind of shit."

"You're right about that," Murphy said. He stepped next to the television and tapped on the image of the mayor. The mayor stood behind the Commissioner, surveying the crowd.

"Look at him," Murphy said. "That's the face of a man whose fate lies in the hands of a psychopathic killer. Here's what I want you to do. You meet with Glazkov at two o'clock this afternoon."

"Oh, hell," Butler said. "Today?"

"Yes, today," Murphy said. "I would have preferred yesterday, but yesterday we didn't have two confirmed serial killings in New York City. Tell Glazkov that I suggest a full media blitz against our darling mayor. Let's make this killer-on-the-loose the *mayor's* problem."

Murphy pointed at the screen.

"You can see it on his face. He's in trouble and he knows it. He's up for re-election next year. Glazkov's people can turn up the heat. I need people on the streets saying that a certain Assistant District Attorney is determined to make this city safe."

Butler smiled and nodded.

"I've already figured this killer out."

"Oh, really?" Murphy said. "Let's hear it."

"He's killed the owner of a bakery and two waitresses. He's a freaking food critic."

Murphy shook his head and checked his watch.

"Two o'clock. Be early—but not too early. And get right to the point. Glazkov is a no-nonsense guy."

"Got it," Butler said.

Butler followed a large man into Glazkov's office. Butler introduced himself and attempted to inform

Glazkov of his background. Glazkov stopped him with a raised hand.

"I know all I need to know about you, Mr. Butler. That is why you are here. I have eyes and ears in many places. You should remember this. Always."

"I see," Butler said. He spelled out Murphy's plan.

Glazkov tapped a finger against his lips.

"This idea has merit. Mayor of New York—this will be an excellent move. For us all. Tell Mr. Murphy I will put things into motion."

"Will that be all?" Butler said.

Glazkov produced two glasses and a bottle.

"Do not be in such a rush. We will not be friends, but we will work together closely. The occasion of our first meeting calls for a drink."

Glazkov showed Butler the bottle's label.

"The finest vodka in all of Russia—and therefore, the finest in the world."

They took a drink.

"Magnificent," Butler said.

"Good," Glazkov said. "I want you to know I require one-hundred percent loyalty."

Glazkov narrowed his eyes and leaned forward.

"And one-hundred percent honesty."

"Of course," Butler said. "We're on the same side. What's good for one is good for all."

"Ah, if it were only so simple," Glazkov said. "I trust your friend Murphy as much as I trust a venomous snake."

Butler had trouble swallowing and went into a fit

of coughing.

"I'm…I'm sorry?" he said.

Glazkov swirled the liquid in his glass before drinking it dry.

"Shane Daniel Murphy," Glazkov said. "Midwestern boy with enormous dreams—and the will and tenacity to make them come true. Does that sound correct?"

"Yes," Butler said.

"Yet, you and he parted company during his rise in the legal world," Glazkov said. "You were not Murphy's first choice to be at his side. Why not?"

Butler rubbed his chin.

"It was my goddamned brother."

"Your brother?" Glazkov said.

"My older brother. He was top of his class at law school and recruited by a Washington firm that represents some major military contractors. They must have checked him out really close—you know, like you do. They found out about me and Murphy. My brother told me that I could step into a good job in D.C. My only other choice was to face a federal indictment along with my good pal Shane Murphy."

Glazkov smiled.

"Very good, Mr. Butler."

"Very good?" Butler said. "What's so good about being blackmailed by your own brother?"

"Because I knew all this," Glazkov said. "I needed to hear it from you."

Butler sighed.

"Mr. Glazkov, you're kind of an asshole."

Glazkov laughed and refilled both glasses.

"I must disagree. I am a World-Class Asshole. Four years ago, Mr. Murphy decided on impulse to involve himself in a street crime."

"I know all about it," Butler said.

"Robert Casper Halliday," Glazkov said. "The boy who would not go away."

"Apparently, he's been targeted by this serial killer," Butler said. "Right now, he's probably sucking his thumb and hiding under his bed."

"That is beside the point," Glazkov said. "He is a target of the local and national media, making his visibility a liability to us. You must make certain that Murphy does not further involve himself with the boy."

"Why would Shane—?"

"I do not care about the *why*, Mr. Butler," Glazkov said. "I am well aware that Murphy has not let his association with Casper Halliday die a natural death. This *cannot* continue."

"I'll let him know," Butler said.

"Good," Glazkov said. "If the Halliday boy continues to draw attention,

"He might have to…be dealt with."

Twenty-Eight

Casper woke the next morning. Bobby was in the shower. He came out dressed.

"Are you going out?" Casper asked.

"I have a case I need to finish," Bobby said. "It's just paperwork. Mark told me to take off a week or two, but...I don't know."

Bobby sighed.

"I have to make arrangements for the memorial service. You can come with me if you want."

"I have something to take care of, too," Casper said.

Bobby was curious, but didn't ask any questions.

Casper entered Chief Dwight Livingston's office. He didn't have an appointment but the Chief didn't mind.

"What can I do for you, Casper?" Livingston asked.

"I want to know what you know," Casper said.

"I'm...not following you," Livingston said.

"The investigation of this serial-killer," Casper said. "I want to be in the loop."

Livingston looked down and shook his head.

"I understand what you're dealing with, son. When Brooke went missing—I would have given anything in the world to lay my hands on the men who took her. But that desire helped nothing. All it did was torture every piece of me: My mind. My stomach. My heart. Good God, it was…it was even poisoning my marriage."

"There was one difference, Chief," Casper said. "You knew *everything*—everything piece of information the department had, *you* had."

"Of course, it was different," Livingston said. "This is my job."

"Some things are more important than titles, sir."

"You're not even eligible to become a detective, Casper," Livingston said. His voice had a concerned edge.

"I don't have time to work my way up the seniority roster, sir," Casper said. "The bastard killed two women at random. My mother—"

"Casper, please—"

"My mother's murder was not random, sir. We know one thing about him. He likes the attention. He's watching the news—"

The voice of Livingston's receptionist sounded over the intercom.

"I'm sorry, sir. It's the mayor. Line one."

Livingston picked up the receiver.

"Chief Livingston."

Livingston listened for almost a minute. He ran a hand over his stressed face and put down the phone.

"I may as well tell you this. It won't be a secret for long," Livingston said. "Over a hundred people showed up outside WNYX this morning with picket signs and bullhorns. That group swelled to over two hundred. Apparently some people blame Miss Callaghan for…"

Livingston paused.

"Kit Callaghan has been fired."

"Holy shit," Casper said.

"Personally, I think it was the right thing to do," Livingston said. "If they can put a lid on this 'Ghost Man' thing, then we can go back to—"

"Wait a minute," Casper said. "This killer is not *stupid*, sir. So far, he's left you nothing to work with. Tell me that's not true."

Livingston said nothing. He ground his teeth.

"He could have killed me a thousand times," Casper said. "But he wants me to suffer—all because I have the same *stupid nickname!* Do you really think he's going to stop, sir? Do you?"

"I have no idea," Livingston said. "But we have every available man on the case—"

"No, you don't," Casper said.

"This is insanity," Livingston said. "We've put security details on you and your father. And on Miss Casey and Miss Hampton. There's nothing else I can do."

"Yes, sir, there is," Casper said. "All I'm asking is to be in the loop on this investigation. I will not do anything to put myself or anyone else in danger. Maybe I'll be no help at all. But I spent hours a day in the Fishkill library studying sociopaths. And psychopaths. And the criminal mind. I guarantee you will have no more tireless and motivated investigator working to take this asshole down."

Livingston smacked his palm on the desk.

"I can't *do* that! I could be *fired.* The entire department could suffer."

"I won't tell if you won't," Casper said.

Livingston closed his eyes.

"Go home, Casper. Spend time with your father. Grieve. Come to terms with what has happened. You're an officer of the NYPD. You will witness a lot of pain and suffering over the course of your career. I know that doesn't help right now. But it's the truth, and you know it."

Casper blew out a breath. He stood and extended his hand.

"I'm sorry, Casper," Livingston said.

"How is your daughter, sir?"

Livingston bit his lip and nodded.

"She's…coming around. Slowly."

"That's good," Casper said. "I'm glad you got a second chance, sir."

Casper took two steps toward the door. He turned back.

"My mother isn't coming back."

Twenty-Nine

Robert Ferrill stood nude in his living room, his feet spread wide like the pose of a superhero. He raised the remote control and changed the channel from one news network to the next.

The city of ten million. The state of twenty million. Add forty million from California.

Over three hundred million in the country — watching as he, the Ghost Man, had his way with the world.

He walked to the bathroom to perform his ritual.

One hour later, his hands were smooth and every nerve tingled in anticipation. He walked into his bedroom and went to work on the mannequin. He removed the shoes. He ran his hands one last time over the pantyhose that had belonged to Karin Armstrong.

Karin with an "i".

Ferrill removed the pantyhose. He clipped the hose to a hanger and placed the shoes on the top shelf of his walk-in closet.

Ferrill opened a shopping bag. He lowered his head into the bag and inhaled deeply. He exhaled.

"Ahhh."

The recent memory washed over him. Her scent. Her exquisite lower body. The warmth of her quivering torso as he pushed himself against her. Her desperation.

Her will to live — in spite of her blood flowing to the floor beneath her.

The precious mother…of the fake Ghost Man.

Ferrill dressed the mannequin in the pantyhose. Slowly. Carefully. Religiously.

He started with the toes. Then the feet. He worked his way up.

Ferrill bucked his hips against the only remains of Katherine Halliday that mattered to him.

Ferrill showered for an hour, washing away his filth.

He dressed and went to his car.

****

Ferrill drove past the house where Mona Casey lived with her mother and small child. He spotted the unmarked police car immediately. He was not surprised.

Ferrill drove past the building where Blair Hampton rented an apartment. The windows of her apartment were dark, but he spotted yet another unmarked police car parked on the street near the entrance.

He drove north, out of the city — near the gated entrance to the home of retired state senator James Hampton. Here, Ferrill spotted an unmarked police car and a plain black sedan bearing Federal license plates. Ferrill did not slow. He took a wide, circular route that brought him near the back of the Hampton property.

Ferrill spotted another Federal Government vehicle in the area.

Ferrill smirked at the vehicle in his rear-view mirror.

So. You won't make this easy. Good. Time to play. What about a diversion, Mr. Halliday?

****

Three nights later

Robert Ferrill loitered outside the company break room. The new girl was apparently slow at everything. Ferrill was present when her supervisor yelled at her three different times, only a few hours ago.

The girl did not stop, but Ferrill saw her confidence falter with every scolding.

This suited his plans, perfectly.

Ferrill stood next to a vending machine sipping a soda when the door opened. Jessica Collins jumped and shrieked.

"I'm sorry, Mr. Ferrill. I thought everyone was gone."

Ferrill smiled and tossed away the soda can.

"I like to see that everyone gets safely to their vehicles," Ferrill said. "It's one o'clock in the morning."

"Aw, you're so sweet," Jessica said. "Now I feel bad that I took so long. I am *so* slow!"

"Not a problem," Ferrill said. "Have a good night,

Miss…"

"Jessica. Jessica Collins."

"Have a good night, Jessica," Ferrill said.

"You too, sir. Thanks again."

Ferrill strolled across the dark lot.

"Oh, *shit!*"

Ferrill stopped and turned.

"What's the matter?"

"I have a freaking flat tire," Jessica said. Ferrill walked over to look.

"Do you have a spare?"

"I think so," Jessica said. "I just bought this car."

Ferrill removed his duffel bag.

"Open your trunk. I have a flashlight and gloves."

"Thank you so much, Mr. Ferrill. I can't tell you how glad I am that you're here."

Ferrill took a quick look in the trunk. He knelt by the flat tire. The passenger side of the car faced away from the building and toward a dark section of the parking lot. He shined his flashlight at the tire.

"I can show you your problem right here."

Jessica knelt beside him and looked at the tire.

She struggled when Ferrill pinned her arms and pressed the chloroform-soaked rag against her face. She fell limp and unconscious.

Ferrill bound the girl's hands and put her inside the trunk. He inflated the tire he had let the air out of less than an hour ago. He walked to his car and changed into his *other* work clothes.

The clothes of the Ghost Man.

Thirty

The time of night dictated that he quickly take care of business.

Robert Ferrill loaded the mutilated body of Jessica Collins into the trunk of her car for the second time. He drove the car to a predetermined spot, climbed out, and walked away—leaving the keys in the ignition. The neighborhood was known for drug-trafficking and homeless junkies.

Ferrill walked five blocks and boarded a late-night bus. He got off the bus two blocks away from his own parked car. Ferrill drove back to the neighborhood where he left the girl's car. He parked far away and watched the car from the shadows.

He didn't have to wait long.

Georgie Cane stumbled down the sidewalk in a long, filthy coat. He stopped occasionally to lean against a building while he cried. He rubbed his arms against the cold and the demons that attacked his mind in the absence of heroin.

Cane saw the parked car. He ambled to the driver's door and jerked it open. He fell into the seat and cried even more at his good fortune.

The keys. The keys are here.

Cane heard a noise. Or thought he did. His head

snapped left and right and then to the rear. Cane reached for the keys with trembling hands. He had no driver's license. He had not driven a car in a long time. Cane had lived on the streets for three years. He dropped out of high school and moved in with friends. He worked manual labor jobs that paid in cash. When Cane's friends introduced him to heroin, no one seemed to care about earning money anymore. And on one occasion, Cane woke up to find his small stash of money gone. A month later, the landlord and two large goons evicted them from the slum apartment.

He could not let this treasure get away from him. Not until he found Nicky C. Nicky C would take care of him. He always did as long as Cane had something to trade. And Cane had something right now. Georgie panicked.

What if it won't start?

Oh, god. Oh, god. Please…

Cane turned the key…

The engine started.

Thank you. Thank you. Thank you.

Cane exhaled when the warm air from the heater hit his face. He pressed his hands against the sides of his head.

How do I find Nicky C? Where do I go?

Cane tried to concentrate while random thoughts and images blasted his mind from every direction.

Cane put the car in gear and inched away from the curb.

Robert Ferrill smiled and walked to a nearby bus stop. Half an hour later he was in his own car. He drove two blocks, pulled over and walked into a neighborhood bar.

"Hey, Bob," the bartender said. "You're running kind of late."

Ferrill rubbed his hands together.

"Yeah. I came home to a damned flat tire. Is it too late for a beer?"

"Never," the bartender said.

Georgie Cane drove around a corner and recognized where he was. A fresh batch of tears flooded his vision. He pulled the car to the curb at an angle and climbed out.

"Nicky! Nicky C!"

Two men in dark clothes sprinted toward Cane.

"Dammit, Cane! Shut your stupid mouth."

"I've got somethin', Nicky!"

Cane rubbed his arm, anticipating the needle that would give him life.

"I've got somethin' good!"

Nicky C addressed his Number Two man.

"Go back to the corner."

The man left.

"Damn, Cane," Nicky C said. "You look like *shit.*"

"I'm sick, Nicky. I'm sick bad."

"Yeah, I hear you, Cane. But I run a business, you know. This ain't no soup kitchen."

"Look, Nicky," Cane said. He wiped his nose on his sleeve.

"I got a car. I got this car. It's a good car."

"Huh," Nicky said. "It looks like a pretty good car. You got the title for it?"

A spasm of pain forced Cane to double over.

"I don't know what that is, Nicky. I got the keys. Here. It's a good car, Nicky. I drove it here."

Nicky C pulled on a pair of leather gloves and took the keys.

"Let me look it over a little. I think we can make a deal."

Cane choked on a sob. Nicky poked his head inside the car. He sniffed. Nicky walked to the back of the car and opened the trunk. His eyes opened wide.

"Jesus Christ!"

"What's wrong, Nicky?" Cane said.

Nicky C was almost hyperventilating. He looked up and down the street, unsure of what to do. He pulled his gun and pointed it at Cane.

"Get in. Get in the car."

"Why are...why are you pointing a gun at me?"

"Shut up and get in the car!"

"You want to drive it—I don't care, Nicky. You can drive it."

Nicky C squealed the tires backing away from the curb. Cane was thrown against the dashboard.

"It runs good, huh, Nicky? It's worth some money, huh?"

Nicky C forced himself to drive sensibly. They reached a dark warehouse district within ten minutes.

Cane leaned against the back of the seat. He moaned. Nicky C reached inside his coat. He took out a skin-pop rig loaded with pure uncut heroin. Cane opened his eyes wide.

"Oh, god. Oh. Thank you, Nicky."

"Take your coat off, moron," Nicky C said.

Cane tugged at his sleeves.

"It's a good car, right Nicky?"

"Yeah. It's a great car," Nicky C said. "I'm going to fix you up for a long time."

Nicky C swapped his leather gloves for a latex pair. He prepared the syringe and pushed the needle into Cane's arm. Nicky C watched for as long as he needed to.

Georgie Cane experienced an explosion of euphoria—

Before he died.

Nicky C walked three blocks before he pulled the phone from his pocket. His Number Two man answered.

"What the hell just happened?" the man asked.

"Nothing," Nicky C said. "You hear me? Nothing happened. Get in your car and come get me."

Thirty-One

Casper came home to an empty apartment. He called his father's cell phone. Bobby picked up on the second ring.

"Hello?"

"What's going on?" Casper asked.

"Are you at home?" Bobby said.

"Yeah."

"I'm down in the courtyard," Bobby said. "Feeding the squirrels."

"What are you feeding them?"

"Peanuts," Bobby said.

"Do you have enough?" Casper asked.

"I think so," Bobby said. "The squirrels might disagree."

"I'll come down," Casper said.

Casper looked around the courtyard. He and Bobby were alone. Casper sat next to Bobby on a bench.

"Not much of a crowd today," Casper said.

Bobby looked up and scanned the windows of the high-rise apartment building.

"None of them want to look at me. Or you either, for that matter. You can't really blame them. It's human nature."

"Yeah," Casper said.

Bobby offered the bag of peanuts.

"Here you go. Make some new friends."

Casper tossed a handful of peanuts in the middle of a semi-circle of five squirrels.

"Speaking of friends, I need to go by my apartment and feed my turtles."

"You have turtles?" Bobby asked.

"Yeah," Casper said. "Two. Bonnie and Clyde."

"Male and female?"

Casper shrugged.

"The girl at the pet store made an educated guess."

"I guess time will tell," Bobby said.

"Yeah," Casper said. "Time will tell."

"Time will tell," Bobby said. "And time heals all wounds. That's what they say, right?"

Father and son stared ahead.

"We won't ever heal, will we?" Casper said.

"No," Bobby said. "Not all the way."

"But we need to...we need to stay close," Casper said. "Me and you. So neither one of us withdraws into a bad place."

Bobby Halliday moved over and put his arm around Casper's shoulder.

"That's right. That won't help anything. We should lean on each other—no matter what."

"And we should buy more peanuts," Casper said. "Because these squirrels are going to send messages to their friends all over the city."

Bobby laughed.

"How long is the lease on your apartment?" he

asked.

"Six months," Casper said. "I have a little over two months left."

"You can move back in here, if you want," Bobby said. "It's up to you. I'll understand if you want your own place."

"I'm not sure yet," Casper said. He looked at his father's face.

"Does it bother you? Being in there...by yourself?"

Bobby turned and looked at Casper. His face showed no emotion.

"Do you want the truth?"

"Of course," Casper said.

"It bothers me," Bobby said. "But not in the way you might think."

"I...don't understand," Casper said.

Bobby Halliday's face became dark. And foreboding.

"I'm going to see that bastard die. It doesn't matter if I catch him, or someone else does. I'm going to see him die."

"I feel the same way, Dad. If anyone deserves the death penalty...but we don't have it."

Bobby stared at the ground.

"He's going to die. I swear it."

"All right," Casper said. "The bastard is going to die."

****

Casper flipped on the light switch inside the door

to his apartment. The only other light came from above the terrarium that held the turtles.

"I'm sorry, guys. Did you miss me? Are you hungry?"

Casper shook the food container over the top of the terrarium. The turtles were indeed hungry. Casper sighed.

"I'm sorry. I already said that, right?"

Casper leaned his head against the top of the terrarium.

"I hope you can forgive me. My mom…"

Casper raised his head. He couldn't say it aloud — even to the turtles.

"I'm sorry."

Casper opened the refrigerator. He took out a beer bottle, opened it, and took a long drink. He held open the door and took out some food that was well past the expiration date. He dropped the containers into the trash can.

Casper jumped when the doorbell sounded. He crossed the room and look through the peephole. He opened the door.

Blair Hampton stood there, her hands covering her mouth. Her eyes were red and full of tears.

"Oh, my God…Casper…"

Blair spread her arms. She fell into Casper's embrace.

Casper closed his eyes. They filled with silent tears as his head pressed against the top of Blair's head. The scent of her familiar shampoo filled his senses. The feeling of Deja-vu and the emotions of the moment made him weak in the knees. He felt more whole—and more *right*— than he had in a long time.

"I'm *so sorry*," Blair sobbed into Casper's chest.

Casper held her tight until her quaking sobs stopped.

"I've…I've been by twice," Blair said. "You weren't here."

"I've been staying with my dad," Casper said.

Blair stepped back. She sniffed and wiped her eyes.

"Are you going to move back…back…home?"

"I don't know," Casper said. "I have a couple of months left on my lease."

Blair nodded. Casper took her hand.

"I've missed you," he said. "A lot."

Blair smiled, weakly.

"I've missed you, too."

"Can I get you something?" Casper asked.

"No. Thank you."

"Do you want to sit down?" Casper said.

Blair bit her lip and stared at the floor. She shook her head. Her tears started again.

"I can't stay, Casper. I had to see you. I *had* to. I wanted to hug you—to hold you. This was so…so *terrible!*"

Casper stepped forward and put his arms around Blair. She pushed him away.

"No. This isn't about me. I didn't come here for you to comfort me."

"Why can't we comfort each other?" Casper said.

"No, Casper. I—"

"Will you stay with me, Blair?"

"Wha…what are you talking about?" Blair said.

"Will you stay with me tonight?"

"No, no, no," Blair said, shaking her head. "I can't…I can't do…*us*, anymore."

"Oh."

"I love you, Casper. But we can't be together. Don't you see? The universe doesn't *want* us together!"

"That's crazy—"

"Oh, *is it?*" Blair snapped. "Death has been chasing us since the day we *met!*"

"That's not true—"

Blair cried even harder.

"Why are you doing this? Why are you making it harder? Can't you just—I have to go, Casper."

Blair put her hand against Casper's cheek.

"I am so sorry."

And then she was gone.

Casper looked down at the street from his balcony. He saw Blair run from the building and climb into the passenger side of a car he didn't recognize.

Casper stood above the terrarium and watched the turtles eat.

"You guys don't know how good you have it."

Thirty-Two

Casper sighed and turned a three-hundred-and-sixty degree circle. He had intended to accomplish several things in the visit to his apartment. But now, he wanted to escape these walls as quickly as possible.

Casper walked to his bedroom and took workout clothes from his dresser drawers. He locked the door behind him and went to his car.

Twenty minutes later, Casper parked outside of Master Kim's gym. He smiled when he saw the car that belonged to his good friend, Mando Gonzalez.

This has to be a good sign.

Casper climbed out of his car carrying his gym bag. He walked through the door. Master Kim met him. He bowed and then embraced Casper.

"I am sorry, my friend," Kim said.

"Thank you, Master," Casper said.

"Are you…are you ready to join us?" Master Kim asked.

"Yes," Casper said. "I want to be here."

Kim paused.

"Are you sure?"

Casper eyed the older man.

"I'm sure."

"Very well," Master Kim said.

Casper entered the training room. Mando crossed the floor and embraced his friend.

"I'm glad you're here," Mando said.

"Thanks," Casper said.

Master Kim led the group of twelve through their initial exercises. Then, he divided them into pairs.

Master Kim paired Casper with the most advanced of his students.

One pair at a time, the students faced off in duels. Master Kim stepped in occasionally to give instruction.

"Good," Master Kim said. "Always remember. Physical confrontation is always a last resort. Reason is always preferred. It is the mark of a sound mind and a sound spirit."

Master Kim pointed at a door.

"Now, Mr. Halliday. You have arrived at an impasse with Mr. Golden. You seek answers that lie beyond that door. Mr. Golden wishes to stop you. How will you proceed?"

Casper bowed to the man he had only seen once before—in this same building. He knew nothing about him.

"I need to pass through that door," Casper said.

"Why?" Mr. Golden asked.

"Because the answers I seek lie beyond it," Casper said.

"I will guard this door with my life," Mr. Golden said.

"Then you will have to die," Casper said.

"Mr. Golden has given you no obvious solution,

Casper," Mr. Kim said. "Now, what will you—?"

Casper took two quick steps toward Andrew Golden. He made a spin kick toward Golden's left ear. Golden blocked it. Casper spun in the opposite direction and landed a kick to Golden's right shoulder. Golden fell to the mat. Casper leapt on top of him and drew back his fist.

Master Kim threw Casper backward. Casper climbed to his feet. Master Kim put his hand against Casper's chest and pushed him against a wall.

Master Kim whispered into Casper's ear.

"You have suffered an inconceivable loss, my son. I understand. But you cannot be here, now. Do you understand?"

"I understand," Casper said. "I have to suffer alone."

"You are never alone. I think of you often. My heart bleeds for you, Casper Halliday," Master Kim said. "Cheng Sun was like a brother to me. But I am the shepherd of many sheep."

"I'm sorry, Master Kim," Casper said. "I'm sorry if I've disappointed you."

Master Kim squeezed Casper's shoulder.

"You haven't disappointed me. You have to heal, and it will take time and meditation. Go to the gym. Go for a run. Work out your anger and frustration with sweat and exercise—not by attacking others."

Casper turned to go. He reached for the door. Master Kim gripped his arm.

"Build bonds with your father. You need him. And he needs you. Grieve as long as you need to. Meditate often. Reclaim your center. It will never leave you. You must put aside anger and hate. They will only lead to more pain."

Casper nodded.

"You have much passion, my son," Master Kim said. "And life has given you far too much to deal with. I see why Cheng Sun loved you like a son."

Casper's head snapped around at that statement. Master Kim smiled.

"Yes, Casper. That is what he asked of me. To teach you as I would teach his own son."

"I miss him," Casper said. "A lot."

"I know," Kim said. "But he is with you, always."

"I know," Casper said.

Casper reached his car and heard Mando's voice behind him.

"Hey. Wait up."

Casper turned around.

"Did he kick you out?" Mando asked.

"Not exactly," Casper said. "I was being an asshole. I shouldn't have come here tonight."

Mando rubbed the back of his neck.

"Bad day, huh?"

"Yeah," Casper said. "I was at my apartment. Blair came by. That was the first time I've seen her since..."

"Since what happened?" Mando asked.

Casper said nothing.

"I'm sorry," Mando said. "It's none of my

business."

Casper shook his head.

"That's not it. I just...I wanted things to be like they used to be. She doesn't."

"Oh," Mando said. "That's too bad."

"I'll be okay," Casper said. "You can go back inside. I didn't mean to screw up your session."

"Are you sure?" Mando said. "I mean, we could get a beer if you want. Maybe destroy a pizza. Sit outside and watch people."

"Some other time, amigo," Casper said. "I'm going to go home and hang out with my dad."

Mando hugged his friend.

"I can't argue with that, Caz. Take care of yourself. Call me, whenever you want. Day or night. I'm here for you."

"Thanks," Casper said, "my brother from another mother."

****

Casper walked into the apartment carrying Chinese takeout food.

"You read my mind," Bobby Halliday said.

"Again," Casper said.

"Keep that under control," Bobby said. He tapped the side of his head. "It can be dark inside."

"It's the detective gene, Dad. And that's all your fault."

"Yeah. I guess it is," Bobby said. He took plates from a cabinet and set them on the dining room table.

The doorbell sounded.

"Are you expecting anybody?" Casper asked.

"No," Bobby said. "Let me know if it looks like a reporter. I'll answer the door holding a gun."

Casper looked through the peephole. It was not a reporter. It was someone he did not expect to see.

Chief of Detectives, Dwight Livingston.

Casper opened the door. Livingston glanced right and left down the hallway.

"Let me in, please," he said.

Casper stepped aside.

"Yeah. Sure."

Livingston stepped into the room. A second later, Bobby stepped in from the dining room.

"Chief Livingston?" Bobby said.

"Hello, Bobby," Livingston said. "I hope I'm not interrupting your evening."

"No," Bobby said. "We were just about to have some dinner. Chinese takeout. Can I make you a plate?"

Livingston looked at Casper.

"Do you have plenty?"

"Sure," Casper said. "I always buy extra. I like having leftover Chinese food in the fridge."

Livingston grunted.

"I do the same thing. Sure, I'm starving."

Livingston sat his briefcase beside his chair at the table. Food containers made the rounds.

Bobby took a bite and then cleared his throat.

"I can go to the living room if you two need to talk."

Livingston looked at Bobby and then Casper.

"No. That won't be necessary. I doubt you two have many secrets."

"No, sir," Casper said. "Especially now."

Livingston pushed his plate aside. He picked up his briefcase and opened it. He stared inside for a few moments. Livingston stood and stared out the window.

"Do you have a beer?"

"Sure," Bobby said. He walked to the refrigerator and returned with a bottle. Livingston took a long drink and exhaled.

"I'm about to break enough laws to have me crucified."

Bobby looked at Casper.

"What are you talking about, Chief?" Bobby asked.

"Listen, Bobby," Livingston said. "I don't want you to think this is written in stone. We've had a new Deputy Commissioner of the Internal Affairs Bureau since Baker retired fourteen months ago. Did you know that?"

"Yes," Bobby said.

"Here's the deal," Livingston said. "At least six uniformed officers got off the hook for illegal gambling. You took the fall because you were working IAB at the time."

"I was guilty," Bobby said. "I never said I wasn't."

Livingston shrugged.

"Maybe it was a good bust—maybe it wasn't. A lot of powerful people didn't want a word about a link to organized crime on the official books. That's why you were pressured into resigning."

"Like I said, I was guilty as —"

Livingston held up his hands.

"Just…just hear me out, Bobby. The official record of your resignation states you were having personal problems. You were stressed out and you couldn't sleep. Do you remember that?"

"Yeah —"

"The new D.C. and I go way back," Livingston said. "I was a groomsman at his wedding. I attended Christenings for all three of his kids."

Bobby stood and ran a hand over his head.

"I don't know what you're getting at, Chief."

"You made a mistake, Bobby," Livingston said. "Well…maybe a couple."

Livingston looked at Casper, whose jaw was hanging slack.

"Nothing changes right now," Livingston said. "It may take a while. It damn sure can't look like a consolation prize…shit. That sounds wrong. We have to catch this asshole. And to tell you the truth, I hope we don't take him alive. I hope a thousand bullets cut him into tiny pieces. I want you back in uniform and back on the force, Robert — if that's what you want."

"Jesus," Bobby whispered. "I don't know what to say…"

Livingston pointed at Bobby's chair.

"We're not done here. Have a seat."

Livingston removed a thick folder from his

briefcase. He put the briefcase on the floor and opened the folder on the table. He gave Casper a quick smile.

"This," Livingston said, "is everything we have."

"Chief," Bobby said. "What the hell are you doing?"

Livingston took a deep breath.

"There's no way I could have foreseen a situation like this. You should have made detective, Bobby. There just weren't enough positions available. I know you were disappointed—and that's why you took the IA job. And then your son…"

Livingston took a moment to compose himself.

"And then Casper saved our lives. My daughter's. And my wife's. And mine. Eight other girls. Shit—maybe the lives of a hundred more girls. Add my parents. Maggie's parents. All those other parents. Brothers. Sisters. Aunts, uncles and cousins. Dozens—maybe hundreds of lives—affected by a young man too young to even attend the academy."

Livingston downed the rest of the beer. Bobby brought another one. Dwight Livingston stared at the floor.

"What Casper did that night played a part in…what just happened to you."

Livingston looked up with tear-filled eyes.

"I don't give a damn what the law says. What kind of man could ignore what Casper did? I can't. And I won't."

"I'm sorry if I acted like an asshole yesterday," Casper said.

"No, you're not," Livingston said.

"But—"

"Don't apologize, son," Livingston said. "I would have done the same thing. Let's get the ground rules straight."

Livingston held up a cell phone.

"This phone is a burner—paid for in cash. No one knows I have it—not even my wife. Don't call me on anything else. Got it?"

"Got it," Bobby said.

"Okay," Casper said.

"As far as covering our asses, I'll state the obvious," Livingston said. "You don't go out together doing anything that looks like an active investigation. You'll get caught. And if you get caught, I get caught."

Livingston stared at Casper.

"If we get caught, I can't pull strings. And your dad's career with the NYPD stays over."

"We get it, sir," Casper said.

"Number two," Livingston said. "Information flows both ways. If you find out something, I want to know it five seconds later."

"Of course," Bobby said.

Casper nodded.

Livingston glared at both men.

"Number three. This is not revenge. I give you information. That's it. This is police work. There are no more promises. If we find him—*when* we find him, we take him down. You will *not* be involved. You will sit right here until I tell you to do otherwise. Are we clear?"

"Yes, sir."

"Yes, sir."

"And number four. Do not *ever* lie to me."

Casper and Bobby nodded again.

Livingston showed them four photos.

"These two photos are from outside the station. These two are from the entrance and the break room. No one can identify this officer."

"Holy shit," Casper said. "He has a police uniform?"

"Apparently so," Livingston said. "We shouldn't be surprised. He's made no mistakes so far. Glasses. Mustache. Hat pulled down over his eyes, red hair. He's in disguise, without a doubt."

Livingston reached for the photos.

"Wait," Casper and Bobby said at the same time. They both leaned over and stared at the photos for a few more seconds. When they sat back, Livingston gathered up the photos.

"Karin Armstrong," Livingston said, "had four years training in self-defense. Detectives at the scene of the murder in her parking garage found evidence of bleach on the concrete and the bumper of the SUV."

"She hurt him," Casper said.

"It's possible," Livingston said.

Livingston laid out three pieces of paper.

"He's killed a bakery owner and two waitresses…"

Thirty-Three

Casper woke to the smell of frying bacon. He stepped into the hallway and saw his father. Bobby was dressed in pajama bottoms and an undershirt. He moved with more energy than Casper had seen in several days.

"Good morning," Casper said.

"Good morning," Bobby said. "Hungry?"

Casper stretched.

"I wasn't. Until my nose told me I was."

"Coffee and bacon," Bobby said. "Works every time."

Casper sat down on a kitchen stool. Bobby flipped the bacon and stepped back from the stove-top.

"I can't believe this," Bobby said. "My career was over..."

"We have a job to do," Casper said.

"Yeah," Bobby said. "I know. But I would scrub toilets for the rest of my life if we could have her back."

"I know, Dad," Casper said. "I would be right there beside you."

Bobby turned and looked at Casper. Bobby's face was void of emotion.

"I know what the Chief said. And I will do everything in my power to protect you and your career. But if I get the chance to watch this murdering bastard die—"

"I know," Casper said. "Let's hope it doesn't come to that."

Bobby turned back to the stove.

"What are you going to do today?" Casper asked.

"I'm going downtown," Bobby said. "I have street snitches I haven't contacted in four years. I'm going to see how many of them are still around. What about you?"

"I don't have any street snitches yet," Casper said. "I'm going to study the material the Chief left us. Maybe I'll find something to follow."

"Okay," Bobby said. "Do you want to do something for dinner?"

"I'm not sure," Casper said. "Give me a call later. I'm going to my apartment and move Bonnie and Clyde over here. I need to empty my refrigerator and pack some clothes."

Bobby nodded.

"Good idea. We can compare notes tonight."

"You're damn right," Casper said with a grim smile. "We're going to get him, Dad."

Bobby stared into the frying pan.

"Yes, we are."

****

Casper stopped his car in front of his apartment. He stepped out and watched the sun sink beyond the horizon. The looming darkness made him more comfortable.

The bright of day belonged to the good guys. Daylight criminals were few and far between. In the boroughs of the city, people moved with confidence. Citizens believed they were safe from the bad people when the sun was shining. And they were almost always right. Police officers walked, rode, and drove the streets with an air of invincibility in the light of day. Natives and tourists walked, jogged, and laughed their way along the city streets. Life was good.

Casper Halliday knew better. He was only twenty-one-years-old. And an NYPD rookie—with a murdered mother.

Casper knew the most important hours of his life would happen in the darkness of the city; when the bad element trolled the streets. When the bad people sought victims to fuel their sick desires.

When madness reigned.

Casper entered his apartment and flipped on the lights. He opened the refrigerator door and put everything perishable into a garbage bag.

Did I really buy this much beer? I can't remember.

Casper opened one of the sixteen bottles and took a long pull. It tasted good. He took another drink. The alcohol hit his brain. He closed his eyes and took a deep breath. He turned on his stereo and played some music—not too loud. Background noise. Music to make him feel like he wasn't alone; that he was still connected to the real world.

"Hi, you guys," Casper said to Bonnie and Clyde. "Have you missed me? I've missed you. Guess what?

You're coming with me to live at Dad's apartment. You'll like it there. I promise. We have breakfast in the morning, most of the time. And we stay up late, watching cop shows. Do you like those? I bet you do. I named you after famous criminals. Nothing personal. Don't worry. I believe you'll both live long, productive crime-free lives."

Casper put his face close to the lid of the terrarium.

"There's a sick son-of-a-bitch out there. He murdered my mother. But we're gonna catch him. I swear—as sure as I'm standing here and an officer of the New York City Police Department. I swear it."

Casper took a second bottle of beer into his bedroom. He took a long drink and sat the bottle on his dresser. He sighed and opened his closet. Casper selected clothes and laid them on his bed. He could hear his neighbor's stereo through the walls. This wasn't unusual—especially on the weekends. Casper didn't mind. They had good taste in music.

The doorbell sounded. Casper reached for his service weapon.

But he wasn't wearing it. He froze.

Was it Blair? Had she come back? Had she reconsidered?

Did she…

Did she love him—enough?

Casper took a step.

Or was it another reporter? Another heartless vulture stalking him to further her own agenda at the expense of his pain? Someone looking to gain from his loss?

Casper stood in the middle of the room, his hands balled into white-knuckled fists.

The doorbell sounded again. And again.

Casper slipped off his shoes. He crept to the door and leaned against the peephole.

It couldn't be. This wasn't possible.

"Casper? Are you in there?"

He knew the voice.

Oh, yes. I know that voice.

Casper shivered. The tremors ran from the top of his head to the soles of his feet. Casper lifted the security chain. He unlocked the deadbolt and opened the door.

She was a mess.

Her hair looked like she had run through a storm. Her expensive dress clung desperately to one shoulder. Her mascara was running.

She was a beautiful, sensual, mess.

"Charlie," Casper said.

Charlie Talbot collapsed into tears.

"Oh, my God, Casper..."

She spread her arms. Casper moved into them. Charlie buried her face in his chest. A door opened two apartments down and then quickly closed.

"Can I come in?" Charlie asked.

"Of course," Casper said.

He backed into his apartment. Charlie walked forward and threw her arms around Casper again. She held him tightly.

Casper closed his eyes.

She's so warm…she feels so good…

Casper felt uncomfortable. He pulled away.

Charlie whispered in his ear.

"Please don't let go."

Casper didn't let go. And somehow…it felt right.

Casper moved his lips and pushed with his tongue. Strands of Charlie's hair had made their way into his mouth. He didn't care.

"I'm so sorry," Charlie whispered.

"I'm sorry, too," Casper whispered.

"Don't you be sorry," Charlie whispered. "Your mother was taken from you. You have nothing to be sorry about."

Casper paused.

"I had no right to interfere with your life," Casper said.

"Why?" Charlie whispered.

"Why?" Casper said.

"I have lots of friends," Charlie said. "How many people can say that?"

Casper said nothing.

"But those friends wouldn't dare interfere," Charlie said. "You *did* something."

"You deserve better," Casper said.

Charlie made a fist and hit Casper's shoulder.

"There you go again!" she said. "You don't know me—we met, like, what? A few weeks ago?"

"Maybe it doesn't make sense," Casper said. "But I *do* know you. I don't understand it either. But I—

"You knew I would blow up," Charlie said. "You

knew I would scream and call you names. I might never have spoken to you again."

"Yeah," Casper said.

"But you did it anyway," Charlie said.

"Yeah," Casper said. "I'm just a rookie. I don't know what the hell I'm doing."

Charlie leaned back and looked Casper in the eye.

"You knew exactly what you were doing. You slapped me in the face with the truth."

"What are you going to do?" Casper asked.

"It's over," Charlie said.

"Good."

"I've checked into a hotel," Charlie said. "I've hired an attorney and filed a protection order."

"Good," Casper said. "Double good."

Charlie looked away. She raised her hand and touched her face with her fingertips.

"I can't believe I let him get away with...hitting me."

Casper said nothing. Charlie looked at him.

"I'm not like that. I've *never* been like that! That's not me."

Casper's face turned to stone.

"He'll never hit you again. I swear it."

Charlie smiled. Her fingers trailed down Casper's arm.

"My precious guard dog."

"Don't put up with his shit, Charlie," Casper said. "I mean it. If he tries calling you or—"

Charlie put her finger against Casper's lips.

"Sh."

Casper's neighbors had turned up the volume on their sound system. The opening refrain of George Michael's Careless Whisper permeated the door and walls.

Charlie leaned into Casper's chest.

"I love this song," Charlie said.

"I do, too," Casper said.

"Of course you do," Charlie said. "Every guy loves this song, but most won't admit it."

"Hmmm, I'm not scared," Casper said. "I like it. What can I say?"

Charlie swayed against Casper's chest. Her left hand slid down Casper's right arm and her fingers intertwined with his. They moved, side-to-side, in time with the music.

Casper closed his eyes. He felt as if his goose bumps had goose bumps. But he was warm, and comfortable, and...excited? He tried to push away.

"No," Charlie said into his chest.

"Cha—"

"Casper?" Charlie said.

"Yes?"

"Will you make love to me?"

Casper shivered so hard he knew Charlie could feel it. His words came in a breathless rush.

"Oh, my God. No, Charlie."

He laughed nervously.

"You're not serious."

"Yes, I am," Charlie said.

"This isn't right. That's not what you want."

"Don't tell me what I want," Charlie said. "And for goddamn sure don't tell me what's right."

Casper flushed with embarrassment when he realized he had said the wrong thing.

"I'm sorry, Charlie—"

Her lips pressed against his. Their tongues touched. Charlie pulled back slightly and licked his lips.

Casper didn't stop her. In what seemed to be only a fraction of a second, they melted into each other's arms. Charlie's lips moved to Casper's cheek. They moved to his neck.

Casper opened his mouth to speak. It took a few moments.

"I think..."

Charlie kissed his neck again. And again.

"You think what?" she whispered.

"I think... you've changed my mind."

Thirty-Four

Casper opened his eyes and stared at the ceiling. It took him a moment to remember where he was, and what had happened before he fell asleep.

He smelled Charlie's perfume. Casper turned his head. The blankets were turned back, and the space was empty. Casper sat up in the bed. He caught another scent—a faint hint of tobacco smoke. The balcony door stood open about a foot. Casper relaxed. He wasn't sure what last night meant, but he didn't want to think Charlie might have dressed in silence and run away in horror and humiliation.

Casper pulled on his pants and stepped onto the balcony.

"Hi," he said.

Charlie sat on one of the two chairs on the small balcony with her stockinged feet against the railing. She raised a bottle.

"I stole one of your beers."

"No problem," Casper said. "Is that my coat?"

"Yep," Charlie said. She pointed at her feet.

"And those are your socks. It's a little chilly out here."

Casper rubbed his arms.

"Yeah, it is." Casper smiled.

"What's so funny?" Charlie asked.

Casper cocked his head to the side and looked at Charlie's thighs.

"Is it a little breezy under there?"

Charlie lowered her feet to the floor and laughed.

"I'm wearing my underwear, you naughty boy."

Charlie dropped her cigarette butt into the empty beer bottle and sat the bottle on the table. She slapped her hands to her cheeks.

"Oh, my God. I can't *believe* I did that."

"Did what?" Casper said.

"Did *what?*" Charlie said. "What I did...three hours ago!"

"I was there, too, remember?" Casper said.

Charlie grabbed Casper's hand. The coat she was wearing fell open, exposing her breast.

"Of course you were, honey."

"I hope I was okay," Casper said.

Charlie smiled.

"Oh...you were wonderful, Casper."

Charlie pulled on Casper's hand.

"Holy shit," she said. "There are scratches all over your shoulders."

Charlie let go of Casper's hand. She covered her mouth.

"My God. I am such a slut-puppy cougar!"

Casper wrapped his hand in Charlie's hair and pulled their lips together. Their tongues intertwined until Charlie pulled away.

"You are no such thing," Casper said. "You are wonderful—and the most beautiful, exotic, desirable woman on earth—"

"Calm down, Casper," Charlie said. "I appreciate your kind words, but—"

"They're not kind words," Casper said. "They're the truth. I can't believe that asshole—"

Charlie shoved the empty beer bottle in Casper's face.

"Get us a beer and a blanket and come sit with me."

Casper returned and spread the blanket over them both. His left hand reached and intertwined with Charlie's right.

"You have a very nice view," Charlie said.

Casper turned and looked at her.

"Yes, I do."

Charlie threw her elbow into Casper's side.

"Oh, stop it. You know that's not what I was talking about."

"Yes," Casper said. "And I'm sure a full third of my rent is because of this view."

"Welcome to New York," Charlie said.

"Have you always lived here?" Casper asked.

"No," Charlie said. "I grew up in Vermont—in a two-hundred-year-old house."

"How did you get here?"

Charlie moved her feet to the railing.

"I moved to Boston. I was accepted to the Berklee College of Music—for violin."

"Wow," Casper said.

"Yeah," Charlie said. "Wow. At the beginning of

my second semester, a professor took me aside and told me I didn't have the skills to become a professional. I wish he had just punched me in the stomach."

"That was harsh," Casper said.

Charlie shrugged.

"He was right. I was the worst one in my class. There were students there who could play circles around me."

"Is that where you met your husband?" Casper asked.

"No. The school allowed me to switch from violin to voice. That didn't work out either—but I completed my sophomore year."

"I'm surprised it didn't work," Casper said. "You have a great voice."

Charlie laughed.

"I have the perfect voice for telling you boys where the shots are being fired."

Casper ran his finger down the length of Charlie's arm and took her hand. Charlie shivered.

"You're giving me goose bumps."

"So, what happens now?" Casper said.

"I'm leaving in a little while," Charlie said. "Do you want me to go now?"

"No, no, no," Casper said. "That's not what I was talking about. I mean, what happens now...between us."

"Oh," Charlie said. She squeezed Casper's hand.

"Nothing has to happen, honey. I think tonight might have helped both of us. We're just two people who are hurting and needed to be close—to reaffirm our connection to humanity. It doesn't have to mean anything deeper than that."

Casper sighed.

"Of course, it helped me. But this wasn't just therapy to me. I'm not wired that way."

"Then I made a terrible, terrible mistake," Charlie said.

"No, you didn't," Casper said.

"Can we just—can we not talk about this right now?" Charlie said. "I'm feeling so good—for the first time in a long time."

"I'm not talking about getting married or anything," Casper said.

"What?" Charlie said. "Married? Jesus Christ, Casper, I'm old enough to be your moth—!"

Charlie's chin fell to her chest.

"Shit. I'm sorry."

"That's okay," Casper said.

Charlie lit a cigarette and blew out the smoke.

"Don't you have a girlfriend? Ha. This is a fine time to be asking that, huh?"

"She doesn't…she doesn't want to see me anymore," Casper said. "Too much stress. Too much publicity. I don't blame her."

"She's quitting the department?" Charlie asked.

"Yeah," Casper said. "She's already gone. She's going back to school."

"That's not such a bad idea," Charlie said.

"No," Casper said. "Her father has connections at the FBI."

Charlie took Casper's face in her hands and kissed

him on the lips. She tapped out her cigarette.

"I'm going to take off. I've had a wonderful evening."

"Me too," Casper said. "You're welcome to stay. It's up to you."

Charlie smiled.

"I don't want your neighbors to wonder about the hussy slinking out of your apartment in the morning."

"Would you stop calling yourself names?" Casper said. "I like to think I have good taste."

"You're right," Charlie said. She kissed Casper again.

"I'm leaving with good thoughts and good feelings. Thank you, Casper."

"Thank you," Casper said.

"Celeste."

Thirty-Five

Charlie dressed and called for a taxi. Casper walked her to the door. Charlie reached for the door knob.

"Wait," Casper said. "I'll walk you down."

"You're not dressed," Charlie said. "I want one more cigarette, and I'm not going to smoke in your apartment."

"It's almost two in the morning," Casper said.

Charlie patted her purse.

"I have a whistle, a can of mace, and a taser."

"Really?" Casper said.

"Really."

"Hey, I just thought of something," Casper said. "If you'd rather not stay in a hotel, you could stay here."

Charlie put her hands on her hips.

"Casper—"

"I don't mean with me," Casper said. "I'm moving in with my dad—at least for now. I have two months left on my lease here. The rent is paid."

Charlie bit her lip.

"That's not such a bad idea."

She hugged Casper and kissed his cheek.

"Good night, young prince."

"Sweet dreams, Princess."

Casper finished dressing. He took a duffel bag from his closet and put it on the bed. He had intended to pack his clothes and Bobbie and Clyde and go back to his parent's...

To his father's apartment. But that was a few incredible hours ago. Casper walked to the kitchen, took a beer from the refrigerator, and sat on the living room sofa. He raised the remote control and scrolled through the channels. Casper paused when he saw a scene showing patrol cars pulling out of a precinct station parking lot. He dropped the remote on the sofa and took a drink.

The program was an episode of Cagney and Lacey, a police drama from the 1980s.

Casper blinked and felt a tear trickle down his cheek.

Cagney. And Lacey. A little trigger—out of the distance.

A late night—on the sofa...watching this show with his mother.

Kathy Halliday's death had not really hit home for Casper. It was still far too insane for his mind to deal with.

He knew the sad emptiness; he felt pain for himself and for his father.

And for the horror she had endured at the end. Casper's memories of her played across the screen of his mind like they were on an endless loop. He re-lived the difficult days when the two of them were alone and afraid. When all they had was each other.

But behind it all, lurking in the shadows, was the knowledge that the monster who took her away…was still out there.

The monster had chosen Kathy Halliday to get at him. All because of a stupid nickname.

His nickname.

Ghost Man.

****

The monster stirred.

He had been dozing in his car. The lights of the taxi reflected off of his rear-view mirror. The taxi pulled into the designated commercial taxi-zone in front of the building's entrance.

Robert Ferrill sat up and adjusted his mirrors.

"There you are…Mrs. Talbot."

A dark shape in the doorway flicked a cigarette onto the public sidewalk and hurried to the taxi.

"Hello…" Ferrill said to himself. His eyes moved to her legs. They were magnificent.

Perhaps that is why she wears no hosiery. What a shame.

Or perhaps our young Mr. Halliday ripped them off of you.

Ferrill checked his watch and sighed. He would live out no fantasies this night. Not only did he have to report for work in a little more than an hour, but he had presented the New York Police Department a little gift.

He had given them their killer, wrapped up in a

bow; a stolen car with a dead girl in the trunk—and a worthless degenerate behind the wheel.

When the taxi disappeared around a corner, Ferrill pulled away from the curb. He would be early for work, but that was not unusual. He was good at his job. Everyone said so. Not that he cared. He didn't.

It wasn't that he was popular because he wasn't. He knew most of his co-workers thought he was weird. Strange. Maybe even a sociopath, which was strange considering his duties. But he did his job and that was all that really mattered. After the first few weeks, no one tried to engage him in small talk. They certainly didn't attempt to hang out with him away from work.

The job gave Ferrill exactly what he needed: a variable schedule. Easy access to hundreds of miles of densely-populated metropolitan area.

And an almost perfect cover. Robert Ferrill was hidden in plain sight.

He was the perfect Ghost Man.

Thirty-Six

Casper lay back on the sofa. When the next commercial came on, he walked to the bedroom and grabbed his pillow. He thought for a moment, dropped the pillow, and picked up the pillow that had cradled Charlie Talbot's head a few hours ago.

Grow up, Casper. Don't be an idiot.

Casper held the pillow to his face and breathed in deeply. He tucked the pillow under his arm and returned to the living room.

His cell phone woke him. Casper picked up the phone and looked at his watch.

4:35.

The number on his phone seemed familiar somehow, but he wasn't sure who it was.

"Hello?"

"Casper?"

"Yeah."

"This is Dwight Livingston."

Casper's eyes widened. He swung his feet to the floor.

"What—?"

"Listen to me, Casper. I only have a minute. I'm locked inside the men's room of a warehouse on the edge of Dumbo. Do you know where that is?"

Casper squeezed his eyes shut and rubbed his forehead.

DUMBO.

Down Under the Manhattan Bridge Overpass.

"Yeah—"

"Look," Livingston said. "You can't come here, and I can't leave."

"I'm sorry, sir. What are you talking ab—"

"We got him, Casper."

Casper leapt to his feet.

"*What!* Where? Where is he?"

"I told you—"

"Where is the son-of-a-bitch?"

"Goddammit, Casper," Livingston snapped. "Calm down. I told you the rules. It doesn't matter where he is."

"Because he's dead."

Casper was almost hyperventilating.

"Dead?"

"Yes," Livingston said. "He was a junkie. A heroin addict. Tracks all over his arms and legs. But it's over."

Casper paced the floor. He grabbed a handful of his hair and pulled.

"That doesn't make any sense—"

"It doesn't have to make sense," Livingston said. "All that matters is he is no longer among the living."

"But—"

"No," Livingston said. "I have to go. Here's what I want you to do. Tell your father what I've told you. Stay home. Keep your eyes and ears on the television. The mayor's office is going to leak this, I guarantee it. He wants this case wrapped up so bad he would kiss the corpse on the lips. I'll be in touch."

The line went dead.

Casper packed his duffel bag. He carried it and the terrarium to his car and drove to his father's apartment. Casper saw light beneath the apartment door. The door wasn't locked. He pushed it open.

"I was wondering where you were," Bobby Halliday said. "I just got home. I was about to call you."

Casper sat down the terrarium and went to the kitchen. He heard Bobby's voice.

"Bonnie and Clyde. Welcome to mi casa."

Casper returned with two beer bottles. He handed one to Bobby.

"Beer for breakfast?" Bobby said.

Casper sighed.

"You're gonna want it.

"I have something to tell you."

****

Casper and Bobby stared at the television. Chief Livingston was right. Reports of the capture of the serial killer preempted all local programming. There was no mention of the killer being dead.

Of course not, Casper thought.

Let the people think if they stay tuned, they might get a look at his face. They might get to look into the eyes of the monster that lived among them. The monster capable of taking delight in watching the life-blood drain from another human being. How fascinating.

Bobby leaned forward and put down an empty bottle, making a total of eight. He rested his elbows on his knees and rubbed his face with both hands. He turned toward Casper.

"A heroin addict? I wouldn't have guessed that in a million years."

Casper shook his head.

"At least he's dead," Bobby said. "And gone. I can't imagine sitting in a courtroom watching the mother—"

Bobby stopped and took a breath.

"I can't imagine watching a judge hand the prick a life sentence. If I had gotten my hands on him, I would have crashed through a barricade to get him into a state with the death penalty."

"I'm not sure it works that way," Casper said.

"Yeah," Bobby said. "Me neither. This is the real deal, though."

Bobby pointed at the television. The mayor stood in front of a podium wrapped in as many microphones as it would hold. The mayor was tight-lipped, but he stood tall and there seemed to be a hint of relief in his expression.

"He's not going to say a damn thing about the guy being a junkie," Bobby said. "That reflects badly on him. No one wants to think about what happens after dark in the bad parts of town. Everybody wants to pretend the junkies and the homeless are hiding like cockroaches— not out looking for victims."

There was a sudden commotion to the left of where the mayor stood. Security personnel circled the mayor. The scene moved away from the stage. A shaky camera moved through a crowd of policemen. With police officers descending upon the renegade cameraman, the camera gained a higher viewpoint. The camera's operator raised the camera over-head. Shouts and curses grew ever closer.

But for two seconds, the view of a white four-door economy car filled the screen. The car's doors and trunk were open. Crime-scene tape surrounded the car.

Two seconds.

Two seconds was an eternity in the digital age.

The screen went dark to the uncensored growling soundtrack of a deep male voice.

"Son-of-a-bitch!"

The news feed returned to the studio desk.

"Jesus Christ," Bobby whispered.

"That was staged," Casper said.

"Your damn right it was," Bobby said. "He's playing this like he's in freaking Hollywood."

****

A few miles away, two men with a different agenda watched a television screen in silence. The man behind the desk looked for a handy projectile. He snatched up a stapler and threw it toward the far wall, shattering the glass of a picture frame. A woman's voice came across the intercom.

"Are you all right, Mr. Murphy?"

"Yes," Shane Murphy snapped through gritted teeth. "Thank you."

Murphy stood and paced the floor.

"They caught him. They caught the son-of-a-bitch. And every idiot in the city is going to believe the mayor had something to do with it. I can't believe this. Can you believe this?"

"No," Bradley Butler said. "That was too damned fast. And too damned easy. I think—"

Murphy raised a hand.

"Shh. The asshole is coming to the podium. Look at him! You'd think he just won the goddamn lottery!"

"He did," Butler said. Murphy gave him a dirty look.

The commotion began. Policemen closed in on the commotion. The shaky camera broadcast its damning video.

Murphy ran toward the screen. He was momentarily unable to speak. He held out his hands in supplication.

"Oh. *Oh…**Oh!**"

Murphy spun and looked at Butler.

"Are you seeing this? Can you believe what he's—?"

Butler stood and stepped toward the screen.

"Oh, my god. He set this *up!* This is a fake as—"

"*Fake!*" Murphy roared. "Fake freaking news. You filthy, propaganda-slinging son-of-a-bitch!"

Murphy crossed the room and fell onto the sofa. He covered his face with his hands.

"He won't get away with it," Butler said. "The press won't let him."

"Yes he will," Murphy said.

"Somebody will talk," Butler said.

"No, they won't," Murphy said. "What would be in it for them? It would be suicide—the career kind, or the other kind. Or both."

"How can you know all this?" Butler said.

"Because," Murphy said. "The mayor did exactly what I would have done if I was in his place."

Thirty-Seven

Robert Ferrill slept for five hours. He showered, shaved, dressed, and left the hotel room. He fumed when he heard his name being called.

"Robert! Hey, wait up!"

Ferrill turned as Eddie Bailey jogged down the hallway in his direction. "Look," Ferrill said. "I don't mean to be rude—"

Actually, I do. Have I not always made it obvious I want to be left alone?

"I had a hell of a night. I'm on my way to the pharmacy. These springtime allergies are killing me," Ferrill lied.

"I'm sorry, man," Bailey said. "I just—did you meet the new girl they hired in the dining room? The pretty Asian girl?"

"Yeah," Ferrill said. "We were introduced. Said 'hi' a couple of times. I hear she's clumsy. Why?"

"You're not gonna believe this," Bailey said. "You know the serial killer who's been all over the news?"

"Yes."

"They caught him," Bailey said with a satisfied grin. "And he's *dead*."

"Really?" Ferrill said. He winced and rubbed his temples with his fingertips.

"That's great news."

"You'll never guess how they caught him," Bailey said.

Ferrill covered his mouth and faked a coughing fit. "Jesus Christ. Are you going to tell me or not?"

"Okay. Okay," Bailey said. "The killer murdered Jessica Collins two nights ago."

Ferrill looked confused.

"…Jessica…"

His eyes widened.

"The new girl? Our new girl?"

"That's right," Bailey said.

"Oh, no…" Ferrill said. "Are you serious?"

"Like a heart attack, Bud," Bailey said.

"That's…that's less than forty-eight hours ago," Ferrill said. "How can you know all this? That doesn't sound possible."

"It was just a fluke," Bailey said. "Jessica had been working here a couple of weeks. When she didn't show up for work and didn't answer her phone, the company sent a couple of officers to her apartment. The building was surrounded by cops. All this was supposed to be confidential, but you know how *that* works. The guy…"

Bailey paused and swallowed.

"He cut her. All over. He bled her to death, just like the last woman. He stole her car after he put her body in the trunk."

"You said he's dead?" Ferrill asked.

"Oh, yeah," Bailey said. "He's dead, all right."

"What happened?" Ferrill said. "A sniper? Did the police gun him down?"

Bailey shrugged.

"That—I don't know. I just got a call from—well, a friend of mine. Of course, he made me swear not to say a word to anyone, but hey, we're a team. Right, Bob?"

"Yeah," Ferrill said.

Yeah. We're a hell of a team. I want to hang you up by your feet and bleed you like a cow.

"That poor girl," Ferrill said.

"Yeah," Bailey said.

"I have to go," Ferrill said.

"Okay," Bailey said. "See you tonight. I hope you get to feeling better."

Ferrill turned without another word.

****

By five P.M. it was evident the news networks had nothing new. They rehashed the old news and sought commentary from anyone who might keep viewers locked to their channel.

"I'm going to get us something to eat," Casper said.

"Okay," Bobby said. "I'm getting in the shower."

Casper looked through the items in his top dresser drawer. The drawer held his collection of disguises since he became somewhat of a media darling four years ago. Casper chose a stocking cap, fake glasses, and a pair of long sideburns.

He walked two blocks to the east and entered a deli. His phone rang. He answered it and walked out of the deli.

"Yes, Chief?"

"I can meet you at your place at eight o'clock," Chief Livingston said. "Does that work for you?"

"Sure," Casper said. "I'm at the deli right now. I'll get you something."

"Sounds good," Livingston said.

Casper answered the door at seven-fifty-five. Chief Livingston hurried into the apartment. Bobby stepped in from the kitchen and offered Livingston a bottle of beer. The Chief accepted it with a smile.

"I don't have a problem. Not yet."

They took seats at the dining room table.

"Here's what we have," Livingston said. "A routine patrol reported the white compact sedan parked curbside in an industrial neighborhood. This was at three A.M."

"We saw the footage of the car," Bobby said. "Thanks to that bit of theater."

Livingston shook his head.

"No comment."

"Could someone have gotten the license plate number from that footage?" Casper asked.

"Oh, yeah," Livingston said. "That information was out on the web in less than twenty minutes. We couldn't stop it. The girl's name was out there in less than half-an-hour."

"Chief," Casper said. "What's your gut instinct? Is this the right guy?"

"It doesn't matter what I think," Livingston said. "We have a dead girl in the trunk of her own car; we don't have official autopsy results, but the obvious cause of death…"

Livingston paused and leaned away from the table.

"She had dozens of two inch cuts. She bled —"

"He bled her like an animal," Bobby said. "Just like…"

"Yeah," Livingston said.

"The junkie," Casper said. "Who was he?"

"George Arthur Cane," Livingston said. "Thirty-one years of age. Dropped out of high school his junior year. Filed Federal income tax for four years. Never made over twenty-five thousand in a year. Two arrests for shoplifting—five years apart. Never married. Sexual orientation unknown."

Casper shook his head.

"I can't wrap my head around it. A heroin addict commits at least four murders and leaves behind no evidence?"

"This murder is only sixteen hours old," Livingston said.

"What do you have?" Bobby said.

"He wasn't wearing gloves," Livingston said. "And we didn't find any. No other clothes or shoes either."

"So, suddenly he goes from perfect crimes to being an idiot?" Casper said.

"Not exactly," Livingston said. "We're holding onto one piece of evidence. Only eight people on the planet know this."

Livingston looked at the others.

"Now, there are ten. There was a two-and-a-half gallon gas can in the trunk with the girl."

"He was gonna torch it," Bobby said. "Right after he got high."

Casper shook his head again.

"No. The guy who did these murders wouldn't take that kind of chance. He would have worn gloves."

"He was a *junkie*, Casper," Bobby said. "Maybe he used to have the IQ of a brain surgeon, but when that demon takes over your mind—"

"No. He was too good. Too careful," Casper said.

"How many addicts have you seen, Casper?" Bobby said. "Face-to-face? Huh?"

"I haven't…not yet," Casper said. "But—"

"It's like looking into hell," Bobby said. "They don't care about you. They don't care about anybody. All that matters is that next fix."

Casper looked away.

"I want it to be him, Dad. Just like you. I would give anything if it could all be over."

"We'll have this wrapped up in a few days," Livingston said. "You have my word. We'll have every possible resource on the investigation. Let's put this thing to rest."

Casper and Bobby nodded.

Livingston stood and stretched.

"If there's nothing else, I'm sure I have a wife—"

Livingston paused and cleared his throat.

"I'm sure Maggie is pacing the floor and wringing her hands."

Casper picked up his pen.

"One thing, sir. Can you give me the bio on the latest victim?"

Livingston opened his folder and flipped through pages.

"Jessica...Collins. Here you go. Keep it. I have copies."

Livingston moved toward the door. Casper scanned the page and flipped it to the back.

"Sir," Casper said.

"Yes?"

"This isn't everything. There's no job history."

"I'm sorry," Livingston said. "Long day."

"Yes, sir," Casper said.

Livingston opened his briefcase and folder and produced one more sheet of paper.

"She wasn't going to be in the running for employee of the year," Livingston said. "Three jobs in five months—the last one less than three weeks."

Casper might have nodded in response. He wouldn't remember.

Because he felt the same tickle at the back of his mind he once felt at the sight of two men at the Red Hook Port Terminal.

Thirty-Eight

Bobby Halliday rubbed his eyes and opened the refrigerator. Casper caught the door.

"Don't worry about breakfast, Dad. I'll grab something."

"I'm covering the office for Mark today," Bobby said. "What are you going to do?"

"I'm going to look up a friend from Fishkill," Casper said. "He was paroled last year. And then I thought I'd make a little road trip—down to Baltimore."

Bobby sighed.

"You'd better be careful, Casper. If you flash your badge down there it could get back to the Chief."

"I know. I just want to be sure, Dad."

"Are you driving?"

"No. I'm taking the train. It'll be an adventure."

"Yeah," Bobby said. "An adventure."

****

Casper checked his directions and parked his car at the curb.

"Yo, man," a teen-aged youth said as Casper locked his door. "Is that a pig car?"

"It used to be," Casper said. "A long time ago. Now, it's just mine."

"And who the hell are you, White Bread?" another boy said. The other five boys snickered.

"I'm a friend of Jerome Slade," Casper said. "Do you know him?"

The boys eyed each other nervously.

"Bullshit," a boy said.

Casper looked at his notes.

"I'm looking for 1162 Downey Circle."

"Big freakin' deal," a boy said. "The little boy cop's got him an address."

Casper stepped up toe-to-toe with the young man.

"Jerome and I did time together at Fishkill. He might not like it that you're bustin' my ass."

A boy waved at Casper to follow him.

"I know Jerome. He told me about a white bo—I heard about you. Follow me."

The young man stopped at the bottom of a set of beat-up concrete steps. The main door was open, leaving a closed screen door.

"Yo! Mister Slade!"

Casper heard floor boards creak inside the house. The screen door swung open.

"What do you want, Housefly? —*Holy shit!*"

Jerome Slade's eyes went wide when he saw Casper. He crossed the porch and leapt down the steps in two strides. He threw his arms around Casper. Casper squeezed the giant man back just as hard.

"Son of a *bitch*, it's good to see you, Ghost Man." Slade said.

Casper slapped Slade's back.

"It's good to see you, too, Jerome."

Slade held Casper at arm's length.

"Look at you. All growed up and proper!"

"Me?" Casper said. He gripped Slade's bicep. "Look at *you*. You're a *beast!*"

The screen door of the house next door burst open. Two little girls in pink dresses ran across the yard.

"Romey!"

"Uncle Romey!"

They screamed as they ran toward Jerome Slade with their hands held wide. Slade laughed and lowered himself to his knees to swoop up the girls into his arms. He stood, still laughing as the girls smothered his face with kisses.

"Yeah," Slade said, closing his eyes and rolling back his head.

"Look at me. I am a *beast.*"

Casper wiped his eyes. The happy scene sent goosebumps down his arms.

"Let me guess. These are your nieces?"

"Yeah," Slade said with a laugh. "This little rascal is June. And this one is April. I can't stand the sight of either one of them."

The girls beat at Slade's enormous arms with their tiny fists while the giant man laughed.

"Uncle Romey, you are bad. Bad. Bad."

"Yes, I am, my love. I am bad. Bad. Bad."

Slade kissed them on the cheeks and lowered them to the ground. They ran to join their mother, who had come out to the porch next door.

"That's my world, right there, Casper," Slade said.

"Everything in the world."

"I'm glad, Jerome," Casper said. "I couldn't be happier for you."

"Mo Tinsley is supposed to be getting out pretty soon," Slade said.

"That's what I hear," Casper said.

"They can't turn him down, man," Slade said. "He hasn't given them a single reason to keep him locked up."

Casper shook his head.

"Stranger things have happened, man."

Slade stepped closer to Casper. He glared at those around them, demanding space. The others backed away.

"You've had some serious shit happen to you," Slade said.

"Yeah," Casper said. "It's been rough."

"I asked around," Slade said. "Nobody knows shit about the psycho that…you know."

"Yeah," Casper said. "So, what have you been up to?"

Slade shrugged.

"Just keepin' my nose clean. I'm bouncing at a, uh…a gentleman's club. The pay is decent. All I have to do is look like a big guy who don't take no shit. I think I do that pretty good."

"Yeah, Casper said with a chuckle. "You do that real good."

Slade pointed at a twenty-year-old custom van.

"That's my ride. It ain't fancy and it ain't fast. But I can load up my sisters and the kids and even a friend of two to take somewhere nice. That's all I care about, Bro."

Casper gripped Slade's shoulder.

"You're gonna be all right, Jerome."

"Thanks, Casper," Slade said. "Are you gonna be all right?"

Casper stared into the distance.

"I hope so, man."

Thirty-Nine

Casper arrived at the train station an hour early. He had gone overboard with his disguise for the day. He approached the ticket counter.

"Do you think I could talk to the train crew?" he asked. "I've always loved trains."

The ticket agent was sleepy and bored.

"I'll pass along your request. I'm sure you realize we get these requests every day—but we have a schedule to keep."

"Yes, ma'am."

Casper did not check a bag. He carried a backpack aboard.

"Hi," the uniformed conductor said. "I understand you wanted to meet the crew."

"Yes, sir," Casper said.

"Come on up," the conductor said. "This is Engineer Miller."

"Wow," Casper said, offering his hand. "How fast are we going to go?"

"Probably about eighty," Miller said. "Faster than driving. And we don't stop very often."

"For sure," Casper said. "How far do you go? Before someone else takes over?"

"D.C." Miller said. "We lay over there and go back tomorrow."

"Cool," Casper said.

Casper took a seat and waited for the conductor to check his ticket. Casper held out his ticket and stared at the conductor's hand.

"Is anything wrong, sir?" the man asked.

"No," Casper said. "I'm just...very tired."

"Yes, sir."

Casper dozed until he was prodded awake at the Washington D.C. Station. He shouldered his backpack and walked inside. He stepped into line at the ticket booth.

"New York City," he said to the ticket agent.

"Departing in twenty-three minutes," the agent said. "Eighty-six dollars. Cash or credit?"

"Cash," Casper said. He peeled off the bills.

"Could I speak to the train crew?" Casper asked.

"It's the middle of the night, son," the bored agent said. "You want to do that shit, come in early, okay? Next!"

Casper stepped onto the boarding pad. He and three other prospective passengers looked expectantly to the south. Eventually, a headlight appeared. Casper stepped back against the long windows of the waiting room. More people came through the doors. Two men carrying luggage walked through the crowd. They wore matching uniforms.

Casper stepped forward. He stood next to a man who carried two duffel bags. One man spoke to the other. The other man did not reply. That man wore a hat that completed his uniform. His head was shaved and virtually untanned. Casper tried not to stare, but there was something else unsettling about the man's appearance.

What is it? Oh, okay.

The man either had no eyebrows, or they were so faint they were invisible. Casper narrowed his eyes and turned, pretending to look behind him.

The man also had no eyelashes. And a scar over his eye.

****

Casper was exhausted, but he felt uneasy. He felt like he had forgotten something. He knew he was not at his best, but it didn't matter. His current self was all he had. He took a lower seat in a coach class car and dozed fitfully.

The familiar tickle in the back of his mind kept him from falling asleep.

It was nothing. But it could be everything.

No eyelashes. And a scar over his eye.

Casper stood and walked the hallways. He smiled and stood aside when he encountered employees along the way.

At 4:55, he came to the doorway marked, "Dining Room". The door marker read "closed". Casper put his hand against the door and pushed. The door opened.

The kitchen staff worked at full tilt. Cooks, waitresses, and wait-staff scurried about, carrying napkins, silverware, water, and coffee carafes to each table. Casper closed the door behind him.

Only one table was occupied.

The train's Conductor sat in the farthest corner—his briefcase open and paperwork spread before him.

Casper nodded at the man. The man glared at him.

"I guess I'm too early for breakfast," Casper said. "I was just hoping to get a cup of coffee."

A young lady rushed a cup of steaming coffee to Casper before he could even take a seat. He sat at the table next to the conductor.

"Thank you."

Casper glanced at the conductor's table.

The kitchen and dining room staff moved around the room. Casper felt a tickle at the back of his neck. He looked over and read the conductor's badge.

Conductor.

Robert. Ferrill.

"Wow," Casper said. "You have some beautiful young ladies working in this car."

The conductor abruptly pushed to his feet, making Casper jump. The conductor closed his folders and slapped them into his briefcase. He stood and left the room without a word.

Casper finished his coffee. He took one last look at the dining room staff, scurrying about in last-minute preparation for breakfast.

The lights from the chandeliers twinkled off of their hosiery. The tickle at the base of Casper's skull became like the prick of a needle. He winced.

That pain was all he had. There was no evidence. None. Zero.

Just like at the docks.

But that isn't what being a detective really meant, is it? Anybody can slap cuffs on the guy holding the smoking gun.

No shoes. No panties. No pantyhose...

Casper was in dangerous waters. And he knew it. He couldn't say anything to his father—not if what Chief of Detectives Dwight Livingston had mentioned was true. Casper knew what it meant to Bobby to get his job back—and another chance to become a detective. It wouldn't bring Kathy Halliday back—but it would give his father something to live for.

And he and his father would get on with their lives, eventually.

Casper stepped to the dining room doors and peeked through the windows. Early risers lined up at the direction of the conductor.

A shy young lady tapped Casper on the shoulder.

"Excuse me, sir. I have to open the doors now."

Casper stepped to the side. Passengers trailed into the dining car. Casper watched the conductor's eyes roam over the young women the way a wolf looks at sheep. Seconds later Casper and Ferrill made eye contact. Casper tipped his cap and left the car.

We'll be seeing you, Mr. Ferrill.

Forty

Casper let himself into the apartment. He dropped his backpack, eased himself onto the sofa, and closed his eyes.

"Casper?"

Bobby's voice sounded from his bedroom.

"Yeah, Dad. It's me."

Bobby walked into the living room, buttoning his shirt.

"That didn't take long," Bobby said. "What happened?"

Casper sighed.

"There was nothing to see. Most of those old service tunnels have been roped off. They've posted security guards around the clock. One of the guards told me the county is going to pump those old tunnels full of concrete. They say they've been nothing but trouble for years."

"Sounds like the wise thing to do," Bobby said.

"Yeah."

"So, have you given any thought to going back to work?" Bobby asked.

"Yeah, I have," Casper said. "Are you getting sick of me?"

Bobby smiled.

"Of course, not. It's been...well, I'm really glad

you've been here."

"Me too."

Bobby sat. Casper leaned forward and kneaded his fingers.

"It's gonna hit...one day...isn't it?"

Bobby struggled to think of what to say.

Casper cleared his throat.

"I mean, one day it's gonna hit—right here."

Casper tapped his forehead. And then his heart.

"And it's going to be real."

Bobby moved to the sofa and put his arm around Casper's shoulder.

"Yeah. That's probably the way it's gonna happen," Bobby said. "I think about it, too, and then I make it go away. It's like I'm sleep-walking. Sleep-walking through a movie about myself."

"Yeah," Casper said.

"I'm here for you, son," Bobby said. "Anytime. Anywhere. Always."

"Thanks, Dad," Casper said. "Same here."

Bobby signed and slapped Casper's knee.

"I told Mark I could give him five or six hours tonight. He's running himself ragged. He turns down more work than he accepts. The agency could use some more investigators."

"I'm sending him some referrals," Casper said.

"Really?" Bobby said. "That's good. You gonna hang out here tonight?"

"Yeah," Casper said. "I'm tired. And I have something to do tomorrow."

"Something top secret?" Bobby said.

"Girl stuff," Casper lied.

"Oh. Okay," Bobby said. "I'll bring home pizza."

Casper slept for three hours. He showered and dressed and picked up his cell phone. He pressed a number and listened. The phone rang three times.

"Hello?"

Casper was startled. He wasn't expecting to hear a woman's voice. He looked at the phone's screen. He hadn't made a mistake.

"I was trying to get in touch with Mando Gonzalez."

"Is this Casper? Casper Halliday?"

"Yes. Is Mando—?"

"Oh my God!" the woman said. "You're for *real*. I thought Mando made you up."

Casper heard another voice in the background.

"Hold on, Casper," the woman said. "I'm going to put you on 'speaker'."

"I don't like being on speaker," Casper said.

Casper heard Mando's voice.

"Dammit, Layla! Did you answer my phone?"

Casper understood now. Layla was Mando's sister's name.

"I *had* to," Layla said. "You weren't here. And it's *Caaasper!* Your imaginary friend."

Mando's voice was nearer now.

"Give me that."

"No," Layla said. She giggled. "I demand that you introduce me to Casper properly."

"Fine," Mando said. "Casper Halliday, this is my older sister, Layla. Layla, say hello and goodbye to my friend, Casper."

"I'm not that much *older*," Layla said. "Ten months and fourteen days, to be exact. Kind of makes you think *someone* might have been an accident."

"I wasn't an accident," Mando said. "Mom and Dad just couldn't wait to try for something better."

"Your name is Layla, huh?" Casper said. "Like that old song?"

Mando cut off Layla's reply.

"Yeah, my dad was a big fan of Derek Frampton."

Casper laughed.

"You mean, Eric Clapton?"

"No, I'm pretty sure it was Derek Frampton," Mando said. "Anyway,—"

Layla tried to interrupt.

"Hey! Hey!" Mando shouted. "I'm telling *my* story to *my* friend on *my* phone in *my* room. Do you have a problem? *Is* there a problem? I didn't think so. Are you still with me, Caz?"

"You bet," Casper said. "Tell me about Derek Frampton."

"Well, you probably don't know this, but Derek Frampton used to play the banjo on this show called 'Hee-Haw'—"

"You're so full of shit!" Layla said.

"So, Derek had this dog—an old, ugly, scraggly dog with one eye, three legs, and a chewed-off ear. She wandered up to Derek's porch one day while he was practicing the banjo. Derek felt sorry for the pitiful thing, so he gave her half of his bologna sandwich. The dog wouldn't leave. So, Derek made her a bed in the corner of his bedroom and named her Layla—"

"You lying little ass-wipe!" Layla said.

"Uhn-uh," Mando said. "Stay back. I'm not finished with the story. So, the next night, Derek comes home after a hard night of playin' banjo on the Hee-Haw, and Layla has chewed up all his shoes and shit in the floor."

"Jose Armando Gonzales," Layla growled. "You are a *dead* man."

"I mean, how ungrateful can you be?" Mando said. "She's given food and water and shelter, and she ruins stuff and shits in the floor. So, Casper, now you know all you need to know about my sister."

Casper heard the sounds of scuffling and laughter. Mando took possession of the phone and turned off the speaker. Casper could still hear Layla.

"I hate you, Mando," she said in a fake sweet voice.

"I apologize for my dear sister," Mando said. "She just graduated, so she has been under a lot of pressure. She was also in a sorority, which we all know only exist to teach nice girls how to drink heavily."

"Like *you* would know anything about a sorority," Layla said.

"Our parents went out tonight," Mando said. "I'm stuck here, babysitting."

"Hah!" Layla said. "I'm the big sister. I'm babysitting *you.*"

"But I'm not the one who has almost emptied a full bottle wine in less than an hour."

"*I...* " Layla said, "am still celebrating my monumental accomplishments, dear brother. Do you want to arrest me, Sheriff Mando?"

"I'm not a sheriff," Mando said. "Hey, Casper. You still there?"

"Of course," Casper said. "This is much better than TV."

"Like I was saying," Mando said. "I have to babysit because *somebody* thinks they are the favorite child—"

"I *am* the favorite child," Layla said.

"Someone actually believes they are a princess—"

"A *Disney* Princess!"

"Excuse me," Mando said. "It wouldn't do for me to leave and have my parents find the Disney Princess passed out in a puddle of vomit—"

"*Gross!*"

"And worse than that," Mando said. "When they got her awake she might start telling stories of what went on at all those sorority parties. My poor parents would have nightmares *forever.* Yes, it's a sacrifice for me, but, protect and serve, you know."

"That's right," Casper said. "Protect and Serve. There is no nobler calling."

"Jesus, Layla," Mando said. "*Another* bottle?"

"These bottles are tiny," Layla said.

"Like hell they are," Mando said. "I know you're used to drinking wine out of a box, but—"

"Was that a joke?" Layla said. "Aw, my widdle

brudder told a joke. How sweet."

"Why even bother with a glass?" Mando said. "Just chug that bottle like a *real* sorority chick."

"Oh, my God, Caz. She's *doing* it. I am *not* mopping up your mess and I'm not holding your hair out of the toilet."

"I am going to drink until I find my Disney Prince!" Layla said.

"Casper," Mando said. "I'm gonna put you back on speaker for a second."

"No—"

"Listen to me, Casper. I want you to meet this girl. I want you to marry her and move her to Kansas, or Montana, or South America. I will send you money every month. I swear."

"Yes! Yes!" Layla said. "I, Layla Grace Gonzalez, the Disney Princess, will marry Casper the Friendly Imaginary Friend of my asshole brother. We shall live on a ranch in Montana and raise My Little Ponies in every color of the rainbow. We will have many, many, many angelic children and eat Skittles for breakfast every day."

"She's not making sense right now, Caz," Mando said. "But remember, I'm going to send you money every month. Cash money."

"I'm not feeling so good," Layla said.

"Go. Get out!" Mando said. "Do not even *think* about puking in my room.

"Do you see what I have to put up with, Caz?"

"Don't ask me," Casper said. "I'm an only child. You can't fool me, though. You love her like crazy."

"Yeah, I do," Mando said. "She won't remember any of this tomorrow. It's a good thing I'll be around to remind her."

"Of course," Casper said.

"She's not really like this," Mando said. "Like she's acting tonight. She's actually pretty shy."

"Obviously," Casper said.

"No. Really," Mando said. "She's smart as hell, and when Layla puts her mind to something—that thing gets done. She's awesome."

"Say, Mando," Casper said. "I hate to screw up the good mood, but I need a favor."

"Sure," Mando said. "Name it."

"I'm going back to work next week," Casper said.

"That's great!" Mando said.

"But I need something done tomorrow," Casper said. "Early. I need an address."

"Not a problem," Mando said. "Wait. Let me get a pen."

"Okay," Mando said. "Shoot."

"The name is Robert Ferrill," Casper said. "Somewhere in the city."

"Ten million people, Casper," Mando said. "All you have is a name? What is this about, anyway?"

"I need...I really can't say much more," Casper said.

"Is that so?" Mando said. "I thought we were bros, Caz."

"We *are* bros," Casper said. "You're my best friend. I don't want to put you in danger."

"We're *cops*, Casper," Mando said. "We met in the

freaking academy. We're going to look danger in the eyes until we retire."

"Neither one of us could have known what was going to happen while we were still rookies," Casper said. "A psychopath murdered my mother, Mando. And not just *any* psychopath. A psychopath who hasn't left one freaking clue! A psychopath who killed my mother because somebody called him Ghost Man. And that got...my mother killed."

There was silence.

"You don't believe it was the junkie." Mando said.

"No," Casper said. "I don't."

"This dude, Robert Ferrill, you think he's the guy?" Mando asked. "Who the hell is he?"

More silence.

"Can't you just get me the address?" Casper said.

"Bite me, Casper."

"What?"

"Are you forgetting all those days and nights from the academy?" Mando said.

"No."

"I think you have," Mando said. "We were supposed to be partners, remember? We swore we wouldn't rest until they made us partners. We did a pinky-swear."

"And how do you take care of a partner?" Casper said. "You do whatever it takes to save his life. And that's what I'm doing right now."

"Bullshit," Mando said. "Who is this guy?"

"He's the guy I think murdered my mother!" Casper said. "And I can't prove anything. Do you feel better now?"

"I want to know why you suspect this Ferrill guy," Mando asked.

"It wasn't some lame-ass junkie," Casper said. "No way."

"They've got the whole damn NYPD on this," Mando said. "Why don't you just wait and see what they find?"

"Because too many people want this case off the books!" Casper said. "The department, the mayor's office, and the Governor's office want this case closed, dead, and gone. What if they're wrong? Maybe the psycho killer starts again. Or maybe he moves to L.A. and starts murdering women there. Or maybe...he goes underground and never kills again. And my mother's murderer is never found. I can't live with that, Mando. I can't. And I don't know if my dad can, either."

"Let me help you," Mando said.

"I can't do that, Bro," Casper said. "We're just rookies, remember? If I ruin my career, then I have the rest of my life to get the bastard. I can live with that. But I can't live with ruining your life."

Casper bit his lip.

"I messed up Blair's life. Do you see what I'm talking about?"

"That's not fair," Mando said. "That was the sweetest bust in the last fifty years. It's not your fault she couldn't handle it."

"It *was* my fault," Casper said.

Mando shook his head.

"No."

"I'm going to tell you something you can never repeat," Casper said. "We lied."

"What?" Mando said. "What do you mean, you lied?"

"I shouldn't even be saying this on the phone," Casper said.

"You're making me nervous," Mando said.

"There were four bad guys on the dock," Casper said. "Blair shot one of them. I killed the others."

Mando blew out a long breath.

"That's heavy, man."

"We couldn't tell the truth," Casper said. "I fired Blair's weapon. So, the story was, *she* killed three. And you know what happened next."

"Yeah," Mando said. "They made her into a superhero."

"Exactly," Casper said. "And it was a lie. She couldn't deal with it."

"That's too bad," Mando said. "But that has nothing to do with me and you."

"Yes, it—"

"I know what 'partner' means," Mando snapped. "All for one and one for all. Like the Musketeers, baby."

"No," Casper said. "You don't have a dog in this fight. That's why I'm asking for your help. I need an address, and then you go about your business."

"If we're ever going to be partners, then we're partners right now," Mando said. "How many Robert Ferrills do you think there are in a city of ten million? You have to give me more than that."

Moments of silence followed.

"I'm flying blind here, Mando. I don't have a single piece of evidence. All I have is a really bad gut feeling about a guy who freaked me the hell out."

"Do you have any more information, or do you want a list of five hundred people?" Mando said. His voice was flat.

"He works on trains," Casper said.

"What kind of trains?" Mando said. "The subway? Freight trains?"

"No," Casper said. "Passenger trains. I don't know everywhere he goes. But I know he works between here and D.C. Maybe farther."

"This doesn't make any sense," Mando said.

"The last victim," Casper said. "Jessica Collins. She worked in the kitchen and dining car of the passenger train for three weeks."

"Shit," Mando said. "Why would he pick somebody he freaking *worked* with? That's just stupid."

"Maybe he's losing it," Casper said. "There's something…something about the damn stockings. The girls on the train wear uniform dresses and stockings— probably pantyhose. All the…the victims have been found without underwear, hose or their shoes."

Mando's eyes narrowed.

"You seem to know a lot more than I do. Who have you been talking to?"

Casper said nothing.

"Did you ride this guy's freaking train?" Mando said. "Dammit, Casper. Your face has been plastered everywhere."

"I rode a train to D.C., got on another one and came home," Casper said. "It was just a hunch. And I wore a disguise."

"You're holding out on me," Mando said. "But you expect me to trust you."

"Nothing has happened," Casper said. "I had a feeling. I rode a train, and got another feeling. Do you want to risk your career for that?"

Mando's nostrils flared as he stared into Casper's eyes.

"Look at me," Mando said. "Look me in the eye and tell me this guy murdered your mother."

"I can't do that!" Casper said. "All I know is I'm as sure as I was about the guys trafficking girls from Red Hook."

"I'll get the address in the morning," Mando said. "I'll talk to my cousin Eddie over at the 110th. He used to be a hacker. But you have to promise me something."

"What?" Casper said.

"Whatever this is—wherever it goes— you don't close me out," Mando said. "I'm serious. If you want to do a little information gathering, fine. But you don't go in guns blazing without me, or I'll never be your partner. You get me?"

"All right," Casper said. "But you need to know something else. The junkie is dead. Ferrill isn't. There's no death penalty in New York."

"I know that," Mando said.

Casper cleared his throat.

"I'm not going to stand in a courtroom and listen to a judge give my mother's murderer a chance to die of old age."

Forty-One

The next morning, Casper waited impatiently for Mando to call. When the phone rang at 10:20, he answered it on the first ring.

"I've got it," Mando said. His voice became a whisper. "I'm not sure what Eddie did was exactly legal. He used to be *deep* into the dark web before he got busted. That's how he ended up working for the good guys. I asked him how he found out where the guy works. He laughed and told me to mind my own business and to kiss Layla for him."

"I really appreciate this," Casper said.

Mando read off the address.

"It's a house," Mando said. "A small one, in an old, quiet neighborhood."

"You went there?" Casper said.

"No. I saw it on the computer. It freaked me out, dude—thinking that monster could live inside that place. Oh, and he's single. No dependents. I have to go, Caz. What are you gonna do now?"

"Just surveillance," Casper said.

"You can't do that in a Crown Vic," Mando said.

"I'm going to rent a car," Casper said. "Something plain."

"Play it cool," Mando said. "If this is really the guy, he hasn't made any mistakes—until he killed too close to home. He even handed us a dead suspect and a victim in one package. This is *way* over your head."

"I'm not going to let him get away," Casper said.

"Look," Mando said. "You can talk to Sergeant Kavanaugh. Hell, you can even talk to Chief Livingston."

"Talk to them about what?" Casper said. "My rookie's instinct?"

"You have detective cred with the people upstairs, bro," Mando said. "Enough to get a raid on this dude's house. We can make up something—a gas leak. Or a call from a neighbor saying they saw smoke inside."

"What if there's no evidence inside the house?" Casper said. "Or even worse, there *is* evidence, but an attorney gets the case thrown out because of an illegal search?"

"No way," Mando said. "Not after multiple murders."

"Then he pleads insanity," Casper said. "You think he isn't smart enough to escape? Worst case—he eats federally-subsidized meals until he's ninety years old."

"So what?" Mando said. "He'll be in a cage like Hannibal Lecter. He'll never see the sun again. Don't do this, Casper."

"I'm not suicidal," Casper said. "I'm just going to watch him—while the rest of the NYPD follows the trail of a dead junkie."

Mando sighed.

"I should have applied to the Sheriff's Department."

"Nah," Casper said. "Tan uniforms and a Trooper's hat? That wouldn't have been a good look for you."

"Shit," Mando said. "I can make anything look good. I can't say the same for you."

"We'll see," Casper said. "I get to pick the grooms-men's suits when I marry your sister. I'm thinking about a 70's disco kind of vibe...lots of pink ruffles..."

"I was making a joke," Mando said. "You can't marry my sister."

"You hide and watch," Casper said.

"Did you hear what I said?" Mando said. "You can't marry my sister."

"The hell I can't," Casper said.

"I have to go," Mando said. "Forget about my sister."

"It's too late," Casper said. "Montana. Ponies. Skittles."

"I hate you," Mando said.

"Talk to you later," Casper said. "Brother."

"Shut up," Mando said.

"Okay. Brother-in-law."

****

Casper picked up the rental car—a dark blue, four-door compact. The closer he got to Robert Ferrill's neighborhood, the faster his heart beat. His hands perspired on the steering wheel. He shuddered when he saw a sign with the street name on it.

Casper drove slowly past Ferrill's house at 1:30

P.M. The lawn was neatly trimmed and tidy. The small front porch had no furniture. A medium-sized four-door sedan sat next to the house beneath a carport.

A white car.

Like the good guys drive.

Right.

Casper parallel-parked down the street as far as he could while still able to see Ferrill's car and driveway. He chose the rental car for its plain appearance and its darkly-tinted windows. After three uneventful hours and two bottles of water, Casper was forced to give up his parking place. He drove to a fast-food restaurant and used the rest room. By the time he returned to the neighborhood, there were fewer places to park. There was more foot-traffic on the sidewalks. Casper parked, but he could only observe Ferrill's residence with his binoculars.

A teen-aged boy and girl, hand-in-hand, strolled past him. Their eyes lingered on the stranger sitting curbside in his car for no obvious reason. Casper picked up his phone and pretended to have a conversation.

Casper worried that someone would report him to the police. That was a potential confrontation he did not want to have.

The sky grew dark.

Perfect.

A good rain would clear the sidewalks and send the lovebirds indoors. Casper checked his watch. He would give Ferrill one more hour to make a move. Casper knew he would have to change rental cars before he returned tomorrow. The thought made him tired.

The teenagers turned toward a house. Casper watched them to see if they looked his way again. He jumped when his phone rang. He checked the display.

Charlie Talbot.

That's weird.

He hadn't called Charlie since the night they spent together in his apartment. He didn't know what to say to her. Charlie had spoken of that night as some kind of "therapy", which left him thinking of himself as a pharmaceutical—something a new-age doctor might prescribe for a depressed thirty-something woman who found herself married to an ex-jock asshole.

Still, Casper thought of that night often—even during the darkness of the last few days.

"Hi, Charlie."

"Hello, Casper."

Charlie's silky, sultry voice washed over him like a hot bath.

"How are you?" Casper asked.

"The asshole moved out of the apartment," Charlie said. "I was there less than two hours when he showed up—in violation of the protection order."

"Did you call the police?" Casper asked.

"You're damn right I did," Charlie said. "That's not going to help his case. Not that he cares. He was freaking *crying*. I swear, that scared me more than if was screaming."

"I'm sorry," Casper said.

"How about you and your father?" Charlie asked. "Are you all right?"

"We're gonna be okay," Casper said. "Thanks for asking."

"I want to ask you about something you mentioned," Charlie said.

"Yeah?"

Charlie sighed.

"Matt knows where I'm staying. I knew he would find me. He doesn't give a damn about the court order. He calls on the hotel phone. I have to sneak out through the kitchen when I leave."

"Can't you—?"

"I don't want to fight anymore!" Charlie shrieked. "I don't want to argue! I don't want to listen to crying or begging—!"

"Have him arrested, Charlie," Casper said. "Some time in jail will straighten him out, I guarantee—"

"He won't go to *jail*, Casper!" Charlie said. "Don't you *get* it? He's part of a good-old-boy network on Wall Street. There are attorneys everywhere. They take care of each other like the freaking *mafia.* Having him arrested would just piss him off and bring more power into his corner. And it might even make him crazier. I don't know what he's capable of."

"What do you want to do, Charlie?"

"Can I use your apartment for a few days?" Charlie asked.

"Of course," Casper said. "I'll bring you the keys. Just tell me where and when."

"I'm sneaking out to a movie with my friend, Linda, tonight," Charlie said. "I can't look at these hotel room walls anymore. I won't be home until after ten. Is that too late?"

"No. That's cool," Casper said. "Where do I meet you?"

"Your apartment is fine," Charlie said. "I'll have Linda drop me off, if that's okay."

"Sure," Casper said. "Call me when you're fifteen minutes away."

Charlie laughed.

"Should we synchronize watches?"

"It's gonna be late," Casper said. "And dark. And you're a very desirable woman."

"And so is Linda," Charlie said.

"I...don't know how to reply to that," Casper said.

Charlie laughed again.

"Do you have any beer?"

Casper smiled.

"I *will* have. Do you have any cigarettes?"

Charlie's voice relaxed.

"Hmmm. As a matter of fact, I do."

Forty-Two

The rain picked up, just as Casper hoped it would. He could use his binoculars without fear of being seen. The windows in the neighborhood flickered with the glow of televisions. Casper lowered the binoculars and rubbed his eyes. He rubbed his neck and leaned back against the headrest.

Casper's eyes opened. He panicked. The hypnotic lullaby of the rain had done its job. He checked his watch.

Dammit.

He checked his watch. He'd lost an hour-and-a-half. Casper raised the binoculars and squinted against the rain. The white car had not moved.

Casper dreaded having to spend tomorrow repeating the exact same surveillance. He would have to switch cars, and still, it would be more difficult to go unnoticed.

"Come on," he growled at the house. *"Leave."*

Another fifteen minutes passed. He needed to pee again. And he had to meet Charlie in a little over an hour. Casper dropped the binoculars onto the passenger seat. He yawned, rubbed his eyes, and started the car.

A white sedan passed him.

Casper snatched up the binoculars again. The carport was empty. He checked his watch.

Ten minutes. I'll wait ten minutes. Maybe he went for a burger. Or toilet paper.

Or to murder someone.

Casper waited ten minutes. Two houses away, a front door opened. Two people ran to a car and drove away. Casper checked his watch again. He waited five more minutes. He put on a windbreaker he kept in the back seat of his car. It was the only protection he had against the rain and he knew the temperature had dropped considerably. His fingers tapped against the steering wheel. He found it hard to breathe. Casper pulled the door handle and shoved the door with his shoulder. He was pelted by cold rain. Casper had one foot on the pavement when he saw headlights approaching from the rear. He pulled his foot inside and slammed the door shut. Seconds later, the white car passed by and stopped beneath the carport.

Casper drew in a ratcheted breath.

I could be dead right now.

His fingers rubbed the grip of his Glock. He raised the binoculars. He waited for the lights of the white car to go out.

They didn't.

The driver's door opened. A man hurried out of the car wearing a dark raincoat. He ran inside the house. Casper checked his watch. He needed to leave. He would be late meeting Charlie—but the headlights and taillights remained lit.

And so did the nagging tickle in the back of his mind.

Casper sent a text message to Charlie and then turned off his phone.

I may be a little late. I'll call when I'm on my way. Sorry.

Casper saw light reflect off of the door to the house. Robert Ferrill popped the trunk lid of the white car and loaded two pieces of luggage.

Bingo.

The car exited the driveway. Casper leaned down until the headlights passed. He sat up and watched the car disappear around an intersection.

I'll wait five minutes.

How many times are you going to do that?

Casper slapped his cheek.

"Cheng Sun," he said aloud.

He had no idea where the words had come from.

Trust yourself. Do not question the voice.

Casper scratched the itch at the back of his neck.

"Okay. Here we go."

The cold rain soaked through his clothes. Casper crossed the street to the far sidewalk. He walked head-down—his hands shoved deep into his pockets. He paused, took one last look around, and hurried up Ferrill's driveway. Casper came to a wooden gate past the carport that opened into a small, fenced back yard. He didn't worry about a dog—not with Ferrill's job.

Casper stopped under the roof of the tiny back porch. The porch contained only a small round table, a single chair, and a wastebasket. The wastebasket was empty. Casper removed his soaked windbreaker. He wrung the water from it and put it back on. He pulled on a pair of latex gloves and tried the back door knob.

Locked. He tried three different windows. None of them would budge.

A dog barked. Casper froze. The bark was distant. Casper listened. No other barking dogs joined the first.

Good.

Casper noted that none of the homes in the neighborhood displayed security system signs. The residents felt safe here. This was a quiet, safe neighborhood.

The perfect place for a killer to hide.

Casper pulled his gun. He held it by the barrel and struck the back door window pane. He winced, waiting for an alarm. Nothing happened. Casper reached inside and unlocked the door knob and the deadbolt. He turned the door knob and pushed. The door stopped against a security chain.

"*Shit,*" Casper whispered between clenched teeth. "Paranoid much, asshole?"

Casper pulled the door closed. He pushed the Glock through the broken window and tried to use the pistol's barrel to lift the security chain. He felt the end of the barrel contact the chain. He pushed.

The gun slipped. Casper lost his grip on the gun. It clattered to the floor. Casper screeched at himself.

"*Idiot!*"

Overcome with desperation, Casper crossed the yard and snapped a limb from a tree. He returned to the door and managed to dislodge the security chain. In the process, a shard of glass from the broken window sliced through the windbreaker, his shirt, and his upper arm.

Casper turned the door knob and stepped inside the house.

Forty-Three

Robert Ferrill inched the car forward on the crowded one-way, four-lane street. He sipped his coffee, the welcome warmth helping the car's heater dry his wet clothes. It was early spring in New York.

One never knew what to expect.

Ferrill's cell phone lay on the passenger seat. It sounded with a series of tones Ferrill never expected to hear—but he was *always* prepared to hear.

He crossed two lanes of traffic, cutting off drivers who lay on their horns and screamed obscenities through lowered windows. Ferrill did not care. He turned left at the next light and pulled immediately to the curb. He turned on his emergency flashers, which did nothing to appease impatient drivers who were forced to go around him.

Ferrill picked up his phone. He activated a video feed and swore a string of obscenities. He keyed in a phone number and floored the accelerator. The car fishtailed away from the curb. Ferrill took the next turn without braking, launching the car in the opposite direction.

"Employee services," came the answer.

"This is Conductor Robert Ferrill. I was on my way to work. I've been sick. I've had to pull over twice to

Eleven

Casper phoned the diner at 9:30, an hour before the end of Kathy's shift.

"This is Kathy. How may I help you?"

"Yes, Ma'am," Casper said. He disguised his voice. "We're having a little impromptu get-together just down the street. Would it be possible to pick up, say, a hundred-and-fifty club sandwiches by ten-thirty?"

"Did you say a hundred-and-fifty?"

Casper laughed.

"Come on, Mom. I'm just messing with you."

"That's not funny," Kathy said. She sounded relieved. "They would have me making those sandwiches and I'm supposed to be out of here in an hour."

"I know," Casper said. "I thought I would order pizza and pick you up."

"Don't you work in the morning?" Kathy asked.

"I have the day off," Casper said. "I had to go in really early today. Something…bad happened."

"Are you talking about that murder in the East Village?"

"Yeah," Casper said.

"I saw that on the news," Kathy said. "They didn't give many details, but it sounded really bad."

"It was," Casper said.

"You can stay over in your room," Kathy said. "Sleep all day if you want. I'll be quiet."

"I'm going to drive up and visit Mo in the morning," Casper said.

"Mo?"

"Mo Tinsley. Maurice," Casper said. "You remember. My old cellmate."

Kathy sighed.

"I remember now. My God, that seems like a thousand years ago."

"Not exactly," Casper said. "I haven't been back to visit since I started at the academy. Mo should be up for parole pretty soon."

"Okay," Kathy said. "We're getting busy again. I need to go."

"I'll be there at 10:30," Casper said.

****

Casper pulled his car into the visitor's parking lot and shut off the engine. He leaned back in the seat. He had been holding his breath for the last few seconds without realizing it. This was the fourth time he had visited since he was released. Each time a strange feeling came over him when he saw the walls, fences, and barbed wire surrounding Fishkill prison. This had been his home for thirty months.

I almost lost it all in this place. Yes, I committed a crime. But it was an extremely unfortunate association that put me here.

wiped his eyes and tucked the shoes inside his windbreaker.

"You're not keeping these, you son-of-a-bitch."

Casper turned to leave.

No. Stop. It's evidence. Important evidence.

Casper returned his mother's shoes to the shelf and ran from the closet. He jerked to a stop when the room lights came on.

****

The voice came from everywhere. Or it came from nowhere. It didn't matter. There were not supposed to be any voices.

"So, you've found me, Officer Halliday."

Casper looked to every corner of the room.

"Does it really matter where the cameras are?" Ferrill said. "I've been watching you since the first piece of glass hit the floor."

"I'm going to kill you," Casper said.

"Of course, you are," Ferrill said. "But let's get a few facts straight before we get so serious. First, I am indeed a son-of-a-bitch. A *crazy* bitch. Can you believe she almost tried to have sex with me? But I was too young and weak—and she was too strong, too stoned out of her mind, and insane. Now that that's out of the way, do me a favor, Officer Halliday. Open the top drawer of my dresser."

"I'm coming to get you," Casper said.

Ferrill laughed.

"You have no idea where I am! Maybe I can limit

your options. Open the top drawer of the dresser."

Casper walked to the dresser and opened the top drawer.

"The rear right-hand corner," Ferrill said. "There's a wooden box. Open it."

Casper lifted the box with trembling fingers. He opened it.

A picture of his father looked up at him. Casper took the small stack of photos from the box and sorted through them.

Blair. Mando. Charlie. Sean. Mona Casey.

And Cody.

"You sick bastard," Casper growled.

"I'll not deny it," Ferrill said.

"You *fucking demon from hell!*" Casper shouted.

"Ah, more accolades!" Ferrill said. "Please stop. You're embarrassing me."

Casper ran back into the closet and grabbed his mother's shoes.

"Ah, ah, ah!" Ferrill said. "Those are mine. I found them."

"And by the way," Ferrill said. "Apparently I'm not the only one looking for you. I don't know this gentleman. Who is he?"

Casper's head snapped around when a large television screen came to life. He took one step closer. And another.

The video showed lifeless eyes staring at the camera. The hole in the man's forehead was perfectly centered. Blood trickled onto a floor that Casper recognized.

The dead man was Matthew Talbot. Casper dropped the shoes.

Oh, God. Charlie…

Forty-Four

Casper ran through the back door. He pulled on the gate three times before it opened. His right foot slipped, driving his knee into the concrete.

"Ahhh!"

He felt no pain. Casper regained his feet and sprinted to this car. He slammed the door behind him and inserted the key into the ignition after four tries with trembling fingers. He picked up his phone and swore as he waited for it to power on.

"Come on...come on!" he shouted.

He had one new text message from Charlie.

Don't worry about it. Linda and I are going to stop for coffee. My phone battery is almost dead. I'm not much at thinking ahead. We'll see you later.

Casper dialed Charlie's number. The call went straight to voice-mail.

Casper pulled away from the curb, the rear of his car fishtailing on the wet pavement. He looked down at his phone and dialed another number.

Sean Kelly answered on the second ring.

"Hey, Casper, what's—"

"Sean!" Casper shouted. "Where are you?"

"I'm at Mona's. Why—"

"Listen to me," Casper said. "Get them out of there. All of you. Mona's mother, too."

"What the hell—?"

"I don't have time to talk, Sean. You'll have to trust me. *Get out of the house!* And stay away until you hear from me!"

"Okay," Sean said. "You got it."

Casper squealed the tires around another corner. He made another call.

"Hey, Cas—"

"Dad! There's trouble. *Big* trouble. Come to my apartment building. Do *not* come inside unless you hear from me!"

"I'm on my way," Bobby Halliday said.

Casper tried to concentrate on the crowded street. He had one more call to make. He jerked the wheel when his phone rang. Casper turned late at the next intersection, sending the rear of his car into the front door of a parked car.

He had no intention of stopping. He pushed the accelerator to the floor and entered the highway ramp. He looked at his phone's screen and answered the call.

"Mando!" he shouted.

"Something told me to call you," Mando said. "What's going on?"

"I might need your help," Casper said. "Can you come to my apartment building?"

"Yeah. I can be there in a few minutes."

"Come on. Don't come inside the building unless you hear from me."

"Shut up. I'm coming," Mando said. "All the way."

****

Linda pulled her car into a ten-minute parking zone. Charlie Talbot leaned her head back against the passenger seat.

"That was one of the best nights I've had in a long time," she said.

Linda laughed.

"Really? A movie and a coffee is a great night?"

Linda's smile faded.

"I'm sorry, honey. That was a shitty thing to say."

Charlie patted Linda's hand.

"Don't be sorry," Charlie said. She sighed. "I'm sure lots of people assumed our marriage was like a fairy tale. My *real* friends can understand when they find out it's not. Thank you so much for tonight."

Charlie grabbed her purse and reached for the door handle.

"I can wait with you," Linda said. "It's late."

Charlie shook her head.

"That's not necessary. This is a decent neighborhood. And these apartments have an excellent smoking section."

"I thought you only smoked when you were drinking," Linda said.

"That's true," Charlie said. "I anticipate a drink or two."

"What if I want to wait around and see who this mystery person is who's willing to lend you their apartment?" Linda said.

"He said he would be late," Charlie said. "I don't know *how* late."

"So, it's a *he*," Linda said. "This is getting more interesting by the minute."

"Linda," Charlie said. "Stop thinking like a porn producer."

"So, he's gay, then," Linda said.

Charlie pulled on the door handle.

"I had a wonderful time, Linda. Thank you."

"You're too gorgeous to be out alone at night," Linda said.

"Aw, how sweet," Charlie said. "Thank you. You're a wonderful friend."

"Yeah," Linda said. "I hope you survive the night."

"Now you're starting to be an asshole," Charlie said.

"Get out of my car," Linda said.

Charlie leaned over and kissed Linda's cheek. "Good night."

"Good night. Idiot."

****

Charlie stood under the awning by the apartment building's entrance. There was a bench, a trash can, and a long-necked receptacle with sand in the bottom to hold cigarette butts. The earlier rain had turned to a drizzle. Charlie was alone. She lit a cigarette and smoked half of it before Linda finally pulled away from the curb. Two young men pushed through the entry doors, laughing and talking. Charlie disposed of her cigarette and walked toward the doors.

"Well, *hello*," one man said.

"Hello," Charlie said. "Are you going to hold the door for me?"

"Of course, beautiful lady. Unless you want to go out with us—an excellent time guaranteed."

Charlie rubbed her eyes.

"I'm sure. But I'm giving a test to an advanced economics class at 7:45," she lied. "Forty percent of my students will fail. It would be better if I was sober when I give them the bad news."

The other young man held a door open.

"She's too smart for us, Mickey."

"Maybe next time," the other man said.

"Yeah," Charlie said. "Maybe."

****

Charlie pushed the elevator button. She entered the empty compartment and pushed the button for Casper's floor. She pushed the button on her cell phone and was greeted by the "low battery" warning. Her head fell back.

"Ahhhh!"

The door opened. The hallway was empty. She walked toward Casper's apartment.

She heard the click of a door behind her. She walked faster. Charlie stopped at Casper's door. She looked to her left.

The hulking figure was covered, head-to-foot. A

hideous mask covered his head.

Charlie opened her mouth to scream as she reached for the door knob.

She couldn't believe the door opened. Charlie ran through the doorway and tried to slam the door behind her, but she tripped.

She tripped over a body. The body of her dead husband. Her head hit the wall.

The madman crashed through the door and slammed it behind him. Charlie couldn't make a sound. She pulled the can of mace from her purse. As the madman's hands reached for her, she turned her head and pressed the cylinder's button.

Robert Ferrill moved his head enough that the mace hit just one eye. His suppressed scream sounded between clenched teeth as he fell to the floor. He wiped his eye with his sleeve and clawed his way toward Charlie. Charlie kicked his head. Once. Twice. Three times.

"Oh, my God! Matt!"

"You fucking *bitch!*" Ferrill growled. Charlie crab-walked backward.

The door burst open. Casper leapt onto Ferrill's back.

"You're a dead man, Ferrill," Casper said.

Ferrill pushed with his legs, flipping himself on top of Casper.

"You and me, boy," Ferrill said. "Two Ghost Men enter. Only one leaves."

The heel of Casper's right hand shot out and

connected with Ferrill's jaw.

"Good one," Ferrill said. He drew the knuckle knife and thrust it toward Casper's face. Casper deflected the knife but it sliced into his shoulder.

"Ayyye!"

Ferrill raised the knife over his head. Casper closed his eyes.

The door burst open again. A dark shape crossed the room. A silver streak passed over Casper's head. There was a sickening sound of something very solid striking flesh. Robert Ferrill's weight no longer pressed against his chest.

Casper looked up into the face of Mando Gonzalez. His friend squeezed the grip of an aluminum baseball bat. Mando's face had a crazed expression Casper had never seen before.

Casper clawed to his feet. Mando seemed to be frozen in time and space.

"Thanks, Buddy," Casper said.

Mando said nothing. Robert Ferrill writhed and groaned on the floor. Casper took the bat from Mando's hands.

"Thanks. You just saved at least two lives. You might need to sit down."

Mando looked like he was going to be sick.

"Okay."

He sank to the floor.

"Charlie," Casper said. "Are you all right?"

Charlie sat on the floor, hugging her knees to her chest and staring at her dead husband. She shook her head.

"No..."

"Okay," Casper said. "It's going to be okay. Mando. Are you still with me?"

Mando nodded.

"Yeah. Yeah." Mando's eyes cleared.

"Ch-Charlie Tall-butt? What the hell is she doing here?"

Casper paused. Mando's eyes moved to the body lying to the side of the door.

"What the...who the hell is that? Is he dead?"

Casper pointed at Ferrill.

"Yeah. Thanks to that asshole and this."

Casper lifted Ferrill's silenced 9mm pistol.

"It's Matt Talbot."

Mando's chin dropped.

"Hooooly *shit!*"

Mando turned to Casper.

"Your shoulder's bleeding. Is it bad?"

Casper winced and pulled on his sleeve.

"Not bad."

"We have to get you patched up," Mando said.

"Take Charlie into the other room first, okay?" Casper said.

"Yeah. Okay."

Mando climbed to his feet and led Charlie through the hallway to a bedroom.

Casper crossed the room to Ferrill, dragging the baseball bat. Ferrill seethed, drawing breath through his clenched teeth.

"What are you gonna do now, boy?" Ferrill said.

"You caught me. For now. I'm going to prison. Maybe. Big deal. No one can stop me. No one can hold me."

Casper paused. He keyed a number into his phone.

"Yeah. Sean. Everything's cool. I have it under control. Sorry to scare you. Yeah. You, too. Good night."

Casper dialed another number.

"Yeah, Dad. Thanks for coming. No, the crisis is over. I'm gonna need your help in a little while, though, if you'll wait. Sure. I love you, too."

Casper ended the call. Ferrill laughed, even though it made his cracked ribs scream out in pain.

"Yeah, it's all over, right? I'm going to kill every one of you," Ferrill said.

Casper bent over the body of the wounded psychopath.

"In a perfect world, maybe…for a psycho serial killer."

Casper stuffed a rag into Ferrill's mouth. He raised the bat and swung it with all his might at Robert Ferrill's right knee. Ferrill's eyes almost popped from their sockets at the pain.

"Ooo, that's gotta hurt," Casper said.

He took the knob of the bat and shoved the rag deeper into Ferrill's throat. He wound up again and swung the bat into Ferrill's left knee.

The killer's eyes rolled up into the back of his head as he lost consciousness.

Forty-Five

The mayor leaned back into the booth. His two closest aids sliced pieces of their identical plates of steak and lobster.

"Oh, my *God*," the mayor said. "That was heaven."

"The best for the best," an aid said. "We've found the killer and the killer is dead. Your approval rating will jump another five points by the time the morning papers hit the streets."

There were two more heavily armed and capable men waiting outside the restaurant.

Between bites, one of the aids spoke.

"Jesus. Look at *that*."

The three men turned, one at a time, to observe two women being seated at a table in the middle of the room. One of the women was quite attractive. The other was absolutely stunning.

The mayor slid from the booth. The other two men dropped their forks and moved to follow him.

"*Relax,*" the mayor said. "Enjoy your meals. I'm going to get a drink."

The aids didn't have to be told twice. They looked at each other and returned to their meals.

The mayor took an empty chair at the bar. He raised his hand. A bartender taking a drink order from another patron saw the mayor's hand and nodded in his direction.

The mayor jumped when he someone grabbed his arm. The aids dropped their forks and jumped to their feet.

"Holy *hell*," the woman said. She reached down and picked up the broken heel from her left pump.

"I'm *so* sorry, sir," she said to the man whose arm she held.

The mayor had never seen a more beautiful woman in his life. He held up his hand toward his aids.

"No problem. No problem."

"I am *so* embarrassed," the woman said.

"Don't be," the mayor said. "It's all just hammers and nails."

The woman threw back her head and laughed, exposing perfect lips and perfect teeth.

"It is, right? I'm sorry I startled you."

"I'm not sorry at all," the mayor said. "You're the most beautiful woman I've ever seen."

The woman smiled, her perfect lips twinkling under the lights.

"And you are very handsome."

"Could I buy you a drink?" the mayor asked. "Maybe I could fix your shoe."

The woman laughed. Her sex appeal intoxicated the mayor like a drug—beyond anything he had felt in quite some time.

The mayor glanced toward the woman's table. Her companion had garnered the attention of two other men.

"Vodka Collins," the woman said. "And maybe a hammer and a screwdriver?"

The mayor laughed.

"I can access all the tools we might possibly need."

He raised his hand. The bartender responded immediately.

"Vodka Collins for the lady. Pretend you're serving the mayor—with the ultimate discretion, of course."

****

The mayor woke up in a strange room. He lay in a king-sized bed, in a room that was obviously luxurious and expensive. An elaborate chandelier hung overhead. Daylight filtered through the drapes. He looked at his wrist, but his watch was missing.

He remembered nothing.

He was alone. And naked. He rubbed his throbbing temples.

The mayor rolled out of bed and walked to the desk. He ran his fingers through his hair as he picked up his watch. It was eleven o'clock. The laminated folder on the desk told him where he was. He picked up the phone and dialed the only number he knew from memory.

"Mayor's Office. How may I direct your call?"

"It's me. I need to speak to Peterson."

"I'm sorry? Who is this?"

"Goddammit, Tiffany! Transfer the fucking call!"

"Right away, sir."

****

Bradley Butler pretended to read the newspaper while he sipped the paper cup of over-priced coffee. He saw the woman walk through the door. The over-sized sweatshirt, baseball cap, and sunglasses did little to disguise the fact that she was gorgeous. She ordered and received a cup of coffee. She sat down across from Butler.

"Good morning," the woman said.

"Good morning," Butler said.

"You have what you needed?"

"Oh, yes," Butler said. "Exquisite work."

"Easy work," she said. "He couldn't even get it up. I was almost insulted."

"Don't worry about it," Butler said. "The drug has side-effects."

The woman smiled, sending chills through Butler's body.

Maybe one day I'll make her a "fringe benefit".

Butler slid the newspaper covering the envelope containing five thousand dollars across the table.

He had what his boss wanted.

Photos. Photos of the mayor and a high-priced call girl in a hotel room.

This was business. Dirty business.

But Bradley Butler kept his personal agenda separate from his professional relationship with Shane Murphy.

I'm on your side, Shane. As long as it benefits both of

us.

Butler admired the view as the woman crossed the room. He put his hand inside his coat, reassured by the feel of his gun and holster.

Mutual benefits, Shane, ole boy.

And don't think for one second I believe Trent Williams' death was an accident.

Forty-Six

The door opened again. It was Bobby Halliday.

"Holy shit, Casper. What the hell—?"

"Dad," Casper said. "Listen to me. You remember Charlie Talbot, right?"

"I...I don't know..."

Casper grabbed Charlie's arm.

"Take her with you, Dad. Take her home. Don't answer the door for *anybody*. Are you listening to me?"

"I'm not going anywhere," Bobby said.

Casper grabbed his father's arm and pulled him close. Casper spoke into his father's ear.

"You're going to get your badge back. But you have to leave. If you don't get Charlie out of here, you're gonna screw up her life, too."

"Yeah. Okay," Bobby said.

"Dad," Casper said. "You didn't see anything. You got it?"

"What?"

"You did not see anything here," Casper said. "Do you understand?"

"I'm not leaving you, son. There's a dead man in the hall and another one rolling around in the floor."

"The dead man is Charlie's husband. The other one...is the piece of shit that killed Mom—"

Bobby pushed against Casper's chest.

"What? What did you say?"

"I'm going to take care of this, Dad."

"How do you know it's him?" Bobby growled.

"I broke into his house. He had her shoes. He had *all* of their shoes."

Bobby shoved Casper away. He kicked Ferrill in the ribs and the gut before Casper pulled him away.

"Listen to me, Dad. I'm going to take care of this."

Bobby struggled.

"I'll kill the bastard with my bare hands!"

Casper shoved Bobby backward. They fell onto the sofa. Casper held his father down. His mouth was at Bobby's ear.

"I need you to get Charlie out of here. And if you want to ever wear a badge again, you need to leave now. We don't have a lot of time. And you were never here. You got it?"

Bobby breathed heavily. He whispered.

"Okay. I got it. I was never here."

Casper stood. He held out his hand and helped his father to his feet.

Bobby Halliday held out his hand.

"Come with me, Charlie."

"No...Matthew..."

Bobby pulled Charlie to her feet. He pulled her toward the door. Her cries were too loud. Bobby put his hand over her mouth. Charlie bit him.

"Let go of me!"

Bobby's angry eyes focused on his son.

"I didn't say it would be easy," Casper said. "Go with my dad, Charlie. Matt's dead—you can't stay here."

Bobby winced and pulled the sobbing Charlie Talbot toward the door. He looked at Casper.

"You and I are going to have a long talk."

"We'll have a lot of them," Casper said.

Bobby shook his finger at his son.

"You be careful."

****

Mando closed the door behind Bobby and Charlie. He pressed his hands against his head.

"Holy *shit*, Casper! What do we do now?"

Ferrill tried to push to his feet, despite his injured knees. He tugged at the gag. Casper leapt to his knees and shoved the gag farther into Ferrill's mouth. He rolled Ferrill onto his belly.

"Do you have cuffs?"

"No," Mando said.

"Get me a zip-tie," Casper said. "Kitchen drawer."

"Right," Mando said.

Moments later, Casper cinched the plastic zip-tie around Ferrill's wrists. He cinched it tight. And then he pulled it some more. He heard Ferrill wince against the gag.

"What the hell, Caz?" Mando said. "Do we call this in now?"

"No," Casper said.

"No?" Mando said. "Do you have enough evidence to put this bastard away?"

"I have all the evidence I need."

"Then, we call it in!" Mando said.

Casper shook his head.

"No. We call it in, and this piece of shit gets three squares and a bed until he's eighty."

Mando shook his head slowly.

"Uh…what are we gonna do, Bro?"

Casper went to his bedroom and returned moments later with a roll of duct tape. He made three revolutions around Ferrill's head with it, securing the gag.

"Okay," Mando said. "I'm still with you, Caz. What are we doing?"

Casper held his cell phone in his hand.

"It's all gonna be okay, Mando. I've been waiting for this."

"I don't know what that means," Mando said. "We're still partners, right?"

Casper nodded.

"You're damn right. Partners. Stay with me."

Casper dialed a number. The phone rang three times. A sleepy voice answered.

"Hullo?"

"Jerome," Casper said. "This is Casper. Halliday."

Jerome Slade moaned.

"It's almost midnight, man…"

"Yes, it is," Casper said. "I need your help."

"Yeah? What's up?"

"I need you and I need your van."

"What kind of shit is this, Ghost Man?"

"Heavy shit. *Deep* shit," Casper said.

"You got my attention now," Slade said. "What is

it?"

"I've got the son-of-a-bitch that killed my mother," Casper said.

"*Sheeiit,* Ghost Man! Are you freaking *serious?*"

"I'm serious," Casper said.

"You're a *cop*, man," Jerome said. "Drag his ass in."

"No," Casper said. "The worst he gets is life without parole."

"Aw, shit..." Slade said. "What you gonna do with him?"

"Give him what he deserves," Casper said.

"Aw, no, Halliday," Jerome said. "I'm not goin' back to the joint, man. No way."

"You're not going to the joint, Jerome," Casper said. "I just need transportation and a wheel man. Anything looks wrong, you cut and leave."

"Shit," Slade said. "I knew you were bad news— four freaking years ago."

"I love you, too, buddy," Casper said. "Take down this address. I need you here as soon as possible. Do you know Brooklyn?"

"I got GPS," Slade said.

"Okay. Cool."

"You're gonna owe me, Halliday. Big time."

"You're damn right, I am," Casper said. "And I pay my debts."

Forty-Seven

Casper's phone rang. He answered on the first ring.

"I'm almost there," Slade said.

"Good," Casper said. "Drive around to the back of the building—to the parking garage and service dock. I'll meet you there and let you in."

The van rolled up to the curb. Slade lowered his window. He nodded toward Mando.

"Who's this?"

"Mando Gonzalez. This is Jerome Slade."

"Hey," Mando said.

"You two better be tighter than twin ticks," Slade said.

"Don't worry," Casper said. "We're tight."

Casper used a card to open the gated entry. Slade pulled the van inside and backed it up to the service dock. Casper opened a set of double doors and pulled out a laundry cart.

"What's that for?" Mando whispered. "This isn't a hotel."

"Maybe we're not the first ones to need to move a body," Casper said.

"Shut *up*, Ghost Man," Slade said.

Casper winced.

"Jesus, Jerome. I'm trying to give up the

nickname."

"Yeah," Slade said. "Good luck with that."

"Come on," Casper said. "We'll use the service elevator. With any luck, we won't run into anybody."

They stepped into the elevator and pulled in the cart. Casper pushed the button for the twelfth floor. When the doors closed, Casper and Slade exhaled.

Mando cleared his throat.

"A white guy, a black guy, and a Mexican guy walk into an elevator."

Slade glared at Mando.

"*What?*" Slade said.

"Sounds like the beginning of a joke, right?" Mando said.

Slade rubbed his eyes.

"Jesus. I'm goin' back to the slam, sure as shit."

Casper shook his head.

"No, you're—"

"Then you tell Señor Axel Foley that this ain't no damn movie."

"Mando—"

"I know, I know," Mando said. "Sorry."

They made it to Casper's door with the cart without being seen. Casper closed the door behind them in time to see Slade's knees buckle.

"Aw, Jesus. This fucker's *dead!* Who is that?"

"We don't have a lot of time, Slade," Casper said. "I was supposed to meet a friend here last night. She's going through a nasty divorce. That's her husband. This other asshole here put a bullet in his head."

"So we got *two* bodies to move," Slade said.

"Yeah," Casper said.

"Going to the same place, right?" Slade said.

"No," Casper said. "That's not the plan. It should be simple though."

Slade looked at Ferrill's legs.

"Man. You do that?"

"Yeah," Casper said. "You ain't seen nothin' yet."

Casper pointed at the unconscious killer.

"We're going to drop Mr. Talbot and the silenced pistol at *his* house. That house has already been broken into."

Casper grabbed a box of latex gloves from the counter.

"Everybody glove-up. Let's do this."

They loaded Matt Talbot's body into the cart and covered it with sheets. Casper opened the door and signaled for the others to come ahead.

They were not as fortunate as before.

Two giggling young women stepped from the tenant elevator. They were Casper's roommate neighbors. Their tiny dresses, high pumps, and somewhat glassy eyes indicated they were returning from a night on the town. The girls stopped in the hall. One of them pushed her hair behind her ear and grinned.

"Hi. What are you doing?"

"Well, until a few minutes ago, we were playing poker and drinking," Casper said. "Then one of our friends stands up, almost falls on his face, and says he needs to lie down. Yeah. He lay down on my bed for about ten seconds before he puked all over my bedspread. We gotta get rid of this — my whole apartment reeks."

"*Ewww!*"

Both girls stumbled backward. They caught each other when they tripped over their heels.

"Sorry," Casper said.

"See ya!" the girls said. They stumbled into their apartment.

The doors of the service elevator closed.

"Damn, you have to be the best liar I've ever seen," Mando said.

"Thirty months in prison leaves you a lot of time to think about not going back," Casper said.

Twelve minutes later, they were back in the apartment. Robert Ferrill was lighter than Matt Talbot, but he was conscious now, and struggled against their grips. He screamed silently into the gag when his ruined legs were jostled. Slade tossed the sheets over Ferrill.

"Wait," Casper said. He ran to his bedroom and returned with a rectangular box. He put the box in the cart. Slade and Mando looked at Casper with their eyes wide.

"What the *hell?*" Slade said. "A *rubber raft?*"

Slade shook his head vigorously.

"No, no, no, no, no. I ain't goin' out on the damn water in no rubber boat! You have lost your *mind.*"

"Relax, Jerome," Casper said. "Nobody's going in the water. I'll explain later."

They spread out the sheets and left the apartment

behind. Casper directed Slade to Ferrill's house. Slade backed the van beneath the carport. They carried Matt Talbot's body into the kitchen.

"Over by the sink," Casper said.

They laid the dead man on his back. Casper opened a cabinet and took out a cup and a saucer. He dropped them on the tile floor next to Talbot's head.

"What the hell, Casper?" Slade said.

"Looks more like a real crime scene, right?" Casper said.

"That ain't gonna matter if there are ten neighbors watching us leave here."

Casper scratched his cheek.

"I don't..."

"You don't what?" Mando said.

"Come in here," Casper said. He walked into Ferrill's bedroom and shined his flashlight into the closet.

"*Oh, my, God,*" both Slade and Mando whispered.

Casper moved the flashlight beam from the mannequin, to the display of pantyhose, to the shelf of women's shoes.

Casper cleared his throat. He picked up his mother's shoes from the bedroom floor and put them on the shelf.

"These...these are my mom's."

Mando's and Slade's jaws hung slack.

Casper wiped his eye.

"This house is full of surveillance cameras. I found his computer setup and trashed it before I left. There are no recording devices, unless he set up a remote server. The live-feed went to his phone."

"Where is his phone?" Mando asked.

"I used your bat on it," Casper said. "The pieces are on their way to the landfill."

"Let's go," Slade said.

No one spoke until they reached the end of the street. Slade tapped a finger on the steering wheel.

"Which way—"

He froze when the whoop of a siren sounded before an ambulance passed in front of them.

"Jesus," Slade said. "I didn't need that."

"Head toward Manhattan," Casper said. He took out his phone.

"Manhattan," Slade said. "I didn't need to hear that either."

"Hey!" Mando said. "Cut it out, man!"

Ferrill was wide awake now, lying in the rear of the van and trying his best to free his hands from the zip-tie.

"Hold on, Slade," Casper said. He climbed through the side door and added another zip-tie to Ferrill's hands. Casper picked up the baseball bat and held it in front of Ferrill's eyes.

"Your game is over, Ferrill. I have a lot of swings left if you push me."

Forty-Eight

Casper climbed back into the passenger seat. Slade turned the van to the right, following the distant lights of the ambulance. Casper turned on his flashlight, shined it on a piece of paper he took from his pocket, and entered numbers into his phone.

"Who the hell are you calling?" Slade asked. "It's two in the morning!"

Casper put the phone to his ear.

"Don't worry, Jerome. It's another good guy."

The phone was answered on the third ring.

"Mr. Cappelletti?" Casper said.

Mando leaned forward between the two seats.

"What the hell, Casper?"

Casper put a finger to his lips.

"Shh."

"Yes," Cristian Cappelletti said. "Who is this?"

"Casper Halliday."

"Do I know—oh," Cristian said.

"I was there that morning," Casper said. "At the bakery. I tackled you."

"Okay," Cristian said. "I know who you are. You were on the news and…Oh, Jesus…your mother…"

"Yes," Casper said. "Look, Mr. Cappelletti—"

"Cristian."

"Cristian. I'm offering you a choice. All I ask is

that you never repeat what I'm about to say to anyone."

Cristian's voice was tired and full of the heavy sadness that would never leave him.

"Why would I say anything to anyone? You and I share the ultimate pain."

"I have the killer, Cristian."

"What?" Cristian yelled. *"Where is he?* Has he been arrested? Are you sure about this?"

"Please, hear me out," Casper said. "I followed a hunch. The last victim had worked for three weeks in the kitchen and dining car of passenger trains operating between New York and Miami. The murder outside of Baltimore made me curious. I rode a train from Penn Station to D.C. and made sure that I met the train crew. I got off that train and bought a ticket to go back north. The conductor on the northbound train set off all kinds of alarms inside my head."

Casper paused.

"I broke into his house."

"What?" Cristian said. "But…you're a cop."

Casper sighed.

"Yeah, I'm a cop. And my mother was murdered."

"What did you find?" Cristian's voice cracked. "In the house?"

"It's all there," Casper said. "The shoes. He took their shoes. And…their pantyhose."

Casper heard Cristian break into sobs.

"So, it's all over," Cristian said in a tortured voice.

"No," Casper said. "It's not over."

"I don't understand," Cristian moaned.

"The bastard's name is Robert Ferrill," Casper said. "If he's arrested, anything could happen. He'll have an excellent attorney; this case will have lawyers fighting over it. Maybe Ferrill's declared insane and not responsible for his actions. Or maybe he sits in a private cell entertaining book and movie offers while he reads romance novels until he dies. You know there is no death penalty in New York."

"Yes," Cristian said. "A decision I was once in favor of."

"We can end this conversation right now, if you want," Casper said.

"No," Cristian said. "Go on."

Casper's voice was like a drone—void of emotion

"I'm not willing to let this demon live," Casper said.

"What are you going to do?" Cristian asked.

"I'm going to make sure the son-of-a-bitch never sees another sunrise. I'm giving you the choice, Cristian. Do you want to be there? If you don't, I'll certainly understand. Just forget this call ever happened."

Cristian paused.

"Where do I meet you?"

"I'll be at the curb in front of your house in fifteen minutes," Casper said.

Mando sighed and sat back in the seat. Casper gave Slade his next direction. Slade nodded once and shook his head while he mumbled under his breath.

The van had not come to a full stop when a dark

shape approached from the front of the house. Mando opened the sliding door and moved to his left.

Cristian Cappelletti put one foot on the running board and pulled himself up. He looked over the back seat and directly into Robert Ferrill's eyes. A streetlight illuminated Ferrill's face. Ferrill's eyes burned with a mixture of fear, hatred, and madness.

Cristian stepped down, turned, and ran three steps before bending over and vomiting onto the grass. He stood, wiped his mouth, and returned to the van.

"Sorry."

No one spoke. Mando handed Cristian a bottle of water. Cristian rinsed his mouth, spit, and climbed into the van.

Casper turned in his seat.

"Introductions later, okay?"

Cristian nodded.

"Yeah."

Casper turned to Slade.

"Head north—out of the city."

Slade checked his mirror and changed lanes.

"Oh, hell, yeah. That's the most sensible thing you've said all night."

They rode in silence until the lights of the city were finally behind them. Cristian sat with his elbows on his knees, rocking gently.

"I can't believe it," he whispered. "This is really happening."

A few seconds passed.

"Oh, great," Mando said. "I think he just pissed

himself."

Cristian turned his head.

"I did not."

"Not you," Mando said. He jerked his thumb over his shoulder.

"Him."

Slade looked at Casper.

"Hey…"

"Don't worry," Casper said. "I'll take care of it."

Casper's directions took them farther away from populated areas. He directed Slade to a dirt road.

"Oh, man," Slade said. "You're gonna tear up my van."

"No," Casper said. "This road isn't bad. It isn't much farther."

"You've been way the hell out here?" Slade asked.

Casper stared ahead.

"Yeah."

Slade slowed the van and stopped. He rubbed his eyes.

"You mapped all this out. And you're a cop."

Slade turned and stared at Casper.

"You're one scary bastard, Ghost Man."

Casper stared into Slade's eyes.

"She was my mother, Jerome. I would trade my life for hers in a heartbeat. I loved her more than life itself. I am not enjoying this. This is necessary. This is justice."

Slade sniffed and nodded.

"Yeah. Here we go."

Forty-Nine

Casper pointed to the place where the dirt road split into two. Those roads were less-traveled. The weeds grew tall on all sides.

"Turn the van around and park right here," Casper said.

"Do I leave it running, or what?"

"Do you have plenty of gas?" Casper asked.

"I got enough to get us home," Slade said. "Unless you got some messed-up plan that's gonna take all night."

"No," Casper said. "I don't think so."

Slade grabbed the door handle.

"Well, let's get it done."

Casper, Slade, Mando, and Cristian met at the back of the van. A train whistle sounded in the distance. Mando and Slade looked at each other—and then at Casper.

"You gotta be shittin' me, Bro," Mando said. "The train?"

Casper pulled open the back doors of the van.

"If you were a psychopathic killer who was finally coming to grips with his crimes, how would you commit suicide?"

"Oh, my God…" Slade whispered.

Cristian spoke in a steady voice.

"Let's do it."

"How far away is it?" Mando said.

"Half a mile. Maybe less," Casper said. "There are three different roads that provide access to the tracks. This road is the farthest away."

"Are you trying to get in a workout?" Mando asked.

"I'm trying to get away when it's over," Casper said.

"Oh," Mando said. "Yeah. Makes sense."

Slade reached past Casper and picked up the box containing the raft.

"I get it," Slade said. "We pull the asshole on this."

Casper snatched the box from Slade's hands.

"No. That's not what this is for."

Slade's shoulders slumped.

"We gotta carry him? A half-mile? If we hold him by those messed-up legs, he'll be dead by the time we get there. We could drag him on that raft—"

Casper shook his head.

"No."

Slade pushed Casper out of the way. He pulled Ferrill close to him and threw the man over his shoulder in a fireman's carry. Slade's face pinched like he'd bitten into a lemon.

"You stinkin'…"

He motioned with his head.

"Go."

Casper grabbed a coil of rope, put the raft under

his arm, and closed the van doors. He started out across
the field.

Five minutes later they reached the tracks. Slade
bent over and tried to ease Ferrill to the ground. Slade's
knees shook and he lost his grip. Ferrill tumbled to the
ground face-first. The veins of Ferrill's neck strained as
his barely audible cries died against the duct tape. The
others looked around. The horn sounds from the earlier
train had come and gone.

"Oops," Slade said. "What now?"

"Go back to the van and be ready," Casper said.
"Nothing has changed, Jerome. If anything doesn't feel
right or look right, get out of here."

"It's a little late for that," Slade said. He turned
and walked away, stretching his neck.

Casper looked at Mando and Cristian.

"Move him inside the tracks."

They pulled the moaning Robert Ferrill over the
rail.

"Hold his hands to this side," Casper said.

Casper took more zip-ties from his pocket. He
fastened two of them together and looped them around
the rail. He attached them to the ties around Ferrill's
right wrist. Casper moved to the other rail and did the
same thing.

Another horn blast sounded in the distance.

"Casper," Mando said.

Casper did not stop what he was doing.

"I hear it."

"That's not what I'm talking about. I got a bad feeling about this. Don't free his other hand."

"He has broken legs and one hand tied to the rail," Casper said. "And you have a baseball bat."

"He's too smart, Caz," Mando said. "Think about it. Four murders that we know of—and no evidence. You got lucky. I guarantee you this asshole prepared for being caught."

Casper looked at Ferrill's face in the moonlight. Despite his position, Ferrill's eyes burned with an evil stare—as if he believed he was invincible. Casper stood and cut a length of the rope. He used it to connect the zip-ties on Ferrill's left wrist to the opposite rail.

"There," Casper said. "He's not going anywhere."

Casper knelt by Ferrill's head. He raised his knife.

"Hey, what are you doing?" Mando said.

"Let's see what the soon-to-be ex-Ghost Man has to say," Casper said.

Casper cut the duct tape and ripped it away from Ferrill's mouth. Ferrill's tongue worked desperately to push the rag from his throat. When the rag fell free, Ferrill loosed a string of expletives until his voice gave way to a coughing fit. His head snapped toward Casper.

"You little shit. You're not smart enough to get away with this. You're going to prison—all of you. You'll be good little gang-bitches until they skin you alive!"

"You're wasting your breath, asshole," Casper said. "Robert Ferrill, for crimes against humanity, I sentence you to commit suicide by train."

Ferrill's nostrils flared.

"Your mother had such a sweet ass..." he said between clenched teeth.

"Shut up!"

Ferrill's eyes moved to Cristian.

"Oh, I remember you...pretty boy. Do you still have your bakery? You want to lighten up on the icing on the cinnamon rolls. They're too sweet. Not as sweet as that sexy woman, though. And you made it oh. So. *Easy*—!"

"*Shut up!*" Cristian roared. In a flash, he snatched the baseball bat from Mando's hand and charged at Ferrill.

"No!" Casper cried. He reached for Cristian but missed his arm. His arm circled Cristian's chest, allowing him to pull enough so that the bat hit the rail only inches above Ferrill's head. Ferrill winced.

"The boy's got energy," Ferrill said. "I'll bet him and Lizzie used to—"

Casper grabbed the rag and stuffed it back into Ferrill's mouth. He reapplied the duct tape.

"Bad idea," Casper said.

The echo of the train's horn came closer. Casper picked up the box and pulled out the raft. He handed the box to Mando.

"Hold onto this."

Casper straddled Ferrill. He raised the man's head and shoved the folded raft beneath him, beneath his back and shoulders. He stepped outside the rails and attached an end of the coil of rope to the string coming off the raft.

"You're giving him a pillow?" Mando said.

"Hell no," Casper said.

Casper stood and walked slowly backward, uncoiling the rope as he went.

"Come on. Time to hide."

Casper had just enough rope to reach a shallow drainage ditch.

"Show-time," Casper said. He looked at his companions. "If either of you wants to go wait in the van, now is the time."

"No," Cristian said.

"Partners forever, partners now," Mando said.

Headlights appeared on the horizon. Casper crouched down. The other's followed.

Closer. Closer. They could hear the roar of the locomotives now.

Mando held out his right hand. Casper raised his right hand that had a white-knuckled grip on the rope.

"Sorry, partner. I'm not letting go of this until it's over."

"Okay," Mando said. He took hold of Casper's left hand. Mando looked over his shoulder at Cristian. He held out his other hand. Cristian grabbed hold—both of them holding tight against the other's sweaty palm.

"Mando Gonzalez."

"Cristian Cappelletti."

"Nice to meet you."

"Yeah. You, too."

Fifty

The heavy freight train powered into the broad, sweeping curve. Wheels and rail screamed from the friction of steel-on-steel, sending tiny, sparkling metal dust into the air. The headlights were past them now. Casper pulled the slack from the rope. He turned around and ran.

Casper felt the resistance as the trigger activated inside the self-inflating raft. The compressed air canister blew a powerful blast into the portable boat—a vessel intended to save lives in an emergency.

But not this night.

Robert Ferrill's body was launched upright. The force drove his torso against the wrist restraints, dislocating both shoulders. The restraints broke, but Ferrill's legs would not support him.

The last thing Robert Ferrill saw was the blaze of headlights.

The roar was deafening.

The train's engineer activated the emergency brakes on one hundred and seven loaded rail cars.

Casper stumbled and fell when the rope went slack. Mando pulled him to his feet.

"Go, go, *go!*"

Cristian reached the van first. He opened the side

door and jumped to the far-side of the bench seat. Mando reached the door. He looked behind him. Casper was spooling the rope.

"What are you doing?" Mando said.

"We can't leave this here!" Casper said.

Mando bounced on his toes, his head moving in every direction. The rope caught on something. Casper jerked on it. Two seconds later he saw what caught the rope.

The rope was tied to a large piece of blue vinyl.

And covered in blood.

"Aw, shit," Mando said. "Are you putting that in the van?"

"We don't have any choice," Casper said.

"Casper!" Slade yelled. "Get your ass in the van!"

"Five seconds!" Casper yelled. He tore off his jacket and spread it on the ground. Casper folded the piece of blue vinyl and put it on top of his jacket along with the rope. He pulled off his bloody latex gloves and dropped them on top before folding everything into a bundle. He put the bundle in the back of the van, slammed the doors, and climbed into the passenger seat.

"Let's go!"

No one spoke until they reached the stop sign at the paved road. Casper lowered his window and listened.

"Sirens," he said. He pointed with his thumb. "They're coming from the other direction."

Slade nodded and turned onto the paved road.

"It's over?"

"Yeah," Casper said. "It's over."

"What's in the back?" Slade said.

"Stuff that needs to find a fire," Casper said.

"I'll take care of it," Slade said.

"Just take us to my place," Casper said. "I'll drive Cristian home."

Slade nodded.

A few minutes later, Mando leaned forward.

"Hey, Casper."

"Yeah?"

"This is it, right? We're just regular cops from now on. No more vigilante stuff. No more judge, jury, and executioner stuff, right?"

"Right," Casper said. "One and done. Over and out."

Mando took a deep breath and leaned back.

"Cool."

Casper had Slade drop them off two blocks from Casper's building. Casper introduced Cristian and Jerome. They shook hands. Jerome shook hands with Mando. Casper took Slade's big right hand in both of his.

"We cut a big cancer out of the human race tonight, Jerome. We couldn't have done it without you."

"You know what they say," Jerome said. "The best friends will help you move a body."

Casper managed a smile.

"Thank you, Jerome, my good friend. I'll be in touch—after the next few days blow over."

"Yeah," Jerome said. "It's gonna be a shit-storm,

all right. Go home."

Slade drove away. Casper, Mando, and Cristian walked toward Casper's apartment.

"Where did you park?" Casper asked Mando.

"I'll ride with you," Mando said.

"Are you sure?" Casper said. "It's been a long night."

"For some reason I'm not sleepy," Mando said.

They were a few minutes away from Cristian's house. Cristian stared out the passenger window. He had not spoken on the drive.

"Are you all right, Cristian?" Casper asked.

"Yeah," Cristian said. He turned to face Casper.

"It's...it's just a lot to swallow over the course of a few hours."

"Yeah," Casper said. "I know."

Cristian looked away.

"It doesn't bring them back."

"No," Casper said.

"Don't get me wrong, though," Cristian said. "I'm glad this happened. I didn't buy that junkie story for one minute. What if the police just made the case work—and closed it? What if we never knew who the real killer was? Or what if he was caught and I had to stare at my ceiling every night knowing that monster was watching cable television and reading magazines? He might have fallen sleep every night believing he'd done nothing wrong—dreaming sick fantasies with a smile on his face."

"I know what you're saying," Casper said. He stopped the car in front of a park, around the corner from

Cristian's house.

"You should probably walk from here," Casper said. "If any of your neighbors see you, you can just say you couldn't sleep and went for a walk."

"Okay," Cristian said. He didn't reach for the door. He stared through the windshield.

"We dreamed of bringing our children to this park. We wanted at least three. Would you believe we decided to buy our house because of this park?"

"Sure," Casper said. "I can see that."

"We walked through here whenever we had time," Cristian said. "We were so busy getting the restaurants up and running. But...we thought we had all the time in the world."

Casper sniffed. So did Mando.

"We talked about hearing the kids laugh as they ran from ride to ride. From swing to slide."

Cristian pointed.

"That concrete area, there—in front of the bandstand? That's where we'd bring them with their tricycles. And then their little bikes with the training wheels. Then the big day when we took off the training wheels, and they wobbled their way from my arms to Elizabeth's. We would clap and cheer and be so proud of them—and then be a little sad because they were growing up so fast..."

"I'm sorry, Cristian," Casper said.

"Me, too," Mando said. Mando blew his nose.

Cristian forced a polite smile and tapped his chest.

"Thank you. I feel your pain, too—it will always live right here. Right next to mine."

"Detectives will probably be knocking on your door by noon," Casper said. "They'll want you to identify…the evidence. This might be difficult because of what you already know."

Cristian shook his head.

"No." He swallowed hard. "When I see her things…it's going to hit me like a ton of bricks."

Casper extended his hand.

"Good luck."

"Thank you for thinking of me," Cristian said. "Goodbye, Mando."

"Goodbye, Cristian."

Casper turned the car around and drove toward his apartment building.

"He's a good guy," Mando said.

"Yes, he is," Casper said.

Mando yawned.

"I'm gonna crash at your place, if that's okay."

"Sure," Casper said.

"I'm off today, thank God," Mando said. "You know what would be a good thing? If those two neighbors of yours saw that you're home, and I stayed over. That fits with the story we told them last night."

"Good idea," Casper said. "You think like a detective. Or a criminal."

"What's the difference?" Mando said.

They walked into Casper's apartment. Mando walked to the refrigerator and took out two beer bottles.

He handed one to Casper. Mando moved to the living room and dropped onto the sofa.

"I have to call my dad," Casper said.

Bobby Halliday answered on the second ring.

"Casper? Are you all right?"

"I'm fine, Dad. The thing is done. It's over."

Bobby exhaled.

"Okay. Are you in the clear?"

"I think so. Yes."

"Is there a story?" Bobby said. "Something I need to commit to memory?"

"Me, Mando, and a few other guys were playing poker and drinking a few beers last night at my apartment. Two of my neighbors saw us. I think we're good."

"Okay. Okay," Bobby said. "Where are you now?"

"Still at my apartment," Casper said. "Mando is staying over. Is Charlie there?"

"No," Bobby said. "I took her straight to the airport. She wants to stay with her parents for a while. She rented a car. I told her I didn't know if that was a good idea, but she said she wants to be alone for a while."

"Okay," Casper said.

"Are you going to tell me why this woman was in your apartment?" Bobby said.

"We're just friends," Casper said.

"Where did you meet her?" Bobby asked.

"She's a dispatcher," Casper said.

"I know that," Bobby said. "So, you've known her for a month?"

"A few weeks, yeah," Casper said.

"You know what?" Bobby said. "I'm getting used to the fact that your life will never make sense to me."

"I don't know what to say to that," Casper said.

"Get some sleep, Casper," Bobby said. "And then get your ass over here."

"Yes, Sir."

"I love you, Son."

"I love you, Dad."

Fifty-One

Casper slept for three hours. Mando remained fast asleep on the living room sofa. Casper showered and dressed. He wrote Mando a note and stepped into the hallway, pulling the door closed behind him.

A neighbor girl from the night before closed her door at the same time.

"Hi," Casper said.

"Hi."

Casper noted her attire.

"Off to the gym, huh?"

"This might not be the best idea I've ever had. Last night was a little rough. Cheryl is still crashed out."

Casper massaged his temples and motioned toward his apartment.

"I know what you mean. A couple of my friends are sleeping it off."

The girl extended her hand.

"I'm Julie."

Casper shook her hand.

"Nice to meet you. I'm Casper."

Julie giggled.

"I know. That's so *cute*."

"Like a basket full of puppies," Casper said.

Julie laughed and then grabbed her head.

"Ow." She giggled some more.

"I guess I'll go before I talk myself into going back to bed. I've never puked on a treadmill before."

Casper smiled.

"Life is just a long string of things that have never happened before."

"That's good," Julie said. "Somebody should put that on a t-shirt. You're a cop, right?"

"Yes. For a whole month."

"Isn't your girlfriend a police officer, too?" Julie said.

"That's...not really happening...anymore."

Julie smacked her forehead with her palm.

"I'm sorry. That's none of my damn business."

"It's okay." Casper said.

Julie looked at the floor.

"I heard about your mother. I'm so, so, sorry."

"Thanks," Casper said.

Julie shuffled her feet.

"I can't imagine..."

"I couldn't either," Casper said.

"I should let you go," Julie said. "Maybe we could get together sometime—you know, my friends and your friends. Have a few drinks. A few laughs."

"That sounds fun," Casper said.

"It's nice to meet you, Casper."

"Nice meeting you, Julie."

Casper started his car and turned on the vent fan, letting the cool air hit his face. He took out his phone and called Mona Casey.

"Hi, Casper!"

"Good morning, Mona. How's it going?"

Mona lowered her voice.

"You had us worried last night. Is everything okay?"

"Everything's fine," Casper said. "Do me a favor, forget I called last night, okay? If anybody asks?"

"Sure. Okay," Mona said. "I guess this is a police thing I'm not supposed to know about."

"I'm sorry," Casper said.

"Don't be sorry," Mona said. "I have to get used to this 'police' thing. When do you think you could come to visit? It's been a while."

"I was hoping I could come right now," Casper said.

"Really?" Mona squealed. "That would be fantastic! Are you hungry?"

Casper laughed.

"No. But I could really use some good coffee and a bunch of hugs."

Mona laughed.

"We have both in great supply. Cody will be so excited!"

"I'll be there in a few minutes," Casper said. "Can I get you anything?"

"Well…" Mona said, "now that you mention it, somebody got my little boy hooked on chocolate milk…"

"Say no more," Casper said. "I could use some myself."

Casper pulled into the Casey's driveway. The door

burst open, and Cody bolted across the tiny lawn. He launched himself into Casper's open arms. Casper twirled them in circles, with a smiling Mona watching.

"Casper!" Cody yelled. "I misted you!"

"I misted you, too, buddy!"

Casper kissed Cody's cheek and shivered from head to toe as the little boy squeezed him with all his might. Casper carried Cody to meet Mona. They all hugged each other.

"It is so good to see you," Mona said.

"God, I've missed you guys," Casper said.

"Come in. Come in!" Mona said.

Mona's mother sat in a recliner in the living room, her left leg propped up in a cast.

"Oh, no," Casper said. "What happened?"

Carla Hayes adjusted herself in the chair.

"It was time to take down the Christmas lights."

Casper spread his arms.

"I would have done that."

"That's what Sean said," Carla said. "But he was busy working and playing tonsil hockey with my daughter—"

"*Mother!*" Mona said.

"Well, it's true," Carla said. "Sometimes things just need to get done—"

"Mom, what's tonsil hockey?" Cody said. "Is that a game?"

Mona blushed.

"Cody, take that sack from Casper and put it in the refrigerator. He brought you chocolate milk."

"Chocolate milk! Yay!"

Cody ran into the kitchen.

"I swear, Mother," Mona said. "I'm going to put you in a home."

"I fell off a ladder," Carla said. "That kind of thing happens every day."

"Yes," Mona said. "It even happens to coordinated people."

"What?" Carla said. "Are you saying I'm not—?"

"You're clumsy, Mom," Mona said. "You've been breaking shit as long as I can remember."

"There's no need to talk like gutter-trash, Ramona—"

"We have a guest," Mona said. "And we're going to have coffee and chocolate milk and enjoy a pleasant conversation. You can be a part of it or you can hop off to your room."

Carla smiled.

"Don't be silly."

Carla reached her hand toward Casper. Casper took it.

"I am very fond of this young man."

Carla looked at Mona.

"I just like to see you squirm."

"You're evil," Mona said.

"I love you, Ramona."

"I love you, too, Mom. Sometimes."

They sat around the dining room table for over an hour, talking and laughing.

"We'll make a play-date for next week, Cody,"

Casper said. "We'll do something fun. Does that sound good?"

Cody threw his hands in the air.

"Yay! Can Sean come, too?"

"You bet he can," Casper said. "I'll talk to him later and find out when both of us can be there."

"Are you going back to work soon?" Mona asked.

"Yes," Casper said. "It's time."

Casper checked his watch.

"I need to go see my dad. This has been great."

Casper gave Cody a big hug. Mona threw her arms around him and whispered in his ear.

"I'm so glad we found you."

Casper cleared his throat.

"I'm glad we found each other. So, you and Sean…?"

Mona leaned back and smiled.

"I think so."

Carla did not stand but opened her arms. Casper hugged her, too. Carla took Casper's face in her hands.

"I think you're an *angel.*"

"You're embarrassing me, Carla. Take good care of that leg."

Fifty-Two

Casper tapped twice on his father's door and pushed it open. Bobby sat at the dining room table with someone Casper had not seen in a long time.

"Oh, my *God!*" Casper yelled.

Maurice (Mo) Tinsley jumped out a chair and met Casper half-way. They almost fell when they collided in a bear-hug.

"You're out!" Casper said.

"I escaped," Mo said.

"No you didn't."

"No, I didn't!"

"Oh, *man*, it's good to see you," Casper said.

"It's good to be seen," Mo said.

Casper pointed at Mo.

"It's celebration time."

"Damn right. I'm ready," Mo said.

"Give me a couple of days to set things up," Casper said. "And we'll eat, drink, and make merry."

"I don't know who Mary is, but I'll give her a try," Mo said.

"No, you won't," Casper said.

Mo just laughed.

"Do you have a place to stay?" Casper asked.

"Yeah," Mo said. "My cousin Deshaun met me at the gates when I got out. I hadn't seen him in years, of course, and we were just kids the last time I saw him. He's twenty-two now—and he's got a good gig on Broadway. He's a hell of a dancer. And we have some…important things in common. I'm staying with him for now."

"That's great," Casper said. "Welcome home."

****

Casper stepped in front of the mirror. He was finally back in uniform. He was nervous about walking into the station because he knew all eyes would be on him.

Casper and Bobby left the apartment at the same time. Bobby smiled as he held the door.

"You sure look good in blue," Bobby said.

"I feel good in blue," Casper said. "I'm glad to be going back."

The body of Robert Ferrill was identified quickly. The discovery of the murder evidence in Ferrill's home reignited the media storm.

Casper thought about the families of Karin Armstrong and Jessica Collins. This news would rekindle their horror, but it was over now.

The monster had been exposed. And the monster was dead.

Casper pulled into the station parking lot. He was early for his afternoon shift. He looked at his phone and considered calling Charlie Talbot.

No. If she's not being interrogated already, it won't be

long—after her dead husband was discovered in Robert Ferrill's kitchen.

Casper took a deep breath and got out of the car.

He was greeted by somber looks and sad smiles. There were handshakes all around, some fist-bumps, and a few hugs. Everyone told him it was good to have him back. Casper found Leo Sanchez in the locker room. Leo hugged him.

"You're still with me, for now, partner."

"Good," Casper said. "Like a comfortable pair of shoes."

"I don't know about that," Leo said.

They climbed into the patrol car. Leo made a few turns that puzzled Casper.

"Where are we going?"

"The big guy wants to talk to you," Leo said.

"Big guy?"

"Chief Livingston."

"Oh," Casper said. This news made him nervous.

Chief of Detectives Dwight Livingston's secretary led Casper into the Chief's office. Dwight Livingston leaned against the corner of his desk. He stared at the three televisions that lined one wall. They were each turned to a different news station. One glance told Casper what the subject was.

Robert Ferrill.

Livingston raised a remote control that lowered the volume on all the sets.

"Hello, Officer Halliday. Come in. Have a seat."

"Hello, Chief Livingston."

The Chief sat behind his desk. He looked at the televisions for a few more seconds and then turned them off. He pointed at them with the remote control.

"Wow. What a shocker, huh?"

"Yes, sir," Casper said. "Crazy."

"I wanted you to know that detectives are on their way to speak to your father. We saw no need to…subject both of you to the evidence found in Ferrill's home."

"Thank you for telling me, sir," Casper said.

"He has us scratching our heads, that's for sure," Livingston said. "I'm sure you've heard about Matt Talbot."

"Yes, sir."

Livingston sighed.

"I'm sure Charlie is in shock. Mrs. Talbot, I mean."

"Without a doubt," Casper said. "I hope she's okay."

"I know they had separated," Livingston said. "And now this…"

Casper leaned forward. His eyes widened.

"Do you think…maybe this monster was stalking *Charlie*? And her husband found out about it—maybe he followed Ferrill to his house!"

Livingston nodded.

"You're not the first to voice that possibility. We're looking into it. It seems like a stretch, but, hell—we don't have anything else at this point."

"I'm just glad it's over," Casper said. "Not just for Dad and me. Those other families. This killer was good.

Too good."

"I can't help thinking that I might have interacted with him," Livingston said. "Maybe a bunch of times. I've ridden those trains for years."

"Hidden in plain sight," Casper said.

"He must have snapped," Livingston said. "Maybe there was something of a conscience left deep inside his head. Still, standing in front of a freight train? That wouldn't be my first choice if I wanted to kill myself."

"That wouldn't even be on the first page of my choices," Casper said.

Livingston picked up a piece of paper and scanned it.

"There were two men in the locomotive; the engineer and the conductor. Their statements were virtually identical. It was 2:57 in the morning as the train entered a broad, sweeping curve. The headlights were not shining directly onto the path of the train. They said it looked like a bald man fell out of the sky. They saw the terror in his eyes. Both men were pretty shaken."

"I'm sure, sir," Casper said.

"There are a couple of odd things about the scene," Livingston said.

Casper held his breath.

"The train suffered no damage," Livingston said. "Of course, there were considerable delays to train traffic. Part of the evidence gathered included several small pieces of heavy vinyl."

Livingston paused and studied Casper's face.

"Oh," Livingston said. "The members of the train

crew mentioned seeing something blue."

"A coat maybe?" Casper said. "It was cold last night."

"A raincoat, maybe," Livingston said. "But the sky was clear at the time. The vinyl was too heavy for a raincoat. It's more like the type rafts are made of."

"Rafts?" Casper said. "That's weird. But I'm a city kid. I've heard that people love to put things on train tracks—stuff like old tires. Or sofas."

"That's true," Livingston said. "Have you ever seen a self-inflating raft?"

"Yes, sir. I saw a bunch of them at the ports."

Livingston held out his arm toward Casper, with his palm up.

"I guess conceivably you could use one of those like…"

Livingston snapped his hand toward himself at the wrist.

"…like a catapult."

Casper shrugged.

"That sounds like something you might see on YouTube."

Chief Livingston leaned back and rubbed his eyes.

"Casper, where were you two nights ago?"

Casper opened his mouth, but then closed it. He closed his eyes for a moment and then looked into Livingston's eyes.

"You told me to never lie to you."

"Yes, I did," Livingston said.

"I cannot answer your question, sir."

Livingston sighed. He stood slowly and looked out the large window behind his desk.

"I've been thinking a lot about retirement lately. I used to have confidence in my decisions. I seem to be losing that. Maybe I'm burning out. That's not how I want to finish my career."

"I'm sorry, sir," Casper said.

Livingston wore a grim smile.

"I don't think you're sorry at all. And I don't think I blame you. That scares the hell out of me."

Both men jumped when a voice came over the intercom.

"Sorry, Chief," the receptionist said. "There's some breaking news…"

"Thank you," Livingston said. He picked up the remote control and turned on the televisions. The volumes were still down, but all three screens showed a remote reporter speaking into a microphone.

The crawlers at the bottom of the screen told the story.

NYC MAYOR WILL NOT SEEK RE-ELECTION CITING HEALTH CONCERNS

Chief Livingston groaned.

"This is bullshit. He has no 'health concerns'. His numbers are higher than ever! What the hell…?"

Livingston's shoulders slumped.

"I'll do everything I can to close this case, Casper. It's what everyone wants. Millions of people want to go to bed tonight believing we can protect them from the

Bad Man. The Boogeyman. The Ghost Man."

"Thank you, sir."

"One last thing, Officer Halliday."

"Yes, sir."

"I want to see your career as an NYPD officer become extremely *boring*."

"I'll try, sir."

Livingston pointed at the door.

"Go to work."

Fifty-Three

When Casper returned to the patrol car, he told Leo the Chief had wanted to let Casper know how his daughter was doing. Casper didn't think Leo believed the story. In the last hour of their shift, Leo and Casper were called to respond to a domestic disturbance. The call involved eight family members, including two who were extremely high on methamphetamine. Leo took a punch to the face and one to his chest. Casper took a punch to his shoulder. One druggie cut Casper's cheek with a fingernail while Casper was wrestling him to the ground.

It was almost midnight when Casper got home. He was exhausted. His visit with Chief Livingston had exponentially multiplied the effect on his nerves

Casper woke up with a headache. He rolled over and looked at the alarm clock. It read 11:15. Casper groaned. He had to be at work at three.

Casper was assigned new days off, and today was the last day of his new work week.

His two days off would be busy. He was taking Cody to an amusement park, followed by a 3D movie and dinner where Mona and Sean Kelly would join them.

The following night was the celebration Casper planned to welcome Mo Tinsley back to the land of the free.

Bobby Halliday was asleep when Casper arrived. Casper showered and fell into bed.

****

Casper stood and stretched. He shuffled out of his door, took two steps, and stopped.

Bobby Halliday sat at the dining room table. His back faced Casper. The day was dark and cloudy, but Bobby had not turned on any lights. Four long, tapered candles stood on the table, their flames back-lighting two framed 8x10 photographs.

On the left was Bobby and Kathy's wedding picture. On the right, the proud and smiling Mr. And Mrs. Halliday posed with their infant son.

Something on the wall to Casper's right caught his attention. He squinted. On the coat hook inside the apartment's door were four blue uniforms covered in clear dry-cleaning plastic.

Casper shivered in silence.

Bobby Halliday cleared his throat. He raised his right hand. The candlelight reflected off of metal. Casper knew what it was.

His father's badge.

"They're giving me another chance, Kathy," Bobby whispered. His voice broke.

"I miss you so much…"

Bobby's head fell into his hands. His shoulders shook with the strength of his sobs.

Stinging tears flowed down Casper's cheeks.

Sadness erupted from deep inside him like nothing he had ever experienced. He was hopeless to contain it. He fought to control the surge of emotions. Grief rose from deep inside him. He was powerless to stop it.

And then Casper realized he did not want to fight it.

Father and son grieved without restraint for the first time.

Separately.

But…

Together.

Fifty-Four

Casper rang the doorbell to Mando's house. He turned his head when two laughing little girls passed by on their bicycles. Casper heard the door open.

"Hey, are you r—?"

Casper froze when he realized he was not talking to Mando Gonzalez. Instead, he stared into the eyes of an extremely beautiful young woman. The woman stared back at him. They looked at each other for a few seconds. The woman slapped her hands to her cheeks.

"Oh, my *God*. Casper?"

Casper nodded.

"Layla?"

"Oh…I am not prepared," Layla said. She stuck out her hand. "I mean, it's nice to meet you, in the flesh. God, that sounded weird. I was not myself on the phone—"

Casper laughed and took Layla's hand.

"The pleasure is mine. Don't apologize. I had fun."

Mando arrived and stood behind his sister.

"I told you the day would come when you had to meet Casper and you would have to explain that you're a wino—"

Layla elbowed Mando in the ribs.

"I am *not* a wino. I told you—I was relaxing and

celebrating my monumental achievements. You, dear brother, were acting like an evil stepmother."

"Whatever," Mando said. "Are you going to ask him in, or leave my friend on the front steps like he's trying to sell us something?"

Layla bowed and swept her arm.

"Come in, friend."

Casper pointed at Mando.

"Don't you look sharp."

Mando ran his hand down his shirt.

"Don't touch me. You'll cut yourself. Oh, it looks like you already have."

Casper touched the scar on his cheek.

"Yeah, things got a little up-close and personal the other night. Are you ready to go? It's a little early."

"I'm ready," Mando said. "Let me grab my coat."

"You kids have fun," Layla said.

"Thanks," Casper said. He turned toward the door and then turned back. He looked at Layla.

"Would you like to come with us?"

Layla smiled and stammered. Her eyes flicked toward Mando.

"Oh, that's nice, but…you wouldn't mind? Really?"

"Of course I wouldn't mind," Casper said. "I'd love for you to come."

Mando stepped next to Layla and whispered in her ear.

"I thought you had a date."

Layla whispered back.

"Shut up."

"Can you give me ten minutes?" Layla asked.

"Sure," Casper said. "No rush."

Casper, Mando, and Layla stepped out of Casper's car in front of Cappelletti's. A valet took the keys.

"Wow," Layla said. "I've heard about Cappelletti's. It's supposed to be wonderful. And expensive. Do you come here a lot? I didn't know cops were rich."

"She talks a lot," Mando said.

"I don't mind," Casper said. "I've never been here. But it's a special occasion."

"I know," Layla said. "Your friend has come back from someplace you don't want to talk about."

"This is great," Mando said. "One little secret that will drive her crazy like a hangnail."

Layla punched Mando's shoulder.

"Dammit, Layla," Mando said. "This is not Pizza Play-land. Act like a grown-up. If that's possible."

The hostess led them to a banquet room. Casper and Mo hugged. Introductions made their way around the room. Mo brought his cousin, Deshaun, and his old friend, Jerome Slade. Layla stared wide-eyed.

"Oh, my. Look at you," Mo said to Layla. "Girl, you are just *delicious*."

Layla smiled and grabbed Mo's arm.

"Oh, I like you," she said. "Are you going to sit by me?"

"Well, of course I am," Mo said. He looked at Casper.

"You'll have to get used to this, Casper. It's going to happen a lot."

Casper blushed.

"We're not...I...we..."

They ordered and talked, drank and laughed throughout the meal. Jerome and Mando pretended to have just met, but in one moment shared a wink. Before the waitress returned to inquire about dessert, Deshaun excused himself. He had a late performance to attend.

"I would love to see you dance," Layla said. Deshaun obliged with a quick twirling move. Everyone applauded.

"Come to the theater anytime, my dear," Deshaun said. "I will get you backstage."

Layla covered her mouth.

"Really? You can do that?"

Deshaun bowed.

"It will be my pleasure."

No one had room for dessert. Casper smiled at the waitress.

"Everything was wonderful, including the service. My compliments to the chef and to you."

"Hear, hear!" the others said.

"I can take care of the check when you're ready," Casper said.

"Right away," the waitress said.

She returned with a puzzled look on her face. She spread her hands and smiled at Casper.

"I thought you were the designated driver. All

I've served you is iced tea."

"I haven't had anything to drink, Miss. What are you talking about?"

"You paid with a gift certificate," the waitress said. She held out her hand. "And here is your change. One hundred and twenty-seven dollars and fifty-four cents."

"Uh…okay?" Casper said.

The waitress left. Casper laid the money on the table.

"That's a nice tip. I'll be right back," he said.

Casper stepped outside the room and looked left and right. He turned left toward the rest rooms. He stopped when he saw a familiar friendly face. The man was speaking to a table full of guests.

Cristian Cappelletti looked up. His eyes met Casper's.

Cristian bowed his head slightly.

Casper smiled and mouthed the words.

"Thank you."

****

Casper stepped into the apartment. It was late and his father was asleep. But Casper's question could not wait.

He pulled a chair beside Bobby Halliday's bed. He reached and shook his father's shoulder. Bobby stirred and rose up on his elbow.

"What is it, son?"

"I'm sorry to wake you, Dad. But I have a

question."

"Sure, Son. What is it?"

"Is there a voice inside your head that tickles the back of your neck?"

Bobby Halliday smiled.

"You're damn right."

I hope you have enjoyed Ghost Man, the second book in the Casper Halliday NYPD Series. If you did, please consider leaving a review. As has been said, the way to an author's heart is through a book review. Thanks for reading!

To find more of Nathan Roden's books, please visit

nathanroden.com

Nathan Roden lives in South Central Texas
with his wife and two in-and-out sons, and more
dogs and cats than is necessary.

For current and future exclusive free content,
and to find out what's going on, visit

www.nathanroden.com

Connect with Nathan:

BLOG: nathanroden.com

FACEBOOK:www.facebook.com/nathan.rode
n.books

TWITTER: twitter.com/WNathanRoden

GOODREADS:
www.goodreads.com/user/show/41141121-nathan-
roden

PINTEREST:
www.pinterest.com/nathanroden/

Made in the USA
Columbia, SC
04 January 2021

30241539R00217